Staying On

'You reeker!' Sahib shouted ten minutes later. Ibrahim had never fully understood the significance of this exclamation but liked the sound of it.

'Sahib wants?' he inquired, going out to where Tusker sat, well wrapped up, in the worm-eaten cane lounging chair. February, in Pankot, although warm and sunny, brought morning chills.

'Wants? Wants nothing. Has found. *Found.*' Flourishing a document. 'Now we'll see. Won't we just see. I'll sue the bitch from arsehole to Christmas.'

Ibrahim nodded approvingly. It was some weeks since Tusker Sahib had threatened anyone with anything from arsehole to Christmas.

Paul Scott

STAYING ON

ARROW

To my old colleague and friend

Roland Gant

whom I regard and thank

Reprinted in Arrow Books 1997

14 16 18 20 19 17 15 13

Copyright © Paul Scott 1977

First published in the United Kingdom in 1977 by William Heinemann
This edition first published in 1994 by Mandarin Paperbacks,
reprinted 5 times

Arrow Books
The Random House Group Limited
20 Vauxhall Bridge Road, London SW1V 2SA

Random House Australia (Pty) Limited
20 Alfred Street, Milsons Point, Sydney,
New South Wales 2061, Australia

Random House New Zealand Limited
18 Poland Road, Glenfield
Auckland 10, New Zealand

Random House (Pty) Limited
Endulini, 5a Jubilee Road, Parktown 2193, South Africa

The Random House Group Limited Reg. No. 954009

www.randomhouse.co.uk

A CIP catalogue record for this book is available from the British Library

Printed and bound in the United Kingdom by
Cox & Wyman Ltd, Reading, Berkshire

ISBN 0 7493 1865 1

CHAPTER ONE

When Tusker Smalley died of a massive coronary at approximately 9.30 a.m. on the last Monday in April 1972 his wife Lucy was out, having her white hair blue-rinsed and set in the Seraglio Room on the ground floor of Pankot's new five-storey glass and concrete hotel, the Shiraz.

The Shiraz was only a step or two away from the little hill station's older hotel, Smith's, whose annexe had been occupied by Tusker and Lucy for ten years. The annexe, known as The Lodge, was a small bungalow in what had once been an adjacent but separate compound, a section of whose dividing wall had been knocked down and a path trodden to create an illusion of connection between hotel and annexe. The old gateway into The Lodge's compound, now known as the side-entrance, gave on to a lane. Immediately opposite was the Shiraz.

If Tusker had been found at once, then, and a message sent across, Lucy would have had the news at just the moment any woman would subsequently have to think of as the most inconvenient at which to hear she had become a widow. At 9.30 she was going under the dryer.

But Tusker lay dead for half-an-hour and might have lain longer if Mrs Bhoolabhoy, who owned Smith's and lived in one of its principal rooms, hadn't become unnerved by the howling of Colonel and Mrs Smalley's dog, Bloxsaw. The howling was not very loud because the dog was locked in Colonel Smalley's garage, but it was persistent so Mr Bhoolabhoy was ordered over to complain on Mrs Bhoolabhoy's behalf.

Mrs Bhoolabhoy, who had jowls and favoured sarees in pastel colours such as salmon pink which emphasized the fairness of her skin, was a martyr to several things, among them, migraine. On mornings when she kept to her room, work at Smith's Hotel came virtually to a standstill. The

5

slightest percussive sound was more than she was prepared to bear. The hotel was hers, Mr Bhoolabhoy merely its manager, whom she had married. Mrs Bhoolabhoy weighed sixteen stone. Her husband was constructed on more meagre lines.

Mr Bhoolabhoy had managed Smith's for years before the woman he married turned up as its new proprietor. He was her third and youngest husband; according to Tusker Smalley probably the lucky one because she was unlikely to enjoy a fourth, being now almost as richly endowed with killing flesh as with life-enhancing rupees. Tusker, who called Mr Bhoolabhoy Billy-Boy, except when they had quarrelled, which sometimes they had to, said Billy-Boy looked like a man who, inured to disappointment, had suddenly glimpsed an immense possibility and begun to organize himself so as not to make the mistake that would block his way to it. Mrs Bhoolabhoy had had no children by any of her husbands. 'He stands to gain,' Tusker had often pointed out to Lucy. 'And he feeds her up a treat. One day she'll drop.'

Actually, Mrs Bhoolabhoy fed herself without either Mr Bhoolabhoy's help or hindrance. His policy was to minimize every risk of incurring her displeasure. These risks were many. On her good days when she waddled about looking into this and that and finding fault he followed in her galleon-wake in his neat well-pressed suit making sure her orders were carried out and the sources of her irritation at once put a stop to. On her bad days he walked on tip-toe and had the entire staff doing the same so that even the guests (when there were any) felt themselves under a cloud and got out of the place as soon as possible after breakfast.

The last Monday morning in this April (April 24th) was such a morning; if anything heavier than usual with the pressure of Mrs Bhoolabhoy's martyrdom which throbbed like a silent fog-warning through the hotel from the shuttered bedroom (the old Number One) where she lay on a massive double bed which she took up most of. Occasionally Mr Bhoolabhoy was detailed to share this bed but had not been the previous night when he had slept in his own

6

room (the old Number Two). The two rooms were en-suite with a communicating door which Mr Bhoolabhoy never bolted his side of but which frequently did not give to his gentle midnight nudge. He had not nudged it the night before. Sunday had been a shattering day.

At 7.30 a.m. he was summoned from No. 2 to No. 1 by his wife's personal maid, a local Pankot woman whom they called by the name she had been given long ago by the British military family who employed her as a little ayah until they went home in 1947: Minnie. Minnie was now plump, middle-aged and grumpy. Mr Bhoolabhoy got no change out of her. She took orders only from Mrs Bhoolabhoy, and not always from her. Mr Bhoolabhoy maintained a cautious attitude to Minnie. Sometimes Minnie complained about him to Mrs Bhoolabhoy, or about what she called Management which came to the same thing. This led to Mrs Bhoolabhoy shouting at him. At other times when Minnie was being unco-operative even with Mrs Bhoolabhoy he got shouted at again.

'You can't win, old man,' Tusker had told him. 'Not with women. Minnie probably fancies you. It gives her a kick to get you into trouble. Obviously you've never made a pass at her. Try it.'

'No, no. It must be menopause.'

'In that case she ought to go into the next Guinness Book of Records. You've been saying that for years. Have another peg.'

So they had had another peg. That was a week ago. Monday evenings were evenings Mr Bhoolabhoy usually looked forward to. However badly Monday started, however badly indisposed Mrs Bhoolabhoy was at breakfast-time, by lunch she had usually recovered sufficiently to take some nourishment and so fortify herself to spend the rest of the gruelling day playing bridge at the Pankot Gymkhana Club. Mondays were not her only bridge days: there could be sessions on Tuesday, Wednesday, Thursday, Friday and Saturday; but never Sunday because Sunday was Mr Bhoolabhoy's day off and her day for checking his records of the hotel's income and expenditure which often

7

contributed to the fact that there could easily be a difference of opinion between them on Sunday evening, a celibate night for Mr Bhoolabhoy and a Monday morning migraine for his wife.

What gave Monday evenings their attraction was not just that Mrs Bhoolabhoy could be counted on to stay late at the club but also that on these evenings Mrs Smalley took herself to the pictures at the New Electric. Once Mr Bhoolabhoy had seen the last evening guest out of Smith's dining-room and ensured that the servants were beginning to clear up and the kitchen-staff to wash up, that cook had remembered to prepare Mrs Bhoolabhoy's midnight snack, that Minnie had properly arranged her mistress's bed and was somewhere within her mistress's immediate call, then he and Tusker could meet over a bottle either at The Lodge or on the verandah of the hotel (where the sound of Mrs Bhoolabhoy returning could be better heard).

Neither man got drunk. Tusker drank more than Mr Bhoolabhoy, but then Tusker was a member – the last surviving member in Pankot, with his wife – of the old school of British and needed his liquor. Mr Bhoolabhoy drank less not only because he had principles (frail at times) but because he loved listening to Tusker who seemed to know so much about such a lot (old scandal, new scandal, local scandal, international scandal, the Profumo affair, the Kennedy assassination, why President Johnson pulled dogs by their ears, why Prime Minister Heath was married to a boat, why it was that the British were pro-Pakistan in the first Indo–Pak war and pro-India in the one just finished, and what Henry Kissinger had said to the dumbest blonde in Connecticut who only wanted to send a message to her momma in Warsaw).

Over the years of their convivial Mondays Mr Bhoolabhoy had gathered a great deal of esoteric information about Presidents, Palaces and People's Democracies. The range of Tusker's knowledge of the world had astonished him, fascinated him. He often wished he could remember one-tenth of what he had learned, been told; and sometimes

8

thought he might have done so if he had got as well-oiled as Tusker. But apart from his principles, his preference for hearing clearly what Tusker was saying, his relative abstemiousness was imposed upon him by awareness of the necessity to aim off for the wind of Mrs Bhoolabhoy's unpredictable Monday night desire.

This tended to depend on how much she had won. More often than not she came home up on the evening in which case Mr Bhoolabhoy had to be prepared to be up to things too. He had to be similarly prepared if she had lost so much in the day-long bridge session that she was feeling unloved and unwanted in an unkind and swindling world. He found this rather touching and on such occasions, after their combined and gigantic climax, they often had a little weep together and exchanged protestations of their beholdenness one to the other and of their resolve to be beholden forever. (Her break-even nights could be very dull.) Too often, though, the combination of money lost, midnight snack, violent intercourse and tears of relief and love, led next day to Mrs Bhoolabhoy's further prostration.

But this Monday was unlikely to draw to a close for Mr Bhoolabhoy with a convivial meeting with Colonel Smalley (Indian Army, Rtd). Today, unless he could wriggle out of it again he was going to have to write the Letter. Obeying the summons delivered by Minnie he entered Room No. 1 and stood nervously at the foot of his wife's bed. The summons had not surprised him because a quarter of an hour before he had heard Mrs Bhoolabhoy moan. He had already warned the servants not to clatter.

'Shall I send for Dr Rajendra, Lila?' he asked in a whisper, and in the English they spoke to one another in because he could not understand her when she rattled away in her native Punjabi.

She mouthed the word no. Her mouth and her moustache were all he could see of her face. She was on her back, both hands pressed to her head.

9

'Dr Taporewala, perhaps?' Then he moistened his lips in anticipation. 'What about Dr Battacharya?'

Dr Rajendra practised western medicine; Taporewala, the ayurvedic. Dr Battacharya went in for acupuncture, and had once cured Mrs Bhoolabhoy of migraine for a whole week by sticking her ample body all over with little pins; which had been a sight to see.

'No doctor,' she said. 'Have you written the Letter?'

'I am about to.'

'Do it. Then bring it. I will sign it.'

'There is no need for you to be bothered with trivial matters of detail, dear Lila. What am I here for?'

'Sometimes this is a question I ask myself.'

Mr Bhoolabhoy tiptoed out then tiptoed in again.

'Lila, it will have to be typed.'

'Naturally.'

'The machine will make a noise.'

'One has one's crosses.'

Mr Bhoolabhoy nodded.

He went back to his own room and then out through the door that gave, as all the bedroom doors gave, on to the dim green windowless dining-room where ragged palms, potted in brass spittoons, stood sentinel among tables shrouded by stained napery. Daylight entered only from the threadbare lounge which had windows on to the verandah. Between dining- and sitting-room Mr Bhoolabhoy had his office, a glassed-in cubby-hole that gave a view of both rooms. This was Mr Bhoolabhoy's sanctuary. A naked electric bulb provided illumination. The office doorway was narrow enough to make it difficult for Mrs Bhoolabhoy to enter, and inside he kept the office cluttered so that if she entered she could not advance far and, leaving, had to back out. He closed the door, closed the section of window that normally remained open for guests to communicate with him (demands, complaints, settlements), sat in his swivel chair, inserted in the elderly Remington a sheet of hotel notepaper plus carbon and flimsy and began, *April 24th, 1972, My Dear Colonel Smalley*. Then stopped.

From Room 7, the closest to the office, was coming the

10

sound of music. He ran softly out, tapped at the door, opened, and surprised Mr Pandey in the lotus position, eyes closed, transmitting or absorbing *prana* to the accompaniment of a morning raga by Ravi Shankar or someone on All-India Radio.

Mr Bhoolabhoy had little ear for any music except Christian hymns. He switched the raga off. Mr Pandey opened his eyes. Bhoolabhoy, by signs, alerted him to Mrs Bhoolabhoy's Monday morning condition. Mr Pandey sighed, nodded his head from side to side, shut his eyes again and resumed meditation, but this time with an expression of concentration instead of beatitude.

Mr Pandey was chief clerk to the lawyers in Ranpur who dealt with Mrs Bhoolabhoy's intricate business affairs. He came up once or twice a month with papers and documents, stayed a day or so and was boarded free so Mr Bhoolabhoy had no compunction about turning off his transistor. His presence this weekend was especially ominous. Among the papers he expected to take back to Ranpur today was a copy of the Letter. Mr Bhoolabhoy returned to his office, tore the paper out of the machine and set things up again but this time with the two carbons he had forgotten the first time; and began again, 'My Dear Colonel Smalley,' and paused, seeking inspiration, reluctantly resumed without it and eventually finished. He ended, 'Yours very Sincerely.'

It was now nearly 8 a.m.

In the days before the Shiraz was built this had been the witching hour at Smith's because it was at 8 o'clock that the night train from Ranpur was scheduled to get in after its long haul up the single track into the Pankot Hills from the plains and, consequently, at that hour that staff and management had been ready for the arrival of guests who had booked and been hopeful of others who hadn't booked and all of whom began to turn up at about 8.30 in taxis, tongas, avid for breakfast during the serving of which the luggage of departing guests would be piled on the verandah so that it and they could go down to the station to catch the midday departure back to Ranpur. This had been the pattern since the days of the *raj*. After the *raj* went there had been bad times, good times, near-disastrous times, times of retrenchment, times of ebullient hope, as Pankot waxed, waned, waxed again in popularity. But for Smith's now it all seemed to be coming to an end.

The night train from Ranpur still reached Pankot at 8 a.m. From 8.30 or so onward, then, from the front verandah of his hotel, Mr Bhoolabhoy could assess the Shiraz's morning intake of guests who had come up by rail by counting the number of passengers in the taxis that drove slowly past the entrance to Smith's compound before making the right-angled turn into the Shiraz's forecourt. There were seldom many. Most of the Shiraz's guests arrived later in the day by private car or by the Indian Airways 'bus that picked them up in mid-afternoon at the airfield down in Nansera.

The building of the Nansera airfield predated the building of the Shiraz by several years and for a while Smith's had prospered. Half-an-hour by air from Ranpur to Nansera and then an hour's chug in the airport 'bus from the Nansera valley up into the Pankot Hills had made the old hill station an attractive proposition for people who found an all night train journey and a six hour one back a high price to pay for a weekend in more invigorating air. The 'bus had used Smith's as its pick-up and put-down point and the airline had set its office up in Smith's compound – a useful concession which had now been transferred to the Shiraz; and unfairly, Mr Bhoolabhoy felt, the fact that the Shiraz now existed, all five storeys of it, attracted more people up than ever before: people in government, in commerce, the idle rich, the busy executives, and now even film stars and directors from the Ranpur Excelsior Talkie Company who had recently shot part of a movie in Pankot and booked the entire top floor of this modern monstrosity.

The presence of movie stars had caused excitement among simple people who hung round hoping for a sight of them and followed their vans and trucks to the location where they were shooting exteriors even though this was way over on the other side of East Hill. Often they had had their trek for nothing because the heroine was a girl given to temperaments and sometimes locked herself into her suite at the Shiraz for the whole day and admitted only her personal entourage, her publicity manager and the gossip columnists.

By the time she got over her temperament the hero was likely to be having one too. There was no shooting for days at a time. The owner of the film company then came up from Ranpur and threatened everyone with proceedings for breach of contract, upon which the director, a young man who was into realism, also had a temperament and declared the location useless. Everyone packed up and went home.

Tusker and Mr Bhoolabhoy had laughed about this only last Monday night, and he was smiling now, recalling it, when Minnie appeared at the office window, holding her hand out. She had come for the Letter. He indicated the paper still in the typewriter and held up four fingers to indicate four more minutes. It was now 8.30.

Five minutes later, unable to delay longer, he took the letter in to Mrs Bhoolabhoy. Five minutes later still he was back in his office, inserting new sheets of paper to rewrite the letter to Lila's taste. It now began, 'Dear Colonel Smalley,' instead of 'my Dear Colonel Smalley.' It was to end not 'Yours very Sincerely, Lila Bhoolabhoy,' but 'Yours faithfully, L. Bhoolabhoy, Prop.' In between, its three friendly and apologetic paragraphs had to be cut to one curt one. Mr Bhoolabhoy had to type the new version several times before he was satisfied that she might approve it. By ten past nine the final curt version was finished.

He took it to Mrs Bhoolabhoy. After she'd read it she held out her hand. He gave her his Parker 61, then helped to prop her up to sign.

'I will take it across now, Lila.'

'Minnie will take it. Call her.'

He did so. He put the letter in its envelope. When Minnie came in Mrs Bhoolabhoy grabbed the letter and gave

13

it to Minnie herself. 'To Colonel Smalley. Immediate.'

Minnie said nothing but took the letter. Mr Bhoolabhoy made to follow her out but was commanded to stay. 'You may massage the back of my neck,' Mrs Bhoolabhoy said. For five minutes he performed this vaguely erotic task. Things were just getting interesting for him when she said, 'Enough. Now go back to the office to be on hand to deal with Colonel Smalley if and when he comes.'

As he left Lila's room Mr Pandey was coming out of No. 7 armed with his briefcase and his breakfast, a single glass of orange juice which he always drank over at the little hut where Indian Airways had once kept an office. Mr Bhoolabhoy followed him as far as the verandah, watched him cross the compound and settle himself, and kept alert for the sound of the transistor. He heard a crackle or two, but nothing more disturbing so remained where he was, his hand on the back of the chair Tusker usually sat in on Monday evenings.

'Always,' he thought, 'I have the mucky end of the stick. But then I am only part of the fixtures and fittings.' These, undoubtedly, had all depreciated in value. The stucco on the walls of the hotel was peeling, the compound had been let go. Mrs Bhoolabhoy's priorities had never been those of her predecessor, old Mr Pillai, Mr Bhoolabhoy's first employer. Her business affairs remained a mystery to him. Mr Pandey knew far more about them than he did. He glared across the compound at the little babu and wondered not for the first time to what extent Mr Pandey enjoyed more than Mrs Bhoolabhoy's confidence.

'Management!'

'Yes, Minnie, what is it?'

Management, it seemed, had to go across at once to The Lodge to complain about the noise.

'What noise?'

'Smalley dog.'

'I hear no dog.' He bent his head. He heard it then.

14

According to her mistress, Minnie said, the dog had been locked in the garage again, either because Colonel and Mrs Smalley had disagreed once again about whose dog it was and which of them should take it for walkies or because Colonel Smalley was being spiteful as the result of the Letter.

'You personally gave him the Letter?'

Minnie said she had given it to their servant, Ibrahim.

'But Colonel Smalley was in?'

Yes. Minnie had seen him having breakfast on the front verandah of The Lodge.

'And Mrs Smalley?'

According to Ibrahim, the memsahib was at the hairdresser. Also according to Ibrahim there would be a row when memsahib got back because Tusker Sahib had just sacked him. He, Ibrahim, was once more no longer in the Smalleys' employment. He had promised, though, to hand the Letter to Tusker Sahib before leaving, which meant right away because he had been told to get out at once and never come back. It was the fourth time in a year that he had been sacked by one or other of them; but this time Tusker Sahib had actually given him his month's pay. Ibrahim was therefore packing his things so that he could station himself, bundle and all, outside the Shiraz, where Mrs Smalley would find him when she came out with her new blue hair and ask why he wasn't at work. Colonel Memsahib (Minnie said) had gone to get new blue hair because she and Colonel Sahib were expecting a visitor any day.

'An Englishman,' Minnie said, holding her elbows.

Mr Bhoolabhoy stood up. 'Then I must prepare a room.' The Smalleys had no spare room at The Lodge. On the rare occasions they'd had a guest the guest stayed in the hotel.

'Dog first,' Minnie said. 'Room later.'

'Damn the dog,' Mr Bhoolabhoy said but just then the distant howling took on a new and louder and despairing note. A shriek came from Mrs Bhoolabhoy's room. Minnie hurried away. Mr Bhoolabhoy hesitated, then ran down the

15

steps and made for The Lodge. Tusker's wrath was more easily endured than Mrs Bhoolabhoy's. And there was just the possibility that Ibrahim had not delivered the Letter into Tusker's hands, but left it in some perfectly rational but inconspicuous place where it would take time for Tusker to find it.

But whether Ibrahim had handed it to Tusker personally or not before departing, sacked, it had certainly been found and opened. Mr Bhoolabhoy recognized it, without its envelope. Tusker lay in the middle of the bed of crimson canna lilies, the letter clutched in his right hand.

CHAPTER TWO

Tusker Smalley's death can be fixed as having occurred at approximately 9.30 a.m. rather than say twenty minutes later when the dog stopped whining and began to howl, causing Mrs Bhoolabhoy to shriek, because the dog, Bloxsaw (the Indian pronunciation of its real name, Blackshaw), was generally recognized as too stupid to be aware of the moment its master's soul departed; and Dr Mitra, Tusker's physician, pronounced the coronary as having been so massive as to have caused death at the moment of his fall.

About twenty minutes before his fall, that is at about 9.10 a.m., Tusker had dragged Bloxsaw into the garage, locked him in, then told Ibrahim that he was dismissed and could clear out right away. He had paid him off. That was at 9.15.

Ibrahim knew it was 9.15. Having taken his money he glanced at his watch to work out how much longer Lucy-Mem would be at the hairdresser and so how long it would be before the business of negotiating his reinstatement could begin. If it ever did. The paying off had been an ominous variation on the theme of getting the push.

For another few minutes Ibrahim hung around, out of sight, anticipating a yelled complaint that the breakfast egg was off, but the only sound was the racket made by the dog using the garage door as a punch-bag. Presently Ibrahim went out by the back to look for the young *mali* (his trump card on this occasion). The *mali* was nowhere to be seen. Instead there had been Mrs Bhoolabhoy's maid, Minnie, looking for him and now handing him a letter.

'Much trouble,' she said, nodding at the envelope.

'Good,' Ibrahim said. He told her he'd been sacked. She covered the lower part of her face, grinning with him, sharing the comedy of life. Then she went. He took the letter to Tusker Sahib at once, prepared for anything from a

17

shied tea-cup to a friendly smile. The Sahib had always been unpredictable, more so since his illness, but it was always better to be sacked by him than by Memsahib. Once Memsahib had sacked him she had a way of not looking, not listening, not seeing him for days as though the mere fact of her having told him to go had caused him to disappear. All his longest periods of technical unemployment stemmed from notice given by Colonel Memsahib. The Sahib, although sometimes threatening violence, was a soft touch by comparison. With Memsahib the war tended to be one of attrition, not confrontation. Even when she was on his side against Tusker Sahib he dealt with her cautiously.

'A letter, Sahib,' he announced, 'Just now come.'

'I told you to get out!' the Sahib shouted. 'You've got your money, so go, now. *Ek dam.*'

'From Management,' Ibrahim said, putting the letter on the breakfast table. 'Shall not trouble household further. Only performing last duty. The world collapses around one's head. So it is written. Salaam Aleikum.'

He retired into the bungalow and waited, listening for the sound of the envelope being torn open out there on the verandah. He guessed what the letter was about. In the servants' quarters both at Smith's and the Shiraz the subject of the future of The Lodge and of Smith's itself had been discussed for weeks; and news – from conversations overheard of plans made by the consortium of businessmen who owned the Shiraz to buy up Smith's and 're-develop' – swapped for news of what was known or guessed about Mrs Bhoolabhoy's latest successes in playing one of these businessmen off against the other with a view it was supposed to being invited to join the consortium herself.

Apart from the Shiraz, the consortium owned a new hotel in Ranpur, one in Mayapore, and another down in Mirat (The Mirat Lake-Palace Hotel). They also owned a small chain of restaurants called the Go-Go-Inns which specialized in Punjabi food. All the businessmen concerned in these enterprises had come from the Western Punjab in 1947 when it became part of Pakistan at the time of In-

18

dependence and Partition, and had arrived in India penni-less, they said. Mrs Bhoolabhoy's first husband was believed to have come from there, having 'lost his all' in the riots between Muslims and Hindus. It was agreed by the ser-vants both at Smith's and the Shiraz that you could hardly find a Western Punjabi, once destitute, nowadays not mak-ing a packet. 'Bloody immigrants,' Ibrahim sometimes called them.

Ibrahim did not hear the sound of the envelope being opened. Bloxsaw was now yelping as well as punching the garage door. What he did hear was a shout, 'The bitch! The bloody bitch!' and the scrape of Tusker's wicker-chair as he rose, no doubt to go and sort Mrs Bhoolabhoy out.

Ibrahim smiled. Since he had been dismissed it was no concern of his that the Sahib leaving by the front and him-self by the back meant the bungalow would now be unattended. He went to the servants' quarters in the rear compound and found the young *mali* trying to repair the leak in the old water-can.

'Leave that,' he said. 'We are dismissed. One out, all out.'

'When shall we be reinstated?'

The *mali* had been employed for only a few weeks. But he knew the score. Ibrahim had briefed him.

'This time perhaps never. Come. Help me pack a few things then pack a few things yourself to make it look good.'

'I also should pack?'

'Of course.'

'Where shall we go?'

'To the Shiraz.'

'We seek employment at the Shiraz?'

'No. We shall take up positions near main entrance to accost Memsahib when she comes out.'

Mali put the watering-can aside but remained squatting on his hunkers. His brown eyes darkened with the effort of concentrating.

'Ibrahim,' he said. 'Why when you are pushed am I also pushed?'

'I have explained it before. There is no time to explain it again now.'

19

'What of pay?'

'What of it? Did I say *I* was sacking you? You are still in my employ, at least until the end of the month. Speak of pay then, not before.'

'If we are pushed, what of shelter, what of food?'

'Given push, not pushed. If you hope to go foreign you must learn pukka English. Stop asking questions and get on with it. Allah will provide.'

The hut where Ibrahim slept lay behind the corrugated iron garage which was a comparatively new construction. As a bungalow The Lodge had always been diminutive, the servants' quarters correspondingly so: six or seven men, women and boys had once had accommodation here, just sufficient for a modest bachelor establishment in the days of the *raj*. Then, there had been several huts and a cookhouse. Only the hut in which Ibrahim slept remained in good repair. The others had fallen into ruin and of the cookhouse there was nothing left except a few blackened bricks. No one had used it to cook for the occupants of The Lodge since the time Smith's annexed it. A modern kitchen of sorts had subsequently been installed inside The Lodge but this was seldom put to major use because – breakfasts and buffet parties apart – the Smalleys usually ate in the main hotel dining-room or had Ibrahim bring trays over.

Tusker Sahib occasionally had crazes for going to the market and bringing back fresh food which he made a hash of, burning the potatoes, over-spicing the stew. Ibrahim was prepared to make tea, toast, cook eggs, squeeze fruit juice, pour from the packets of cornflakes, oversee the stocking of the refrigerator with butter and milk, and in winter have a go at making the morning porridge which kept his master's and mistress's old bones warm. If either was ill he could and did turn his hand to anything in the line of nursing and commissariat. Years younger than both he felt for them what an indulgent, often exasperated but affectionate parent might feel for demanding and unreasonable children whom it was more sensible to appease than cross.

He had spoiled them both three months before when

Tusker Sahib had been taken seriously ill for the first time in his seventy-odd years, and Dr Mitra had ordered him to bed, either in the hospital or at home, preferably the hospital. 'Bugger hospital,' Tusker had shouted. 'Come to that, bugger bed. Ibrahim'll look after me, so will Lucy if she can get her arse off the chair.'

One of the pleasures of working for Tusker Sahib was the further insight it gave him into the fascinating flexibility and poetry of the English language. Since his youth in Mirat, since his boyhood even, it had never failed to stun him with its elegance. Only those few months in Finsbury Park, London N, had caused him any disquiet. The language had sounded different, there. But the place was stiff with Greeks.

For days after Tusker's confinement to bed he had gone round muttering, 'Bugger bed, and get your arse off the chair.' For days, too, he and Lucy-Mem separately or together shopped for the ingredients of the good nourishing-broth which would keep Tusker's strength up without overheating his blood. Separately or together they had slaved over the rarely used electric oven at The Lodge that was either not hot enough or too hot, somehow not in either their separate or combined competence, a regular djinn of a stove, one moment exhaling smoke and flames and at the next as cold as Akbar's tomb; while in the bedroom or on the verandah Tusker Sahib lay either incomprehensibly docile – like a man (Ibrahim thought) who knew he'd left it too late to go to Mecca or, at other times, pronouncing anathema, against the broth, his wife, Ibrahim, Dr Mitra, and the Shiraz whose tall shadow darkened The Lodge's garden in the mornings until the sun got high enough for the five-storeys to emit heat rather than cast shadow, and cut The Lodge off from the cool breeze that sometimes came at midday in the warm weather. Chiefly, though, Tusker pronounced anathema against Mrs Bhoolabhoy whose chief *mali* was supposed to tend The Lodge's garden as well as the kitchen-garden and the ragged flower pots in the hotel's own compound. Ibrahim belonged to Tusker and Lucy; but the *mali* and the sweeper had always been

21

Mrs Bhoolabhoy's responsibility, their services paid for in the rent.

Throughout Tusker's illness the old *mali* hadn't worked at The Lodge. The grass began to need cutting. The canna lilies began to wilt. The jungle was advancing.

'What does Mrs Bhoolabhoy think I am?' Tusker cried one day. 'A sleeping beauty? What's she going to do? Wake me in a hundred years' time after hacking her way through her own bloody thickets? Who does she think she is? Prince bloody Charming? Just wait till Billy-Boy gets back. I'll have both their guts for garters.'

'What is Sahib saying?' Ibrahim asked Colonel Mem-sahib.

'Nothing. It is only his delirium,' Lucy replied. 'But we must do somehing about the *mali*. The state of the garden is beginning to retard Colonel Sahib's recovery.'

Ibrahim disagreed. He had worked for the Smalleys for several interesting tumultuous years and wasn't ready yet to lose them. They were the last survivors of Pankot's permanent retired British residents. This and the fact that he himself was England-Returned gave him a certain cachet among the other servants. If Tusker died now Lucy-Mem might go Home. He judged that Tusker's anger about the state of the compound was the main thing that kept him on the boil, and so – alive. Tusker was a man who needed irritants. Often he invented them. Here was one ready-made. From a peaceful orderly scene of a *mali* cutting grass and watering canna lilies Tusker might have turned his face away, and to the wall.

Sometimes, feeling himself both demeaned and exalted, Ibrahim threw a can of water on the lilies. He even picked a few marigolds for Tusker's bedside vase. Cut the grass he would not. He was a head-bearer, not a gardener; and in any case he agreed with Tusker that Mrs Bhoolabhoy's *mali* had always cut the grass, if only by steering the old machine while his tenpence-in-the-shilling assistant dragged it on ropes.

'It's in the lease!' Tusker shouted one day. Exasperated and ignoring Ibrahim's advice to do nothing until Mr

Bhoolabhoy was back from his mysterious trip to Ranpur, Lucy-Mem went to confront Mrs Bhoolabhoy, something Ibrahim couldn't remember her ever doing before.

'I never interfere with business matters,' she once said to him in her small light voice. 'I have no business brain at all.' Ibrahim took this with a pinch of salt. Memsahib was a devil when it came to checking change and prices on shopping lists. And most of the concessions Tusker Sahib wrung out of Mrs Bhoolabhoy, Ibrahim knew, originated in what Lucy described as her own 'addled little brain'. Without that addled little brain there would have been no new refrigerator two years ago, no repair to the garage door the same year, no new seats on the twin thunder-boxes which stood side by side on a dais in the bathroom like viceregal thrones and which the liar of a sweeper declared he had evidence of having been used at times simultaneously.

So when Lucy-Mem went to confront Mrs Bhoolabhoy about the case of the disappearing *mali* he almost expected her to return with a *mali* in tow.

'Old *mali* seems to have resigned,' she told him, 'and hired himself out to the Shiraz. Beyond that I simply don't know. I suppose we must wait and see.'

He expected her to say, 'Surely you could have told us old *mali* had gone?' But she didn't, and on second thoughts he realized he hadn't expected it. Sahib and Memsahib were extremely interesting examples to him of the almost total self-absorption that overtook old people such as them. Both lived, really, in worlds of their own. If either had bothered to ask him what had *happened* to old *mali* he might have told them. But all Sahib had done was grumble that the *mali* hadn't turned up, and all Memsahib had done was listen with half-an-ear until the moment when it struck her that it was bad for Sahib to grumble so much.

It wasn't of course true that old *mali* had resigned. He had been sacked, unofficially as part of the process of what Mrs Bhoolabhoy called retrenchment, officially because she had decided that he was selling part of the produce of the kitchen garden to the bazaar from where at times of inex-

23

plicable shortage Mr Bhoolabhoy had been unwittingly buying it back. This was not proven against old *mali* but Mrs Bhoolabhoy was convinced of the fact and when Mrs Bhoolabhoy was convinced of a fact one had to assume that a fact was what it was. There was no appeal against her judgment. All old *mali* had actually ever done, though, was appropriate his fair share of what he had hoed and sweated to grow. The kitchen garden had occupied most of his time, what was left over, Mrs Bhoolabhoy complained, had for years been lazily spent cutting the grass at The Lodge. The *mali*'s departure for the Shiraz left the Hotel with only the assistant *mali*, a youth with a lame left leg and a blind right eye who just about managed to cope with the weeds in the Smith's flower-beds of which, between stony paths, there were now but vestigial traces. It was believed that Mrs Bhoolabhoy was only awaiting an opportunity to sack this wretched fellow too. It was typical of her, Ibrahim thought, that she should have told Lucy-Mem that old *mali* had resigned.

Old *mali* was sacked on the day Tusker Sahib was taken ill, which was the day after his friend and drinking companion, Mr Bhoolabhoy, went down to Ranpur ostensibly to execute commissions for Mrs Bhoolabhoy : a rare enough event for the servants to wonder whether in fact he had been sacked too; or had left her at last for another woman.

For instance, the nautch-girl, Hot Chichanya, who sang at the Go-Go-Inn in Ranpur and was said to be the daughter of a Russian mother and an Afghan father. The head bearer at Smith's had seen a clipping of a newspaper photograph of Hot Chichanya pinned to the inside of Mr Bhoolabhoy's almirah door and one by one all the male servants had entered the manager's room during his absence to get an eyeful.

Mr Bhoolabhoy's interest in Hot Chichanya dated from the time she came up to Pankot to sing in the first cabaret produced in the Shiraz's Mountain View Room (of which it was reported she complained that there was hardly any room, less view and no god-dammed mountain). The servants at the Shiraz said she had a voice like a frog but breasts like melons. In the clipping these showed to advantage in spite of the poor newsprint.

The staff at the Shiraz had also reported to the staff at Smith's that Hot Chichanya was insatiable and kept by her bedside an illustrated edition of the Kama Sutra printed in Hong Kong, to inspire her lovers if they showed signs of flagging at 3 a.m. when the sound of her raucous voice and stamping bootshod feet and the cracking of the red leather whip she used in a number called Koshak-dance had more than once disturbed and brought complaints from other guests, particularly parents visiting the boys who were getting a sound English-style public school education at the Chakravarti College which was housed in the old Summer Residence.

The complaints had no effect. Hot Chichanya was in the protection of two young men, both thin, who were nephews of a senior member of the consortium of owners. All her lovers, rumour had it, were thin. The scrawnier the better, and age no object. Mr Bhoolabhoy could not be ruled out as a candidate. He had attended the cabaret twice. Now he was in Ranpur, where Hot Chichanya performed nightly.

'Poor Bhoolabhoy Sahib,' the Smith Hotel cook said when it dawned on them what the manager might be doing. 'Has he the strength?'

When he got back from the plains three weeks later, although silent he looked content; like a man, cook said, whose objective had been achieved. It was noted too that on the first Sunday following his return he did not go to St John's Church, of which he was a pillar. Francis (Frank) Bhoolabhoy was a cradle Christian. What Mrs Bhoolabhoy was no one knew. She had been married so many times that her original family name seemed lost in antiquity. She showed no interest in any religion, in any kind of hereafter, only in the here and now and in how this might be arranged to her advantage.

On the morning of his return Mr Bhoolabhoy spent two hours in Mrs Bhoolabhoy's room but the persistent sound of chat suggested conversation of a business not an amorous and certainly not a confessional nature. Emerging, he went about his normal routine with his usual air of muffled energy, the difference being that when he sat over his type-writer or whispered a rebuke to someone who had dropped a plate his eyes were on neither.

'He has been having his end away,' the aged head bearer said, using one of Ibrahim's expressions. 'God be thanked, there is hope for all of us.'

Removing the soiled socks, shirts and underwear which Mr Bhoolabhoy had brought back from his trip, the dhobi's boy spent a moment or two on each garment, testing for new scent, conclusive evidence of a wild Khurdish night with the cabaret artist. He had learned from his father that dhobis were expected to maintain a tradition of being the first to detect the smell of adultery in any household. But only once did he discover an aroma not comprised of Mr Bhoolabhoy's natural body odour and the familiar smell of the Hamam soap Mr Bhoolabhoy favoured. He got, just, a whiff of something uncharacteristic when checking a pair of smart y-fronted underpants, but the smell was quickly traced to the fact that the pants were new, still full of dressing, obviously bought in Ranpur and not washed before use. Was the purchase of new underpants significant in itself?

It wasn't until the evening of this day that Mr Bhoola-bhoy gave silent notice of the fact that his wife must have told him both about the *mali*'s dismissal and Tusker Sahib's illness. No member of the staff had mentioned either to him. They preferred him to find things out for himself. At five o'clock he strolled into the rear compound, inspected the kitchen-garden, then as if going to visit the invalid went to the gap in the wall which gave access to and a view of the compound of The Lodge, and stood for a while, hands behind back, observing the uncut grass, like a man looking at the scene of a recent disaster which he'd heard tell of, was inquisitive about but not responsible for.

Ibrahim, stationed where he could see but not be seen watched Mr Bhoolabhoy. He had known from early morning that Mr Bhoolabhoy was back but had said nothing to the Smalleys because it was one of those days on which for no clear reason none of them was speaking to the others unless it couldn't be helped. Such days occurred less frequently than the days on which it was simply the sahib and memsahib not speaking to one another except through him or one of them not speaking to him except through the other; but there was no real accounting for these days of mutual tripartite silence. They simply happened.

So he hadn't reported Mr Bhoolabhoy's return but had expected and looked forward to the visit the manager would presumably pay his old friend on hearing he was still not properly on his feet after a serious illness. He kept watch too, because he did not want to miss the row there was bound to be about the garden. His disappointment when Mr Bhoolabhoy turned away from the gap in the wall and went back to the hotel was profound. 'Chicken,' he thought.

He got up. Memsahib hadn't yet emerged from her siesta. Sahib was on the verandah, asleep over the papers he'd taken out of the scratched black deed box which for the past few days had been the cause of so much fuss and bother.

'It's in the Lease!' Tusker had cried on the day he'd been transferred from bedroom to verandah and saw the full extent of nearly three weeks of neglect. 'Bring me the box.'

'In the Lease or not in the Lease, dear,' Memsahib replied, smoothing his balding head between spoonfuls of broth, 'you're not to worry. Wait until Billy-Boy gets back. When he hears *mali* has resigned I'm sure he will quickly hire another. What is the point of worrying about the garden if it stops you getting well enough to enjoy it when you're better and something's been done about it?'

'You talk like a perfect fool. Always have done.'

'Yes, I know, Tusker. It's my own funny little way of making sense.'

'Are you going to bring me the bloody box or not?'

'Broth first. Bloody box later. But not today. If we eat up all our broth and then sleep like a good boy, who knows we might have a nice arrowroot biscuit with our afternoon tea, mightn't we, Ibrahim?'

'No arroot, Memsahib. Only Giyeftiff.'

'Then a nice digestive, Tusker dear.'

'It appals me.'

'What does?'

'A woman of nearly seventy talking like a kid of seven.'

Later that day, after taking tea and a plate of digestive biscuits into the bedroom where Tusker had retired in a fit of pique after lunch, Ibrahim carried Lucy-Mem's tea on to the verandah and found her sitting, gazing at the long grass, her ankles neatly crossed, her hands folded neatly on her lap.

'Thank you, Ibrahim,' she said without looking at him.

There was a run in one of her stockings. Her shoes had as good a polish on them as he could work up considering how long she had had them. She had a faraway look in her eyes if looking back into places she'd walked in her long-ago shoes.

The day after being accused of talking like a child she helped Ibrahim settle Tusker on the verandah, then went indoors, came out again and gave her husband the deed box and the key and left him to it to go shopping in the cantonment bazaar.

'You reeker!' Sahib shouted ten minutes later. Ibrahim had never fully understood the significance of this exclamation but liked the sound of it.

'Sahib wants?' he inquired, going out to where Tusker sat, well wrapped up, in the worm-eaten cane lounging chair. February, in Pankot, although warm and sunny, brought morning chills.

28

'Wants? Wants nothing. Has found. *Found.*' Flourishing a document. 'Now we'll see. Won't we just see. I'll sue the bitch from arsehole to Christmas.'

Ibrahim nodded approvingly. It was some weeks since Tusker Sahib had threatened anyone with anything from arsehole to Christmas. The threat was never carried out. Ibrahim had been metaphorically booted from one to the other many times but never physically even over a shorter distance. The thing was, Sahib was on the mend. Passion had revived in his body. Poor frail body. Not a patch on what it once was. Judging by the photographs in the living-room which showed a rather portly upright man, smartly uniformed, and earlier a younger man of medium height arm in arm with his little memsahib. In all the photographs the face looked well-fleshed, inclined to chubbiness and (Ibrahim imagined) a reddish complexion, the expression stern, certainly unsmiling. Now, although Tusker Sahib sometimes laughed loud and long, frequently burst out with that explosive derogatory Ha! and could often be discovered alone, smiling to himself and cracking his knuckles, the face was pale, the skin slack. Brown spots blotched his hands and arms. The English, once they began falling physically apart, did so with all their customary attention to detail, as if fitting themselves in advance for their own corpses to make sure they were going to be comfortable in them. A waste of time, really, since nowadays they all got cremated, a fashion that filled what was left of Ibrahim's Islamic soul with horror, and for which he blamed the Hindus among whom the English had lived too long for their eternal good. Let alone short-term good. 'What has become of the world,' Ibrahim wanted to know, 'when a fat money-grubbing Punjabi woman can cause a Christian Sahib a moment's disquiet?'

It was in his mind to say something of the sort to Tusker but just then Dr Mitra appeared to see how his patient was doing and Ibrahim was ordered off to get coffee for him, which he grinned at while boiling; boiling twice to make it doubly disgusting the way the doctor deserved to get it. Ibrahim detested Dr Mitra who spoke to him as so many high-toned Indian nobodys spoke to their own and other people's servants: as if they were no better than coolies touting for headloads at a railway station.

To Ibrahim the difference between being treated by men like Dr Mitra as if he were merely a machine and an anonymous one at that, and being sworn at by a Sahib like Tusker showed the distinction between a real sahib and the counterfeit. The same kind of distinction between a real memsahib and a self-appointed one was apparent when you compared Lucy-Mem with Mrs Bhoolabhoy.

Ibrahim regretted the passing of the days of the *raj* which he remembered as days when the servants were treated as members of the family, entitled to their good humours and bad humours, their sulks, their outbursts of temper, their right to show who was really boss, and their right to their discreetly appropriated perks, the feathers they had to provide for the nest when the nest they presently inhabited was abandoned by homeward-bound employers. Ibrahim had been brought up in such a nest. He still possessed the chits his father had been given by Colonel Moxon-Greife and a photograph of Colonel and Mrs Moxon-Greife with garlands round their necks, Going Home, in 1947. He had also inherited and preserved the two letters which Colonel Moxon-Greife had written to his father from England. Finally he had inherited the silence that greeted his father's two letters to Colonel Moxon-Greife inquiring about the possibilities of work in England for young Ibrahim, now going on twenty.

'Coffee, Sahib,' he announced, clattering the tray in front of Dr Mitra and got nothing in reply except a warming word from Tusker who said, 'What kept you, you old bugger? Pour the bloody stuff out then.' Which Ibrahim gladly did after first bending close to Dr Mitra and using an expression learned from an old friend whose father had looked after a family in French Pondicherry murmuring, 'Tuay maird, Sahib?' Dr Mitra nodded, not understanding, then said, '*Bus, bus,*' as Ibrahim slopped in the under-boiled goat's milk which he hoped was full of the germs of tuberculosis and amoebic dysentery.

30

Back in the kitchen he clattered pans. Mitra was the kind of man who would end up in Finsbury Park, London, N, removing people's gall bladders when they only had appendicitis. Mitra was Sahib's choice but Ibrahim trusted no Indian doctor to treat a white man. At a pinch a Muslim doctor would do, but a Hindu doctor never. The nearest European doctor though was down in Nansera, and he was an Austrian and a Catholic and the Catholics were worse than the Hindus because they believed in human suffering and uncontrolled birth-rates. The Hindus at least had offered a free transistor to every Indian having a vasectomy. But carrying a transistor had at once become unfashionable among the younger men. That lawyer's babu, Pandey, whose transistor was enormous, must have lost his marbles.

Lucy-Mem returned before Dr Mitra had gone. Ibrahim feared they would ask him to stay to lunch. They enjoyed company. But Mitra went and Lucy-Mem walked down to the side entrance with him. When she got back she came into the kitchen and said, 'Ibrahim, it's bad for the Sahib to have the box.'

'No, Memsahib, good.'

'Doctor Mitra says not good. For blood pressure very bad.'

'That is because Doctor Sahib does not understand Colonel Sahib's psychology. Colonel Sahib is not a Virgo like Memsahib.'

'What?'

'Not a Virgo. He is born under the Ram sign of Aries. He must always be butting-in, taking charge, solving non-problems, vindicating self and own beliefs.'

'That's just astronomy, Ibrahim.'

'Astrology, Memsahib, not astronomy.'

'Astronomy, astrology. No *box*, Ibrahim. Tonight I shall hide the box. Tomorrow if he asks for it you will say, *nai malum baksh.*'

'And sound bigger fool than I look? No, Memsahib. Box is good for recuperation. With box good juices flow. Without box juices cease. Sahib turns his face to the wall and all is up with him and with us.'

'No box,' she repeated. She vibrated in every frail bone. Her eyes were bright lavender, her skin like cracked bone china.

In the morning her eyes were grey again, like her hair which needed another blue-rinse. Not smiling at him she said in her lightest smallest voice, 'Perhaps you are right about the box. If he asks you you may give it to him. I am going to the chemist for his prescription.'

Within ten minutes of her going Tusker asked for the box and the key. Ibrahim gave them to him. Then he went into the bedroom. He gave Lucy-Mem's best pair of black high-heeled court shoes a special shine and replaced them on the steel rods at the bottom of the almirah. He dubbined the sensible shoes she had not worn since she and Tusker last went for a tramp, both wearing their tweeds, carrying stout sticks and accompanied by the dog they had inherited from the Blackshaws who had tried retirement (from Tea) in India but lost heart about it and gone home.

After washing his hands he replaced worn-down mothballs with new ones among the little pile of cashmere twin sets in the second drawer of the chest. He examined each woolly vest and more delicate items of underwear, inspecting them for snags and setting aside any that could do with attention either from Minnie's needle or his own expertise in invisible mending. Finally he opened her jewel box and removed the diamond ring and the diamond regimental brooch which she wore only on special occasions such as Ladies' Night at the Pankot Rifles Mess, poured a small measure of the gin into a medicine glass, dropped ring and brooch in and left them to clean themselves.

After they had soaked for ten minutes he dried them carefully, returned them to their velvet boxes then swigged the gin. The shadow of the disapproving Prophet fell on him.

'Waste not want not,' he said aloud. The sun shone again.

Aglow, he went out on to the verandah and stood arrested. Tusker Sahib was pale as death. The document in his hand shook. His mouth worked.

'Sahib?' he ventured.

Sahib took no notice. The document continued to shake, the mouth to work. Alarmed, he went down into the compound and stood where he could keep a watch on Tusker and a lookout for Memsahib. Seeing her returning he ran to meet her.

'I was wrong, Memsahib. Box bad.'

'Oh.'

She stood still. True memsahibs never panicked.

'Well, Ibrahim, we live and learn. How bad?'

Ibrahim raised his shoulders.

'Let us go together, Ibrahim, and see.'

She led the way. Arrived by Tusker's side for a moment Ibrahim thought the Sahib had gone. He sat slumped, eyes shut, mouth open. But suddenly he opened one eye.

'Oh dear,' Lucy-Mem said. 'Have I woken us from our little nap?' She clasped her hands under her chin.

'We were not having our little nap. We were thinking our little thoughts. Plotting our little plots and planning our little plans.'

'Plans for what, Tusker dear?'

'Murder.'

'And who is to be the unhappy victim?'

By way of reply he handed her the document, a single sheet of paper, a letter in fact, which she complained she could not read without her spectacles.

'Then that explains it. You didn't have the bloody things on last time.'

'Last time, Tusker?'

'Last time. When you said, "How nice," or "that's a relief" or some such footling thing.'

'If I commented on it dear I must have read it. And if I read it then I must have had my glasses on. So stop fretting. Read it to me and remind me.'

She gave the document back; rather, had it snatched from her arthritic hand.

33

'Dear Colonel Smalley,' Tusker Sahib suddenly shouted, as if he'd now decided she was deaf as well as short-sighted. ' "Mr Bhoolabhoy has explained your objection to proposed rent-increase. Agreed therefore to renew tenancy of Lodge from July 1st, 1971 to June 30th, 1972 on same terms and conditions as stated in clause 2 current agreement now otherwise expiring. Please countersign and return copy this letter enclosed both parties attaching letter to expiring agreement making no further need further formalities this year." Signed, "Mrs Bhoolabhoy, Prop." '

'Well?' Lucy asked.

'Well? You call that well?'

'You were pleased at the time. Chuffed in fact.'

'Chuffed? What kind of damnfool word is that?'

'One of your words, Tusker. Doesn't it mean pleased?'

'It may or may not.' He was still shouting. 'But I'm not pleased now. You were supposed to check this letter. I didn't know you couldn't *see* it. How could I know a thing like that when all you said when you gave it back – I remember now – was, "oh, well done, Tusker".'

'Wasn't it well done?'

'The bitch cheated us. Two heads are better than one you're always saying. You've said it for years. You've brainwashed me into thinking it. You've made me *rely*. So it's us that's been conned. Us, not me. *I'm* not taking the responsibility.'

Lucy-Mem drew up a chair and sat down. Ibrahim squatted nearby, ready to give advice if asked. After all it was a family crisis. As if sensing this in some remote corner of its dim brain the dog shambled out from its place behind Tusker's chair, collapsed at Lucy-Mem's feet and gazed mournfully from one to the other.

'I'm not very bright over business matters,' she said. Tusker opened his mouth to speak but she ignored this and went on: 'If you want me to understand in what way Mrs Bhoolabhoy has conned us you'll have to explain it in words of one syllable.'

'How the bloody hell can anyone do that when the two key words are current and agreement both of which have more than one syllable to start with? I've just read the damned letter out clearly enough. Can't you even take it in now?'

'Tusker, all I can take in is that you are raising your voice to me, abusing me, I won't say in front of the servants because we have only one.'

'It looks as though we're going to need another, doesn't it?'

A long pause: Tusker glaring, Lucy fingering her string of seed-pearls, Bloxsaw panting, Ibrahim holding his breath.

She let go of the pearls and stroked Bloxsaw's head. The dog turned its blood-shot eyes to look at Ibrahim as if to share the caress with him.

'I can't think what you mean, Tusker, after the way Ibrahim has slaved for us while you've been poorly.'

Ibrahim inclined his head to one side. Then waited. Behind Colonel-Memsahib's gentle manner he recognized the familiar steel. Himself an old devotee of Hollywood films, as she was, he knew Memsahib was about to go into her Bette Davis bit. He had seen her at it when she thought herself alone, strutting up and down, arms folded, waggling her old bottom, muttering in that unmistakable voice. If the Sahib had another attack here and now and she was the only one with him and he asked for his pills she would remain (*that's* what she was thinking) just where she was, stroking Bloxsaw's head, eyes wide open staring at the canna lilies, pretending not to notice his distress, his fight for breath, his struggle to get out of the wicker-chair and fetch them himself. She would go on sitting fondling the dog, alert for the sound of collapse. Then after a minute or two she would go inside and call out in a calm voice, 'Ibrahim? Ibrahim? Fetch Dr Mitra immediately will you? Tell him the master is ill. Very very ill.'

For a moment, though, the master seemed very well. He said, 'What on earth are you talking about?'

'Well Ibrahim did, didn't he? *Slave.*'

'So what?'

'So how can you talk about getting another servant?'

'Yes, I see.' With exaggerated marks of patience and of suffering fools he folded the letter and put it back in the box and turned the key. 'Personally,' he said, 'I have always assumed that another means an other. One other. Not a different one, not one in lieu of one already. An other. Another. A *mali* for instance. To cut the sodding grass. Except that we're not hiring one except over my dead body.'

'Well yes, I see. I misunderstood. And you're quite right. The grass is Mrs Bhoolabhoy's responsibility. So you've always said, and so it is, it's in the lease.'

'Not any more.'

'How can that be, Tusker dear?'

'Because we haven't had a lease since last July. We've only had that conning bloody letter. The one I've just read out to you, very clearly and distinctly.'

Tusker put his head back and shut his eyes. Lucy-Mem raised her shoulders in mystification, and made a funny little face at Ibrahim.

Encouraged he said, 'What the sahib is saying, memsahib, is I think that Proprietor's letter last year renewing tenancy until June 30th next referred only to renewal of terms and conditions as stated in clause two all other clauses not being renewed, for example perhaps clauses stating proprietor's responsibility for exterior and interior decoration and upkeep of garden. Isn't it?'

'Why, Ibrahim!' Lucy-Mem exclaimed, clapping her hands together in surprise. 'How quick you are. Isn't he Tusker? Is that what the letter means? I should never have seen that.'

Ibrahim beamed, then beamed at Tusker but found the eyes open and an expression on Sahib's face that indicated no good.

'Yes,' Sahib said. 'How quick. Too bloody quick by half. So he can get out quick, too. Get up from there and get out. Bloody scoundrel!'

'What have I done, Sahib?'

'I'll tell you what you've done, as if you didn't know. You've been disloyal. You didn't see the position like that

36

in a split second. You've probably damned well known since last year. I can picture the lot of you laughing like drains. You and that thieving lot down there that Madam Bhoolabhoy calls servants. Ha!'

Ibrahim was on his feet now. 'What the Sahib says, the Sahib says. But what the Sahib says is not in accordance with facts. How could I be knowing such things? How could those you call idle fellows be knowing? Also has not the grass been cut since last July until only recently with *mali* gone to the Shiraz? Was bathroom not white-washed last December and seats renewed?'

'Whitewash! Ha! Too true. Whitewash. Wool over the eyes. Cunning bitch. I said get out.'

Ibrahim appealed to Lucy-Mem.

'Sahib says get out. From here, yes, but from here to where?'

'To bloody Mecca for all I care,' Tusker said.

'Mecca,' Ibrahim said, letting his shoulders droop as if exhausted by the very thought of such a journey. 'Muslim old people's excursion. Twilight coach trip. Depart Harringay 0800, with packed lunch of curry puffs and crates of Watney's Pale. Sing-song all way to Southend and back and Kiss Me Sailor hat. What is Sahib taking me for? Day-tripping bugger-fellow?'

Most of this was muttered. With dignity he went inside. With dignity he paused to listen.

'How could you, Tusker? How could you treat Ibrahim so unkindly?'

'He's listening you bloody fool.'

'What does it matter if he is? But he never. listens. He has too much pride. You can't treat Ibrahim like a *servant*, Tusker. He is, I know, but then he isn't. And he's a well-travelled man, a man of the world.'

'Illegal immigrant. God kicked out. That's my opinion.'

'*Pride*, Tusker. That's what I'm talking about. You have no pride any longer. Don't interrupt. And because you have no pride neither of us does. We should have gone home.'

'And who was it who wanted to stay on?'

'You wanted. I agreed. We should have gone home at least after those years in Bombay. We should have gone home after the débâcle. Now it's too late.'

'What do you mean, débâcle?'

'You know exactly what I mean, Tusker.'

'I don't. I've been married to you for more than forty years and I still don't know what the bloody hell you're talking about.'

'At the moment I'm talking about pride. And you have hurt Ibrahim's.'

'You never do that of course, do you? Oh, no. Who was it sacked him last then? Tell me that? And who sulks with him for days after he's been sacked by you, eh? Um?'

'If you had pride, Tusker, instead of sitting here raving and ranting and working yourself into a tizzy about a box full of old paper, you'd write a firm but polite note to Mrs Bhoolabhoy inquiring about her intention in regard to the state of the garden.'

'And have her draw my attention to that letter? Make me look a perfect fool? She conned us. Think I'm going to give her the satisfaction of knowing I've cottoned on at last but know I can't do a bloody thing about it?'

'Then forget about the garden until Billy-Boy comes back.'

'I'll forget about it, don't worry. And a fat lot of use that hen-pecked little sod is if the bitch has made up her mind. Don't think I don't know she has, and why. She's letting the whole place go to pot deliberately. So let it go to pot. Let the bloody grass come in through the windows. I don't care. I'm tired. I'm going to bed.'

'Then I'll help you, Tusker.'

'Don't bother.'

'It's my duty to bother.'

'In your interest too, eh? That's more like. What's to happen to you if I drop dead?'

'That's not something I care to think about, Tusker. Come on. Upsadaisy.'

Ibrahim went his barefoot way through the kitchen and

squatted on the narrow verandah at the back. He lit a Charminar. What, he wondered, was a daybarkle? Daybarckle, Day Barkle? Night Barkle? Whatever it was he fancied he was in the middle of one.

Five minutes later, hearing her footsteps, he nipped out the cigarette and blew the smoke away above his head but remained squatting until her presence became positive and commanding. He got up slowly, his shoulders still drooped, but not quite abject.

'Thank you, Ibrahim. You have done my shoes so beautifully – and my little bits of jewellery too, no?'

He inclined his head. She must have been looking at them. Why?

Her misshapen old fingers twitched at her beads. She said, 'You must, must be patient with Sahib. We must both be patient. Very patient. You must please forgive him for what he said. Doctor Mitra is very worried. And I am worried. The Sahib simply isn't himself. At least – he is more not himself than usual. May I confide in you, Ibrahim?'

He put his hands behind his back, this being the best stance in which to receive a confidence.

She began: 'When a man who has always been active—' – her eyes changed colour – '—and suddenly finds himself inactive he tends, how shall I put it, to exaggerate every teeniest tiniest little thing, *malum*?'

'*Malum*, Colonel-Memsahib.'

'He sees mountains in molehills. Broth – for instance. Long grass. Tired canna lilies. The way the Shiraz Hotel casts all that wretched shadow when the sun comes up. So that the dew stays longer than it should. And the dew staying longer means more nourishment reaches the roots of the grass. *Malum?*'

Ibrahim tilted his head but frowned slightly to convey his understanding that he was in the presence of a superior intellect.

She fidgeted.

'Let us walk,' she suddenly announced. He accompanied her into the back compound.

CHAPTER THREE

'We are people in shadow, Ibrahim,' she said, then stopped
her slow pacing and glanced up at the glass and concrete
structure that had helped put them there. 'And the dew
does not so much nourish us as aggravate our rheumatism
and our tempers. I need a young man. A boy will do. Do
you know one?'

Ibrahim blinked. 'Memsahib?'

'A stout youth. You must surely have among your vast
acquaintanceship in Pankot such a one. I will pay him
reasonably. Rather, I will pay you for procuring him and
you will pay him for me. The Sahib must not know of this
arrangement, although I might persuade him to increase
your wage to reduce the cost of the boy to me.'

The mind boggles, Ibrahim thought. She is an old lady.
He said in a low voice, 'What sort of boy, Memsahib?'

'Oh, any sort, so long as he is strong and willing and not
too expensive, and dependable, and could report for duty
say three days a week. If necessary he could live here to
be close at hand when needed. But yes, I see one snag—'

He wondered which of the many snags she had seen to
such an arrangement. She went on:

'There is the question of tools. In this connection tools
are essential. We had better do nothing until Mr Bhoolabhoy is back. It is all very difficult. Mr Bhoolabhoy may
have to be a party to the arrangement. Almost certainly he
will. *Arrangement.* Let's not call it deception. Yes, Mr
Bhoolabhoy will have to be a party to it. In fact the boy
must appear to be Mr Bhoolabhoy's boy, quite apart from
the question of tools, which I do not have, but Mr Bhoolabhoy must lend his. You understand, don't you Ibrahim?
I couldn't afford to hire the boy and also hire or buy the
tools essential to him to do his job. And another thing.
This, please understand, is only to be an interim arrange-

ment. The boy's hopes of a permanent position should not
be raised. An interim arrangement, yes, that's the way to
put it. An interim arrangement to help Sahib recover his
own health and strength and not dissipate it worrying about
this and that. His blood pressure is very high. It is danger-
ous for him to exert himself physically and emotionally.
But I have to think of my own peace of mind, too, so if during this convalescent period I could obtain the services of
such a boy, regularly, to give me peace of mind, then when
Sahib is fully himself again I could confess everything,
explain that he was really my boy, not Mr Bhoolabhoy's.
Well, not mine alone, Ibrahim. Ours. Yours and mine.
Couldn't we between us find and use such a boy?'

'Memsahib,' he began, automatically finding the word
somewhere in the still centre of his whirling mind.

'I mean he could be of service to you too, in odd ways.
But mainly to me. A boy capable of cutting grass, tending
the flowers, especially the lilies. I don't want to lose my
husband, Ibrahim. And if I'm not to, then the grass must
be kept neat and the canna lilies watered. You were wrong
about the box. You've admitted that. You are wrong when
you think being able to be cross about the garden helps
him. It doesn't. It hinders him. He's not capable of sustain-
ing shocks, nor capable of surviving while in a constant
state of petty annoyance.'

The penny had now dropped. Ibrahim felt both relieved
and disappointed. Uninterested for himself in a boy, the
situation he'd first assumed she was outlining would have
added piquancy to life; but Memsahib simply wanted a
mali. Such anti-climax.

'I know of such a boy, Memsahib. Young, strong, willing.
My younger sister's brother-in-law's nephew, recently getting push because of rising cost of living and international
inflationary spiral.' In fact he knew of several boys who
might answer to that description, who technically didn't but
could be fitted to it. It was just a question of going down
to the bazaar to cast his net. And the proposal could turn
out to be financially attractive. One might presume to
make a small profit.

41

'How much would such a boy cost, Ibrahim?'

He named a figure, and added, 'Plus keep.'

'Oh, dear.'

'There is another perhaps cheaper boy I've heard of, not so bright, but very strong and willing.'

'That would be better. But there is still the problem about food. You know what a close eye Colonel Sahib keeps on the house expenditure.'

Ibrahim blinked again. It was Memsahib who really kept the eyes, but he had to admit he'd occasionally come across Tusker poring over her accounts and bills and muttering. After which they usually had a row. So he also had to admit there could be difficulties about feeding a boy whom Tusker was to be deceived into believing was employed by Smith's. Although the time-honoured arrangement was – because there were no proper cooking facilities in The Lodge's servants' quarters – that Ibrahim's food should be cooked and if required eaten in the servants' quarters of the hotel, the Smalleys provided basic rations in the shape of monthly doles of flour, tea, salt, sugar, cooking oil, and paid a subsistence allowance to enable him to buy what meat and vegetables he needed.

His food was usually cooked by Minnie with whom he had an understanding on various matters; an understanding respected by her colleagues. It was a cushy enough billet. He was able to save most of his monthly wage. There was always buckshee rum from the stock at the hotel. Each year, at the Id, Tusker Sahib and Lucy-Mem presented him with something new to wear. His laundry was satisfactorily dealt with by the hotel dhobi-wallah in exchange for a packet or two of Charminar cigarettes. It was like belonging to a Union without having to pay the dues.

But his most treasured possession, immaculately preserved, was the last remaining set of long white tunic and trousers which his father had worn on mess nights in the days of Colonel Moxon-Greife, and into which he had long since grown, and worn once or twice on the rare occasions when Colonel and Mrs Smalley were guests at the Pankot Rifles Mess. Personal servants, although no longer *de rigueur*, were nevertheless a status symbol. As such you stood behind your Sahib, or your Memsahib, got nicely pissed in the kitchen, passing to and fro, and anyway had the thrill of doing things in the way your father had done them and his father before him, even though the Sahibs and Memsahibs at the long gleaming table were mostly as black as you were yourself.

Tusker Sahib had given him a cummerbund and turban ribbon woven in the colours of the Mahwar Regiment. He had worn his regalia last at the New Year, when all the junior officers, a few of the senior officers and even some of the officers' ladies got quite merry celebrating the recent victory over Pakistan. Tusker and Lucy-Mem were the only British people at the table, and Ibrahim was proud, really, that of all that gathering his own Sahib was the only one who got superbly drunk in the way he remembered his father describing the way Colonel Moxon-Greife always got drunk.

'First, my son,' his father told him, 'Colonel Sahib speaking with much vitality, but in a very discreet way, understand? Then towards end of the dinner he stops speaking at random, and sits at attention. Speaking only when spoken to, but always speaking to the point. Hand always on glass. Glass always being refilled. He sits at head of table. He is President of the Mess. Never do I have to help him to stand when time comes for this. He is rigid. "Mr Vice," he says, standing, meaning Mr Vice-President, who is then also standing and giving toast of The King-Emperor. All then drinking. Colonel Moxon-Greife then sitting down. After that immovable. We take him out in his chair. It is special chair with iron circular attachments, through which poles are passed, so that it becomes like dooli. Some fellows come in with poles. The poles are passed through the rings. We carry him out and across the road to his bungalow. I put him to bed. At six o'clock next morning he is on parade. A real burra Sahib. On Ladies'

Nights he drinks only little little less. So that he walks back with Memsahib across road to bungalow.'

Ibrahim had never been to the Pankot Mess except on Ladies' Night and since he'd been employed by Tusker and Lucy-Mem, Tusker had been only once to the Mess alone, and come back disappointingly sober. It had been different in January, when Ibrahim accompanied them both and stood behind Lucy-Mem's chair, in his regalia, watching Tusker Sahib knocking it back on the other side of the table and then, becoming rigid, suddenly raising his glass and saying in his loud clear English voice, 'Ma Gandhi, God Bless her,' and receiving what sounded to Ibrahim like murmurs of approbation and a grin from Colonel Menektara at the head of the table but which Lucy-Mem described afterwards, on the way home, as mutters of disapproval and smiles of embarrassment. 'You don't know India, *yet*!' Tusker had cried. '*They* knew what I meant. *Ma*, Mother. Mother India. For Chrissakes.'

For a day or so after the mess night Tusker had been alternately subdued and quarrelsome. For a while, subsequently, on an even keel. Then came his attack. Memsahib had had to seek Ibrahim's help because Tusker was taken ill in the early hours of the morning while sitting on one of the viceregal thrones; was slumped, unconscious, half-on half-off, his pyjama trousers round his ankles, white legs spread.

Ibrahim had been embarrassed, not only at the sight of the Burra Sahib in such an undignified position, but before then, because although at one o'clock in the morning when he heard Lucy-Mem calling and knocking on the door of his hut he was where every good bearer should be who had to be up at cockcrow – on his charpoy – Minnie was under him and at last showing signs of taking charge, which was something you had to let Minnie do if you weren't to get the cold shoulder and soggy chapattis for the rest of the week.

'Coming, Memsahib!' he cried when he realized who it was. The overstatement of the week. Withdrawing, stifling Minnie's anticipated shriek of outrage with one hand he hissed in her ear, 'Be quiet. Intruders.' Then covering Minnie with one blanket he wrapped another round himself, groped his way in the dark to the door and unbolted it. Memsahib's torch blinded him.

'Please help me, Ibrahim. Burra Sahib is very ill.' She seldom called Tusker Burra Sahib except at times of crisis. She tottered back down the path, in her dressing-gown, while Ibrahim struggled into shirt and trousers and then followed her.

'In there,' she said. 'I've rung Dr Mitra. But otherwise I don't know what to do. I mean for the best. Whether to move him. In any case I couldn't easily do it by myself. Would you please take a look?'

One of the odd things about The Lodge was that although between the bathroom and the bedroom there was a doorway there was no door: instead a pair of swing-to louvred half-shutters such as cowboys in western films pushed through. When Ibrahim first came to the Smalleys it was explained to him that if he entered the bedroom and saw a towel draped over these shutters it meant that the bathroom-cum-WC was occupied. There was a towel in position now. He hesitated to enter.

'Don't worry, Ibrahim. Forget the towel. But the towel is touching. Almost a sign of grace.' Her voice had changed pitch and intonation, surely. Who was she being now? 'I'm sorry, you can't know what I'm talking about. It's just that he must have been feeling ill when he got out of bed. Quietly, not to disturb me. Not that I was properly asleep.' One of the twin beds was shrouded by a mosquito net which in Pankot was never necessary but which Memsahib liked. She pushed through the shutters. And there Sahib was. 'It's how I found him when I woke and began to worry. I rang Dr Mitra. Did I say? But if there's anything we can do before he gets here we ought to, unless it's too late. Tusker? Bring me a blanket, Ibrahim. I should have thought of a blanket.'

He brought a blanket. He helped her drape it round Tusker's head and neck, himself eased the shoulders away from the wall so that as much warmth as possible could reach

45

his back. Above the smell of scented disinfectant there was a faint smell of excrement. Flush toilets had been fitted at the main hotel. Below these thrones were only sanitation pans which the sweeper removed through a hole in the outside wall. Mrs Bhoolabhoy could sit to her heart's content on a pukka loo. Sahib and Memsahib had to make do with these old thunder-boxes. Colonel Memsahib personally made sure that they were immaculately kept and gave the sweeper baksheesh for polishing the new mahogany-stained seats. But, in Ibrahim's opinion, when flush-toilets were installed in the hotel they should have been put in at The Lodge as well. Flush-toilets were part of the Christian religion, like sitting in your own dirty bath water. In the Yookay even if there was only one bath and one WC in a house big enough for twelve people (like his brother-in-law's house in Finsbury Park) they had for the English the status of shrines.

When first coming to The Lodge, Ibrahim had mentally labelled the twin-loos His and Hers. And it was from His – after Tusker had suddenly groaned, opened glazed eyes and murmured 'Where am I?' and Memsahib had cried out, 'Here Tusker dear, with me and Ibrahim' – that Ibrahim had removed Tusker and carried him (light as a feather he seemed for so hot-tempered a man) well wrapped in the blanket (which had had to be burnt next day along with his pyjamas) and placed him gently on his bed.

For the next three hours he had been alternately running between bedroom and kitchen, boiling water for tea, for a hot-water bottle for Burra Sahib's feet which were deathly cold, making coffee for Lucy-Mem and for Dr Mitra, pouring tots of brandy, or squatting on the verandah within call smoking one of Tusker's India King cigarettes (a present from Colonel Menektara) because his own were back at the hut (and Minnie no doubt no longer was, so he felt entitled to scrounge).

When Dr Mitra left at about four o'clock Ibrahim was deputed to light his way to his car. Unthanked he made his way back. Memsahib called, 'Ibrahim.'

He went into the bedroom.

'Sahib wants a word.'

Ibrahim stood by the bed. A little of Tusker's colour had come back, but not much. His eyes were closed.

'Here is Ibrahim, Tusker dear.'

The eyes remained closed but the left hand was slowly raised. After a moment Ibrahim took it.

'I told him it was you who carried him to bed, Ibrahim,' Memsahib said when they were back in the living-room. 'I'm afraid he's still too weak to thank you. It's his heart. Not too serious an attack, but we may have a long hard haul. I'm not sure, you see, that when Dr Mitra advises a week in the hospital tomorrow he will be – co-operative.'

Ibrahim had his hands behind his back. Her own were suddenly pressed one to each cheek of her unmade-up sharp old little face.

'Memsahib sleeping now. I will bring tea and arroot. Arroot very good for sleeping.'

'Arrowroot.'

'*Han,* arroot.'

Ten minutes later he took the tray in. She was in bed, but sitting upright under the mosquito net, which was parted so that she could watch Tusker who was now asleep.

Ibrahim murmured, 'Ibrahim dossing down in living-room rest of night, keeping watch. Memsahib sleeping.'

Curled up in a blanket in front of the fireplace which was still warm with the embers of the pine-log fire lit that evening he kept nodding off. Whenever he woke he crept into the bedroom. She had kept her bedside light on, but covered the shade with a cloth. There was just sufficient light to see that all was well, that both slept: Memsahib upright against her piled-up pillows, under that cascade of cobwebbed net playing in her dreams, perhaps, Miss Havisham in Great Expectations, still waiting for her groom.

At 5 a.m. he kicked out the last spark of the wood fire in case at dawn there was a mysterious association of ideas and The Lodge burnt down because she had dreamed it.

These images and recollections passed through his mind as he stood with Lucy-Mem in the rear compound. His heart had begun to melt but he hardened it again. She was playing with the beads, telling them off, calculating by means of a handy abacus slung round her withered old neck the cost of a new *mali*.

She said, 'Oh what a tangled web we weave, once we practise to deceive. Even for the best of reasons and for but a limited time.'

She was perhaps waiting for him to make some foolish and generous declaration about the problem of the boy's meals. Actually there was no problem. More casual visitors shared the food in the servants' quarters at the Hotel than even the astute Mrs Bhoolabhoy could guess.

'Of course,' Memsahib said, 'since this boy's services would only be needed a few days a week the question of feeding him is not so complex. Wouldn't he be satisfied with his wage? He has some other part-time occupation? I'm referring to the cheaper boy, the one not so bright but strong and willing.'

'The cheaper boy is cheaper, Memsahib, because at the moment all but destitute unlike the other boy who although given push has wits about him and can pick up this and that and the other. Cheaper boy I think is more deserving case. He is the kind of boy we call always at the back of the queue. Very quiet boy. But loyal, honest and sturdy.' He would have to find a boy who roughly fitted the description.

Memsahib fixed her gaze at a middle distance. She said, 'Sturdy boys take a lot of feeding.'

He was about to say that by sturdy he meant a wiry non-meat eater but stopped himself in time. He hoped she would not ask his name or whether he was a Mohammedan or a Hindu. He said, 'If such a cheaper boy is given the wage Memsahib has in mind and one good meal a day he would work every day in the garden until it is tidy and easier to keep up.'

'Yes,' she said, then folded her arms and began to stroll again. 'But it would have to be made clear to him that it is only temporary employment. And in any case, Ibrahim, no steps must be taken until Mr Bhoolabhoy is back and I have had the opportunity of establishing what the situation is. If it then seems that the only thing for it is to hire a *mali* ourselves, without Burra Sahib knowing, Mr Bhoolabhoy will have to be a party to the little deception because of the question of tools. In fact—'

She came to a standstill.

'In fact, even Mrs Bhoolabhoy may have to know about it. What a wretched thought. But if for weeks there has been no *mali* and suddenly there is a *mali*, Colonel Sahib will not only be pleased, which is the object of the exercise, but may even be cock-a-hoop and when he is better, well enough to go to the hotel for a meal, he might be tempted to say something to Mrs Bhoolabhoy about her having backed down.'

Suddenly she chortled.

Ibrahim smiled. 'Memsahib?'

'Backed down! Can you imagine the sight of Mrs Bhoolabhoy backing down?'

She chortled again. Ibrahim laughed. She had one hand near her throat, the other on her hip. Now she gave a full-throated laugh, then tapped him on the arm. 'We can't think of everything. Let's forget Mrs Bhoolabhoy. The thing is to get Sahib well first. And we must be diplomatic. Very diplomatic. I shall rely on you to a very considerable extent, Ibrahim. If it seems there's really nothing Mr Bhoolabhoy can do about a *mali*, then I'd prefer not to discuss things with him further. It would be better if you discussed them.'

'Memsahib means in regard to use of tools?'

'Well that, yes, but before discussing tools you would have to say that since I think Burra Sahib will never get fully well again while the garden continues in the state it is, I am prepared – so long as Burra Sahib remains in ignorance of the fact – prepared out of my own resources – to see it put right. After that we should have to see. It is a question of one step at a time.'

'Also a question of money. Memsahib spoke of the

49

possibility of persuading Colonel Sahib to increase my own wage.'

'To reduce the cost of the boy to me,' she said almost inaudibly but promptly.

'Memsahib I am not fully understanding this.'

'It only means that to pay the *mali* you would be getting some money from Sahib as well as from me. But a rise is a rise is a rise. Come the day when we no longer need *mali* you would have that extra money for yourself. *Malum?*'

'*Malum*, Memsahib.' He was sure there was a snag somewhere.

'Dear Ibrahim.' Not looking at him she pressed his left forearm. 'What should I do without you? What would either of us do? Just tell me the moment Mr Bhoolabhoy returns, so that I can have a word with him in private.'

But he was unable to do this because on that day no one was speaking to anyone. And although it was Memsahib's turn to take the dog for a walk and she could have doubled this duty with that of going down to Gulab Singh, the chemist, it was he who in the end had had to do so. She had sat on in the living-room after breakfast writing letters at her escritoire while Tusker – shawled – sat out on the verandah reading a book from the Club library, making notes in the margins which the librarian had more than once asked him not to do, and saying Ha! to break the monotony. Both were deaf to one another, to Ibrahim, and now to the tiresome whining and padding to and fro of Bloxsaw between living-room and verandah and garage (which was his home, there being no car there). All Bloxsaw wanted was to be taken notice of, but they weren't speaking to Bloxsaw either. In the end to stop himself going mad Ibrahim fetched the lead, viciously attached it to the collar muttering 'Shaitan! Shaitan!' then dragged the reluctant beast down to the cantonment bazaar to the Excelsior Coffee Shop in what was still called War Memorial Square, which wasn't a proper square at all but the place where the road from West Hill met the one from East Hill.

As usual there were several idle people clustered round

the base of the memorial, among them the Englishman whose long matted red hair reached to his shoulders. He had been in and out of Pankot long enough now for no one to take much notice of him. He had no shoes. His only possessions were a canvas bag, a pair of torn trousers and a blanket – all as filthy as himself.

'Seen our English Hippie?' Tusker had asked Lucy shortly before his illness.

'I've seen a hippie.'

'That's what I asked.'

'He can't be English.'

'He is. I spoke to him.'

'*Spoke* to him?'

'Why not? Tipped him a rupee too. He gave me a lovely smile. The sort that says, Sucker! Comes from Liverpool. He's into what he calls mudditoyshun.'

Sometimes, out of curiosity, if the hippie was there, and came begging at the coffee shop, Ibrahim threw him a few paise. The strange young man was adept at catching them in mid-air but never seemed to resent scrabbling in the dust for those he muffed. Today he just sat with his back to the memorial, either asleep or drugged to the eyeballs.

'Management is back,' the cook at Smith's told him when he called in to pass the time of day, to delay his arrival back at the silent Lodge. 'Ah,' Ibrahim said, and presently returned home. But it was still a day of silence. She waved him away when he ventured near her escritoire. Tusker Sahib was still busy with the library book. Bloxsaw was now too exhausted to care whether he was taken notice of or not. The creature hated the walks with the same sulky passion it whined to be taken on them. Hysterical when locked anywhere it lost all initiative when free. He had never known a dog so intent on getting in sack-time. It had now collapsed on the verandah panting like a pack-dog that had been harnessed to a sledge and driven through a blizzard. It would probably sulk for the rest of the day, like its master and mistress.

51

Mr Bhoolabhoy did not come over to see his old friend who had been ill until after dinner when perhaps he hoped Tusker would be in bed. But Tusker wasn't. He was in the living-room still annotating the library book. The deed box was on his chairside table. Memsahib sat opposite, her spectacles on the end of her nose, knitting one of the awful pullovers which Sahib grumbled about having to wear. Since Memsahib took months to knit a pullover, and knitted it in full view of Tusker Sahib, Ibrahim never understood why it wasn't until he got it for Christmas that he complained about the pattern and colours.

Ibrahim was in the kitchen preparing the trays for bed-cocoa when he heard Mr Bhoolabhoy arrive. He held his breath, waiting for the storm which he was supposed to have averted by tipping Memsahib off that the Manager was back. But the storm never came. 'Have a drink, old Billy-Boy,' he heard Tusker say. 'When did you get back then? Had a gay old time in jolly Ranpur did you? Ibrahim!'

He went in. They were all re-settling in chairs. He was told to bring glasses, beer, gin and lime juice.

'And some biscuits, Ibrahim,' Memsahib said in her gentlest manner, as if they had been having a lovely companionable day.

'Oh, I'm fine, now,' Tusker was saying to Mr Bhoolabhoy.

While he busied himself preparing the tray he paused every so often, anticipating the moment when the subject of the garden could no longer be ignored.

'Where are those drinks, then?' Tusker shouted.

'Coming, Sahib.'

He took the tray in, poured what he was ordered and handed the glasses round. Billy-Boy was describing the new hotel in Ranpur, and the Go-Go-Inn. Tusker was smiling, smiling. Between his chair and Mr Bhoolabhoy's was the chairside table with the deed box still on it. Memsahib asked him whether he had been to the pictures and if so what had they been showing.

Extraordinary. Ibrahim returned to the kitchen and then pottered about from kitchen to bedroom, turning back the

52

sheets, ensuring there were no old towels in the bathroom that should be in the dhobi basket. He dragged the work out for as long as possible, longing for the moment when the word *mali* was mentioned. He would have to pretend to Memsahib that he had not known Mr Bhoolabhoy was back, if she was cross with him in the morning and accused him of being the cause of the row that would surely begin at any moment.

He retired to the verandah. But there was no row. At ten o'clock Mr Bhoolabhoy said goodnight, they waved him off and then told Ibrahim he could lock up. They went into the bedroom. He locked up, cleared the glasses and then sat out on the rear verandah waiting for Minnie to give some sign of life.

The rear verandah was blocked at one end by the wall of the bathroom and presently from there he heard a peculiar sound. An astonishing sound. He could hardly believe it. He must be mistaken. But within a few moments it was beyond dispute. The sound was coming through the little air-grille high up in the wall. The sound he heard was the sound of Colonel Sahib crying.

'Oh, Tusker, Tusker,' Memsahib's voice came drifting through. 'What are you doing? What is the matter? You mustn't be upset. But who is to speak if you do not speak and you oughtn't to speak. What does it matter about a little bit of grass, my silly, silly, Tusker, what does it matter? What is grass? Forget grass. Billy-Boy will see that the grass is cut, I'm sure, and even if he doesn't, who cares whether it is cut or not so long as it is not cut for both of us, and so long as we're together?'

'Oh, Lucy,' Tusker Sahib said, and Ibrahim got up and left.

In the morning when she gave him the shopping list and a letter to post by airmail, she said, 'I think we must mount *Operation Mali*. Malum?'

'*Malum*, Colonel-Memsahib.'

CHAPTER FOUR

The new *mali*'s name was Joseph and he was a Christian.

'Orphan boy,' Mr Bhoolabhoy said. It was Mr Bhoolabhoy who had found him, a fact which potentially gave a touch of authenticity to the deception because when Tusker Sahib said to Mr Bhoolabhoy something like, 'I see after all there's a new *mali*' and Mr Bhoolabhoy agreed that there was he could add that his name was Joseph an orphan-boy from Ranpur whom he, Mr Bhoolabhoy, had found in pitiful circumstances, badly in need of some employment. The touch of authenticity was only potential because it depended on Tusker Sahib opening up a conversation about the new *mali* in that kind of way.

But he didn't. He didn't open up a conversation at all, with anyone. One of the great disappointments of *Operation Mali* was that on the morning Joseph at last arrived and began to cut the grass at The Lodge, Tusker said nothing. He continued to say nothing. To him, *mali* seemed invisible. Which was patently ridiculous. Day after day, while Tusker sat on the verandah, Joseph slaved away at the grass in full view of the master of the house who was now busily engaged in writing in an exercise book. Even when the two were within speaking distance – Tusker on the verandah and Joseph kneeling in the bed of canna lilies just below, nothing was said.

Memsahib said nothing either – either to *mali* or to Tusker about *mali*'s presence. When she and Ibrahim were alone she sometimes said things like, 'Your *mali* is doing well,' or, 'Your *mali* seems a nice quiet boy,' and then changed the subject. This was quite understandable to Ibrahim. In order to please Tusker she had had to deceive him and to cleanse her mind of this deception she was having to deceive herself by thinking day after day of Joseph as a boy with whom she had nothing to do, even though it was

54

she who was going to foot the bill out of funds whose nature Ibrahim did not inquire into. (The housekeeping? Her appetite, never great, seemed less than ever. She now ate like a bird.)

It was Tusker Sahib's own kind of self-deception that puzzled and fascinated him. It was as though – after making all that fuss – he had decided to occupy a world in which neither the garden nor the *mali* existed.

Otherwise the operation had so far worked out well. It had been mounted with the precision that Lucy brought to most of her activities, including knitting which however awful the final result she was prepared to spend hours over, unravelling row after row if she saw a slipped stitch or decided that the tension was uneven.

On the morning after Mr Bhoolabhoy's evening visit, she disappeared for twenty minutes at an unusual hour and, returning, taking Ibrahim on one side, explained that she had executed her part of the arrangement by establishing with the manager that in the foreseeable future the Owner had no intention of replacing the *mali* and might even sack the blind, lame youth. He confirmed that, yes, Mrs Bhoolabhoy did seem to take the view that since last July she had been under no actual obligation to supply a *mali*, and that one could only await developments.

'So the rest is now up to you. Last night, Ibrahim, Burra Sahib was very upset because Mr Bhoolabhoy did not even raise the subject of the garden. It's a pity we did not know Mr Bhoolabhoy was back, otherwise I could have had a word with him before he came across. But it can't be helped. I wish it could. I find these little plots and plans foreign to my nature, to my preference for the way of dealing with things. There was a time when we, when *we*, did not have to go in for such things, a time when as my poor father used to say—'

'God rest father's soul, Memsahib,' he said. He knew she was an English clergyman's daughter.

'—used to say, An Englishman's word is as good as his bond because he is known throughout the world to be an honest man.'

55

'Honest because British, Memsahib.'
'Yes, Ibrahim. But that is all so long ago.'

Yes, Mr Bhoolabhoy had said, the sacked *mali*'s tools could be made available. He could even suggest a boy, able, willing if not very bright.

A not very bright boy would be ideal, Ibrahim thought. Mr Bhoolabhoy explained about Joseph. He had found him asleep in the porch of St John's Church one Sunday morning. The Christian community in Pankot, mostly Eurasians, but with some Indians, such as Francis Bhoolabhoy himself, had for some years now not been large enough to warrant a resident chaplain. Once a month the Reverend Stephen Ambedkar came up from St Luke's in Ranpur to conduct Sunday services and the day Mr Bhoolabhoy had found Joseph asleep in the porch had been such a Sunday.

Mr Bhoolabhoy, a lay-preacher and churchwarden of Pankot's old English C of E church, took care to be there very early on the Reverend Stephen's Sundays, so did Miss Susy Williams. Miss Williams, member of a Eurasian family once well-known in Pankot – its sole surviving member except for a much fairer-skinned and younger sister who had hooked a GI during the Second World War and had last been heard of in Cincinnati – had not only inherited a talent for hairdressing from her mother who in the days of the *raj* had listed most of the memsahibs of Pankot among her clients, but also acquired a talent for music and flower-arrangement. She played the piano at St John's (the organ had long ago seized up and there was no money for its repair) and also decorated the altar. On the Reverend Stephen's Sundays she and Mr Bhoolabhoy arrived within half-an-hour of one another, Mr Bhoolabhoy first, because he had the keys, and Miss Williams just before 8 a.m. They both brought picnic breakfasts which they ate in the vestry.

Finding Joseph asleep in the porch and having elicited the fact that he had come up from Ranpur in search of work, had no home, was hungry, and believed in the Lord

Jesus, Mr Bhoolabhoy gave him a chapatti and a cup of tea from his thermos. Then he got on with his jobs. When Miss Williams turned up, laden with flowers, the boy had disappeared but Mr Bhoolabhoy found him later on his knees pulling grass away from one of the old hummocky overgrown graves, trying to tidy it up, to pay for his meal. Later he helped Miss Williams with the flowers, filling the vases with water and cutting the stalks. He said he had once done this for 'the sisters' in Ranpur. Miss Williams was very pleased with him; but while her back was turned, doing the last vase, he disappeared again.

Mr Bhoolabhoy had then gone down to Ranpur and it was not, he told Ibrahim, until this very morning, when he went up to St John's to make sure his fellow lay-preacher and assistant warden, Mr Thomas, the Eurasian manager of the New Electric Cinema, had kept things in order that he had met the boy again, that he found Joseph again, not asleep in the porch but on his knees once more, working on his sixth grave with an old pair of clippers which Mr Thomas had lent him.

By now Mr Bhoolabhoy had learnt a little more about Joseph. The only sisters he knew of in Ranpur were those who ran the Samaritan Hospital, which was a nuthouse, and, calling there one day with a message from Mr Ambedkar who was high church enough to maintain an ecumenical relationship with Rome, he inquired of a boy called Joseph, fearing that he might be an escaped inmate. The sisters knew only that he had turned up one day and for a week or two in return for a meal and a bed made himself useful in the patch of garden and by cutting and arranging the flowers for the Reverend Mother's desk. Then he had suddenly not been there. They learned nothing about his history which he himself seemed to have forgotten or decided was irrelevant. They had given him some new clothing as well as bed and board and a postcard of the Sacred Heart, the picture the Reverend Mother had once found him contemplating in her study.

Simple but harmless, honest and willing, was how they had summed him up; and if Mr Bhoolabhoy ever saw him again he must be sure to tell him the sisters remembered him and would welcome him back should he need shelter for a week or so. 'A wandering child of God, with a passion for things that grow,' the Reverend Mother said as she and Mr Bhoolabhoy parted.

Ibrahim thought Joseph sounded more ideal than ever.

'Memsahib will want to know, what of pay?'

Mr Bhoolabhoy shrugged. He had never offered Joseph money. Mr Thomas had given him a few paise for running errands. Miss Williams had given him a rupee or two for painting the cane furniture in her bungalow. Food, shelter, convivial occupation – these were what interested Joseph and he seemed prepared to take them where he found them. He should not cost Mrs Smalley much, Mr Bhoolabhoy declared, and he was glad enough for the boy to have an opportunity, however temporary, and would be happy to pretend to Tusker Sahib that the boy was a member of the hotel staff, if that was what Memsahib wanted.

'What about Madam?' Ibrahim inquired, tilting his head in the direction of the Hotel and its Owner.

'Leave Madam to me,' Mr Bhoolabhoy replied, which struck Ibrahim as very funny. If he mentioned the business to Mrs Bhoolabhoy, though, perhaps she would find *that* funny – the thought of Tusker Sahib thinking she'd backed down when all the time he was paying for the *mali* himself. The idea of Mrs Bhoolabhoy being amused by anything wasn't easy to entertain but if anything could amuse her this might.

'I will speak to Memsahib right away then, Manager Sahib.'

'Don't you want to see the boy first? He's in the churchyard. I'll take you up.'

'Memsahib first, boy second. There is no need for Manager-Sahib to trouble himself further, except over tools. If Memsahib likes the sound of the boy I will go to the church and speak to him.'

Memsahib did like the sound of the boy but didn't want to see him either. She said she relied on Ibrahim's and Mr Bhoolabhoy's judgment.

58

'The question is, how much will he want?'

'Memsahib will say the amount she can afford?'

'The least amount he would work for. What do you think that might be?'

He named a figure.

'But Ibrahim, that is almost as much as the first boy you mentioned would probably want. You spoke of another who wasn't so bright but was strong and willing and would be cheaper. How much cheaper would he be than this third boy you and Mr Bhoolabhoy recommend?'

It was unwise to confuse an old lady.

'This *is* the cheaper boy. Only I did not know when I first mentioned him that Mr Bhoolabhoy also took an interest in him.'

'The most I can afford is five rupees less a month than you suggest he might want. If he works very well we might reconsider.'

'And food, Memsahib.'

'Initially you must see him fed, Ibrahim, but you won't be out of pocket. The first thing is to get him. On trial. If he gives satisfaction then you may confirm to him the wage offered and when your next pay day comes round I will give you what is necessary to pay him plus whatever seems fair as a little subsistence allowance.'

'Come,' Ibrahim said to Joseph. 'Bhoolabhoy Sahib wishes to see you. There is a prospect.' And Joseph, as though summoned by a disciple, had risen from the grave-side and followed Ibrahim to Smith's. Ibrahim was pleased with the look of him because it was a malleable look. At Smith's Mr Bhoolabhoy opened the old *mali*'s shed and revealed to Joseph the treasures stored there. The boy stood at the entrance as though it were holy grotto. When he entered, urged by Mr Bhoolabhoy and Ibrahim to do so, he went first to the wooden shelves where old *mali* had left several pots of geranium cuttings which had died for want of attention. Or had they? The boy fingered one and finding a green bud amid the sear leaves muttered something to himself. Then he ran his hands over a pair of garden shears which were rusty. Finally he knelt and examined the old lawn mower which still had ropes attached where the grass box should have been, if it had ever had a grass box.

'Come,' Ibrahim said again, and led Joseph and Mr Bhoolabhoy to the gap in the wall beyond which stretched the untended grass. Seeing that Tusker was ensconced in the old wicker-chair on the verandah, asleep or not asleep, Ibrahim said, 'Manager Sahib will show Joseph what is required?' Upon which Mr Bhoolabhoy led Joseph into The Lodge's compound while Ibrahim stayed behind.

They did not go near the verandah but if Tusker's eyes were open he couldn't have missed them. Bhoolabhoy Sahib stood in the middle of the lawn gesticulating. Joseph stood as if rapt, then knelt and touched the grass. Bhoolabhoy pointed at the bed of canna lilies but neither of them went near. Then they came back and Joseph went at once to the shed, untied the ropes and slowly pulled the machine out into the sunshine. After examining it he searched among the shelves in the hut, found a can of oil, some sandpaper, an old brush, a rusty worn-down knife. He cleaned the knife first and then began to clean the blades of the mower. All these actions were performed in silence.

'Okay, we're in business,' Ibrahim said.

By midday the machine was clean, bright and slightly oiled and Joseph without a word trundled it into the compound of The Lodge and set it down on the grass. One push proved that the grass was too long for the way the machine was set. He had brought a spanner from the shed and now bent to adjust the blades. He adjusted them several times before the mower was running smoothly and quietly. Grass sprayed from the blades like a green fountain leaving beneath a fourteen-inch-wide strip of yellowing turf. Joseph knelt to inspect this strip, smoothing his hand over it, then gathering a handful of cuttings to inspect them.

Ibrahim left him to it. It was nearly time to collect the trays for Sahib's and Memsahib's lunch. He kicked off his chappals and climbed up to the verandah. The Sahib was awake but not looking at Joseph. The delightful purring sound of the mower beginning the job of cutting the lawn did not seem to be reaching him. Neither was it reaching Memsahib who was inside at her escritoire writing more letters. It was still apparently reaching neither of them when he brought the trays and Joseph was still hard at work. Ignoring the boy he went to get his own midday meal. When he returned to collect the trays the sound of the mower was no longer to be heard. The boy must have given up and, like the old *mali*, looked for a place to get in some sack-time.

But the boy was, after all, still hard at work, sweeping the cuttings from the section he'd mown and gathering them into neat piles. Looking forward to some sack-time himself, Ibrahim nevertheless squatted down in his favourite place of observation. Memsahib was in bed asleep and Sahib was dozing in his chair. Ibrahim watched the boy scoop the cuttings into a piece of sacking and cart them off somewhere. He watched him go back and forth and presently, through heavy eyelids, watched him prodding the shorn grass with a fork. Whatever did he think he was doing? Prodding the lawn with a fork when only a small section of it had been cut?

He waited until Joseph looked in his direction and then beckoned him over. He had to do this twice before the boy got the message. He speared the fork into the turf and came across. Joseph went behind the bungalow and waited for him.

'Why are you prodding the grass with the fork?'

Close-to he saw that Joseph was drenched with sweat.

'To make breathe.'

'You are telling me grass breathes?'

'All living things breathe.'

Ibrahim's heart was touched. The boy himself had scarcely any breath.

'Come, you have done enough for a while. You'd like a cuppachar?'

CHAPTER FIVE

That evening over a meal Minnie had cooked for them Ibrahim told Joseph all he felt it necessary for the young *mali* to know: that the old *mali* had gone to work at the Shiraz, that Mrs Bhoolabhoy was a difficult woman it was best to keep away from; that the English Sahib had not been well and might not speak to him but that if he did he should say that Mr Bhoolabhoy had asked him to put the garden straight. Meanwhile he was to take orders only from Ibrahim. The Sahib and Memsahib had been *pukkalog* in the days of the *raj*, had been in India for forty years and although still pukka they were often very peculiar, like most old people. Sometimes they did not know what time of day it was.

'They are not having clock?' Joseph asked.

'They have three clocks. One in the kitchen, one in the living-room and one in the bedroom. They each have a wristwatch. I also have a wristwatch, made in Switzerland, shockproof, waterproof, jewelled movement, purchased in Oxford Street, London, Yookay. When you say people aren't knowing what time of day it is it is an English way of saying they are a bit cracked.' Ibrahim tapped his forehead.

'Sahib and Memsahib are *pagal*?'

'Sometimes.'

'Have they been to the sisters?'

'It is a different kind of *pagal*. English kind.'

'You have been foreign, Ibrahim?'

'I am England-Returned.'

'Ah.' A pause. 'Are the gardens in England beautiful? They say they are the most beautiful gardens in the world. I should like to work in such gardens.'

'You wish to go foreign?'

'To see and work in such gardens, yes. Hyde Park. Sinjames. Kew. Ennismore.'

'Ennismore?'

'One of the sisters is writing to a lady living in these gardens. I am posting the letters. She helped me to read the envelopes. But it was very difficult for me.'

'If you work hard in *this* garden, if you give satisfaction, who knows what will come of it, Joseph? You might become regular employee, get good pay, save up. This is what my brother-in-law did. He was bearer to an officer-sahib in Mirat. Bengali officer.' Ibrahim paused to hawk and spit. 'Also he married my elder sister. Then he went foreign. He was waiter in a big restaurant in London. Getting many tips because a well-trained man, son of man like my own father who was personal bearer to Colonel Moxon-Greife, from the time Colonel Moxon-Greife was only Captain Moxon-Greife, right until Colonel Sahib and Colonel Memsahib went home. But that is another story. I was telling you about my brother-in-law, making many tips, saving, saving.'

'To buy own restaurant?'

'No, to buy shop, also to send money to my sister. In shop he is working very hard and making good profits, so then buying house big enough for sub-letting. You understand sub-letting?' Joseph shook his head. 'Big house, many rooms, accommodation for many people. All Indians. All living Finsbury Park.'

'Ah,' Joseph said again. 'Park.'

'So when he is prosperous man he sends for his wife my sister. So then she is going foreign too and I go foreign with her to guard her on the long journey and to see brother-in-law again and all his many relations who also had gone foreign.'

'Tell me about Finsbury Park, Ibrahim.'

'Fins-burry, not Fintzbri. About Finsbury Park there is nothing to tell. Apart from the maidan it is all shops and houses and too much of traffic. I did not go foreign to look at the maidan. I did not go foreign to become shopkeeper.

I went foreign to guard my sister and for the experience. Experience is more valuable than money. Here you will be getting a lot of experience. Also food and shelter. If all goes well, even a little money.'

Ibrahim waited. An intelligent boy would ask: How much? At least, a smart boy would. So far, though, Joseph had struck him as a boy who was intelligent enough about the things that interested him, but not smart. The next few seconds would show. If Joseph asked: How much? he would have to be watched. And, clearly, he was puzzling a question out.

'Ibrahim,' he said at last, 'will all go well if I do the work well?'

'That is a good question. I am glad you have asked it. The answer is, not necessarily. I have always done my own work to the best of my ability. But often I get the push.'

'Push?'

'The push. Get pushed out. Chucked out. Sacked. It can happen any day.'

'But you are still here,' Joseph said, after considering the situation.

'There is a thing called re-instatement.'

Joseph frowned, trying to concentrate.

'Put it this way, Joseph-*bhai*,' Ibrahim murmured because he had caught a glimpse of Minnie's shadow and knew she was listening in to this man-talk. 'If it is a day when the Sahib does not know what time of day it is, he may say, Ibrahim, bugger-off, let me see no more of you. You are sacked, fired, given push. So I shrug, I say, "If God so wills." Then I wait for Memsahib to return. I say, Memsahib, I am leaving. It is Sahib's *hukm*. So she goes to him and says, "Tusker, how can we manage without Ibrahim?" To her also he says bugger-off.'

'What is this buggeroff?'

'It is a very old English phrase meaning *jeldi jao*. Likewise piss-off. These are sacred phrases, Joseph, never to be used by you or me when speaking to *Sahib-log* but I will teach you some of them.'

Joseph nodded his head.

'So I bugger-off. But that night there is no cocoa to warm their bones and lull them rockabye to sleep. And in the morning there is no *chota hazri* to wake them up, no porridge to set them up for a cold winter day. I am not making it, Memsahib is not making it because although she has not buggered-off in one sense she has in another. Presently Sahib may be making it, being stubborn, but when he makes it it is no bloody good because of that *shaitan* of a stove, so soon he comes looking for me. In my quarters he finds all my things gone. So he comes looking for me here at Minnie's. "What are you doing here?" he asks. "Waiting for Pay," I say. "Why should I pay you when you are not doing your bloody work?" he asks. So then I know I am reinstated. If sacked by Memsahib then it is not so easy. Being a woman she can brew tea and cook porridge better. Two or three days may go by before Sahib again comes looking. "Memsahib has burnt her hand," he says. Some such excuse.'

The boy nodded again. Ibrahim lit a Charminar. It was satisfactorily established that Joseph neither smoked nor drank alcohol. His appetite had been lustier than expected, though. And Minnie had been very flattered by the way her food had been scoffed. (A point to watch. Joseph was a good-looking boy.)

'Ibrahim,' he said, 'What happens if you are pushed by both Sahib and Memsahib?'

'Given push, not pushed. Get idiom right.'

'What happens if you are given push by Sahib and Memsahib at one and the same time?'

Ibrahim looked at him thoughtfully. He said, 'Suddenly you are a philosopher as well as a gardener? You are entering realm of metaphysics? Joseph Einstein is it? Versed in the theory of time and relativity? Haven't I just made it plain that Sahib and Memsahib are always at loggerheads and that sometimes they do not even know what time of day it is, even in Pankot?'

'But Ibrahim, this is what puzzles me. Supposing they neither of them know what time of day it is on the same day and forget to be at loggerheads and push you together? Who then makes the porridge?'

'Not you, Joseph,' Ibrahim said quickly, scenting a danger. 'If I am given the sack you are also sacked. I am not asking you to make porridge, only to cut the grass and tend the canna lilies. You are not a Smalley-Sahib boy, you are Ibrahim's boy. You are my boy.'

Joseph looked at the floor, on which they were squatting round the remains of their meal. Presently Minnie, who was eating her own supper behind the curtain that separated one small room from another, shouted:

'So now in your old age you are wanting a boy.'

'What nonsense are you talking?' he shouted back.

'You call it nonsense?' she cried. 'When clear for all the world to hear you tell him he is your boy?'

'All the world? Suddenly you are all the world? One world, one big ear working, one mind not working?' Pause. 'Take no notice, Joseph. She is annoyed with me because I am sitting here talking to you instead of telling her the meal must have been cooked in Paradise. But I am talking to you as a father, Joseph. Malum?'

Joseph glanced up. The eyes were still sombre, the look guarded.

'Not a Father. Not a Brother. Not orphan-school type teacher-wallah,' he added hastily, inspired to intuit something from the boy's manner. 'Pukka father. Father of son. Also Employer. By arrangement with Bhoolabhoy Sahib.'

Joseph's eyes cleared. He thought for a while and then said, 'In a week or two, Ibrahim, grass cuttings making good compost if kept well-watered. In hot weather coming, very good to make burra canna-lilies. Strew compost among lilies, so keep moisture in earth. Canna lilies then growing much tall and beautiful. Will that be doing well?'

Again Ibrahim waited for the subject of How Much to come up. But it didn't. He said, 'It will be doing well, Joseph-*bhai*. The Sahib is very fond of the canna lilies.'

66

It took Joseph six days to cut the grass section by section, carry the cuttings away to his compost heap in the rear compound and spear each mown section with the garden fork. Sometimes, warned by Minnie that Mrs Bhoolabhoy was in a bad way that morning, Ibrahim made sure that the boy did something quiet. But to be told not to mow did not seem to worry him. He was a methodical worker. There was always something he could find to do. On the seventh day instead of resting he thoroughly cleaned the machine, sharpened and lowered the blades and then traced out parallel swathes on what was again looking like a lawn. He watered it and then began on the edges with the shears.

Midway through the seventh day Tusker decided he was well enough to take a walk. Towards the end of February the sun in Pankot is quite hot, but the air is still brisk. Tusker wound one of Lucy's knitted scarves round his neck, took stick in one hand and Lucy-Mem in the other and descended the verandah steps. Summoned, Bloxsaw slowly followed them along the path to the side entrance. They did not look at Joseph and Joseph did not look at them. When they came back an hour later the only member of the trio to take notice of Joseph was the fool of a dog who went barking and snapping at him as if he were an intruder never seen before.

'Heel, sir!' Tusker shouted. 'Heel, sir!' and banged the stick on the gravel path while Memsahib entered The Lodge dissociating herself from this display of male masterfulness.

Meanwhile Bloxsaw yapped and snapped and skittered round poor Joseph's ankles. Joseph kept still. Suddenly the dog whined, tucked its tail between its legs and ran indoors yelping.

Ibrahim observed this scene from a distance. Later he put the question. 'What did you say to the dog, Joseph?'

'Only I said, Bless You.'

'Ah. That too is a sacred phrase. But I know a better one. You can use it when speaking to the dog. One day I will teach it to you.'

It was March the First.

'The winds of March that make my heart a dancer,
The telephone that rings, but who's to answer?'

In this month of March Lucy-Mem always played 'These Foolish Things' on her gramophone, an ancient HMV radiogram which would only play 78s, which was neither here nor there because Lucy only had 78s, a veteran collection of records bought during the war from some of which the mere ghost of a sound came out, but it was a ghost Ibrahim loved to hear her conjure, which was something she now tended to do only when alone. Occasionally people like the Menektaras asked her to play an old Inkspots or an old Judy Garland, and then she would oblige. But Tusker always laughed, and the Menektaras found the records amusing too, which Ibrahim knew Lucy didn't. The record she loved best, and Ibrahim knew she loved it best because she never played it for anyone but herself (although it was also played for him, listening on the verandah or in the kitchen) was Dinah Shore singing 'Chloë'. Apart from the movies he shared with Memsahib her passion for the sort of music connected with those movies, and with the Moxon-Greife household where there had been a gramophone similar to Lucy-Mem's and a pile of records similar to hers which they used to play when they had young people in who liked to dance after dinner and he had hidden himself near the verandah and watched and listened. When Memsahib played 'Chloë' she always stood very still, with her eyes closed. Sometimes she played it several times over and from his listening place he would pause in his work and nod his head in time to the old tune. Oh, bumpa-bumpa-bumpa-bumpady-day-do. Bumpabumba bumpabumpadi-daydoo. Oh through the black of night, I gotta be where you are. If it's wrong or right, I gotta go where you are. I'll roam through the dismal swamplands (bump), Searching for you. If you are lost there let me *be* there too.

'What is worrying you, Ibrahim?' Minnie had asked him once after such a session and she came round at midnight.

'Sadness of world,' he replied.

March the First this year was the day Tusker went out for the first time entirely on his own. Being the first of the month it was also accounts day for Memsahib and pay-day for Ibrahim. When Tusker had gone, accompanied by Bloxsaw, Ibrahim waited in the kitchen for the familiar sounds of Lucy-Mem opening her escritoire, then the drawer in which the metal cash-box was kept. Hearing both sounds he put the kettle on to make her the mid-morning pot of coffee. He laced it as usual with Golconda brandy to put her in a good mood for the reckoning after which he would be summoned to answer questions, listen to her homily about the rising cost of living and the need to watch expenditure, and finally receive his monthly wage.

On reckoning days, she was at her most formidable. Burra Memsahib *assoluta*. From his vantage point near the kitchen doorway he observed her meticulously controlled and studied act at the desk with admiration, also with some impatience and a delightful apprehension of the possibility of a row of the kind they both knew how to conduct if it developed.

Initially, no words were exchanged except, 'Coffee, Memsahib,' and 'Thank you, Ibrahim, just leave it there.' He placed the tray within reach of her left hand. Her right hand never let go of the elegant black and silver ball-point with which she rechecked the totals of bills paid before entering them on the right-hand side of her housekeeping book. She used the left hand to pierce the bills on a spike and, intermittently, to pour the coffee and carry the cup to her pursed mouth. He noticed that she was able to add up a column of figures as quickly when sipping as when not sipping.

Occasionally she made separate notes in a red memo book. She made these in shorthand, a form of lettering he recognized for what it was and regretted he had never learned. Today she was making fewer shorthand notes than usual. She was also having uncharacteristic trouble adding up. Had he overdone the brandy, this time? He waited until she had got her sums right then entered, coughed, and said, 'More hot coffee, Memsahib?'

She shook her head so he took the tray back, rinsed the pot and cup, ear cocked for the summons to pay-parade.

It came. He marched in, saluted, took the money in his left hand and the pencil in his right to sign the wage book with his usual flourish. He saluted again.

'The lawn,' she said, retrieving wage book and pencil. 'Burra Sahib – I *think* – is very pleased about the arrangements Mr Bhoolabhoy has made for the lawn. He's looking much better. I am pleased too. Really very pleased.'

'Yes, Memsahib.'

'It is so curious about illness and health. Small things, little things, they make all the difference.' She resumed her spectacles and searched on the top of the escritoire. Finding what she was looking for, an envelope, she handed it to him and murmured, 'For the garden, Ibrahim,' and allowed her hand to stay, so that for a moment their fingers were in contact.

'And tonight,' she went on, 'I shall go to the pictures.' She handed him some more money. 'Please book my seat for the second show.'

'Yes, Memsahib. Memsahib, it is only Wednesday.'

'I know. A rare day for me to go. But I have not been, as you know, since Colonel Sahib became ill, and tonight he too will be doing something unusual for a Wednesday. He and Mr Bhoolabhoy are to be – convivial, I gather because Mrs Bhoolabhoy has a special bridge party. Mr Bhoolabhoy is coming here, after dinner. Perhaps you would keep an eye. Very very small chota pegs for Colonel Sahib.'

Ibrahim put his hands behind his back.

'Memsahib is going alone to the pictures?'

When she did so he called a tonga for her, accompanied her, sitting up front with the driver, ostensibly to make sure no harm came to her. It was then usually understood that he would be out front to meet her when the show was over and accompany her home. It was also understood that in the interval Ibrahim had seen the picture himself from a seat in the front benches which he seldom had to pay for because he had a friend at the side entrance.

It had been just so, long ago in the days of the Moxon-

Greifes in Mirat, when he was a boy. Oddly enough the Moxon-Greifes' evening for the cinema had been a Wednesday, and when he was old enough, his father – their bearer – had begun to send him down to the box office with money for the seats and a chit signed by the Sahib. All Ibrahim had had to do was run into the cantonment bazaar, and to the Majestic, present chit and money and run back with the tickets which he gave either to his father or to Naik Hussein, the Moxon-Greifes' driver who had become a movie fan too, out of sheer boredom at having to wait or be back in time with the car to be at the entrance when the Moxon-Greifes came out. Hussein had learned to fill in the time by slipping into the front rows reserved for servants and babus. And one day, finding Ibrahim watching people go in (corrupted already by the scent of an enchantment suspected but experienced only in still pictures outside) Hussein took him in with him.

They did not see the end of the film because Hussein was punctilious about leaving in time to have the car at the entrance before the show ended. Ibrahim ran the short distance home, faced his father's wrath but was saved from its consequences by Hussein who pointed out that to attend a foreign-language movie (which he himself couldn't follow at all) was as good as doing homework in the English the boy was already learning and showing an aptitude for in the class reserved for the sons of attached non-combatants at the regimental school. The Moxon-Greifes had arranged Ibrahim's attendance, so when Hussein described film-going as homework his father didn't have a leg to stand on and in fact took an early opportunity to mention it to Mrs Moxon-Greife when she inquired how Ibrahim was getting on.

Thereafter Ibrahim was allowed to sit next to Hussein at the front of the car on picture-going nights. Sahib and Memsahib must have been amused by his devotion to what they called the silver screen. They discussed the picture with him on the way home, speaking both in Urdu and English. 'The end was disappointing, don't you think?' Mrs Moxon-Greife very often said. Ibrahim did not like to

71

say that he and Hussein never saw the end of a film. Sometimes he begged to be allowed to stay but Hussein wouldn't leave him a moment unaccompanied. He had caught up years later, sitting in front of his brother-in-law's television set in Finsbury Park, watching the old movies. Thus he had seen at last how Greta Garbo died at the end of *Camille*, how Bette Davis died at the end of *Dark Victory* and sat desolate on a chair in the Tower at the end of *Elizabeth and Essex*. In a London cinema he had watched Vivien Leigh running through the mist at the end of *Gone With the Wind*.

Lucy-Mem was more accommodating about time than the Moxon-Greifes had been and less nimble on her feet anyway. She was given too to gossiping in the foyer, so that now Ibrahim had ample time to see the fade-out, go with the crowd, earmark the waiting tonga and approach the front, ready to escort her. On the tonga-ride home, he in front, she behind, they talked about the movie. He liked doing that because it gave him an insight into the things that moved her and the things that made her laugh or of which she disapproved or got bored by. He was longing to accompany her again. Like her, he had not been to the movies since Tusker Sahib was taken ill.

So, hands behind back, he put the question. 'Memsahib is going alone to the pictures?'

'Oh,' she said. 'Oh, Ibrahim. You want to go too.'

He nodded his head from one side to the other: a gesture which in this case meant, As Memsahib wishes.

She smiled, took off her spectacles. 'Why not? Indeed why not? After all, we have both earned an evening off. And we can surely trust Burra Sahib to guard his health, and Mr Bhoolabhoy to see that he guards it. So yes, Ibrahim, let us tonight both go to the pictures. Do you know what is on?'

'Repeat showing, Butch Cassidy, Sundance Kid. Paul Newman, Robert Redford.'

'Yes, of course. We saw it last year, but such good actors. Second House, then Ibrahim. My usual seat if possible.'

He saluted again. In the kitchen he inspected the contents

72

of the envelope marked 'For the Garden'. At the agreed number of rupees a month for the ten or so days of February Joseph had worked it was one rupee short. He had expected Memsahib to cut it even finer. That she both had and hadn't confirmed his opinion of her as a lady of style.

Just as he was about to leave the bungalow to work out how much percentage it would be reasonable to claim for himself before handing the balance to Joseph he heard the gramophone start up. He peeped in. Memsahib was backing gracefully away from the machine, gently turning and twisting her body, her arms round an invisible partner, balanced a little precariously on the soles of her long-ago shoes.

'Oh how my heart has wings.'

CHAPTER SIX

While Ibrahim was out booking the seat and Tusker was still out with Bloxsaw, the *dak* came. Among the few bills and catalogues was an airmail letter from the Blackshaws in England: a proper letter in a proper envelope, not one of those wretched new-size air-letters it was difficult to open without tearing part of the message. The reason for the envelope was that something had been enclosed: a newspaper snipping from *The Times*.

> LAYTON. On February 19th at his home, Combe Lodge, Combe Magnus, Surrey, after a short illness, John Frederick William, Lt-Col. (IA Retd) Pankot Rifles, beloved husband of the late Mildred Layton (née Muir), dear father of Sarah and Susan, grandfather of Teddie, Lance and Jane, greatgrandfather of Boskie. Funeral private. No Flowers please, but donations if wished to the Cancer Research Fund.

Phoebe Blackshaw had written: 'I'm afraid we've reached the stage of life when we look at the Obits first. Directly I saw the word Pankot it occurred to me that you and Tusker must have known Colonel Layton and his family or at least known of them. Not being real Pankot people ourselves the name only rings vague bells, perhaps as people you sometimes referred to. Anyway there it is. How is dear old "Bloxsaw"? And how are your dear old selves?' Having delivered that last glancing blow, Phoebe rambled on full of herself as always. If Phoebe's letters were not now virtually the only ones Lucy could expect to have from home she would have considered them tiresome in the extreme.

When Tusker came back from his walk he seemed in a good mood. He asked cheerfully, 'Anything nice in the *dak*?'

'Only a letter from Phoebe.'

'Usual guff I suppose. What's the drill for lunch, old thing?'

It was ages since he had called her that.

'Has your walk made you hungry, Tusker dear?'

He said it had but that he didn't want broth, nor a tray from the restaurant. He didn't want to go to the restaurant either. The very sight of Mrs Bhoolabhoy waddling from bedroom to kitchen and back again with one of her bloody headaches turned him off. He hadn't seen Mrs Bhoolabhoy since his attack. He didn't care if he never saw her again, the old bitch.

He ruffled Bloxsaw's dumb head, and hesitated. Was he at last going to mention the garden?

'We could go to the Shiraz for lunch,' he said.

Her heart fluttered.

'Oh, Tusker. It's so expensive.'

'Bugger the expense.'

'What about tonight?'

'Can't tonight. Billy-Boy's coming over for a noggin, remember?'

'That's what I mean, Tusker. The Shiraz for lunch would be lovely if we can really afford it for once, but it will worry me if you overdo things. Shouldn't we go to the Shiraz another day, when you don't have to cope with Billy-Boy in the evening?'

'What's the point when it's now I'm hungry? Thirsty, too. Ibrahim!'

'Ibrahim's out, Tusker. What do you want? I'll get it.'

'A gin if there's any left. Where's the idle old sod gone?'

'Well I thought that as you're spending the evening with Billy-Boy I'd go to the second house at the pictures, so he's gone to get my ticket. Is that all right?'

'What could be wrong? You usually do go.'

Not for a long time, she was about to say, but didn't because the nice mood he was in might not last through the small argument such a conversation could easily lead to. So she gave him a very weak gin, changed her twin set and shoes and at twelve-thirty they went across to the

Shiraz and up in the lift to the Mountain View Room where he complained about the table first offered and then about a gravy stain on the menu the waiter handed him.

But he was obviously enjoying himself. The Srinivasans waved. Bobbie and Nita Ghosh came across for a word. The Desais, arriving, stopped by and chatted long enough for Lucy to fear that Tusker would invite them to join him at his expense. The Desais were the richest free-loaders in Pankot. And not once, going to Europe, had they come back with one single little thing from the modest list they usually asked Lucy to give them. Moreover, they were the only two of Tusker's Indian friends who had neither called nor sent flowers. Well, almost the only two. If she put her addled little mind to it she imagined she'd be able to think of several others who would make the same kind of fantastic excuses Mrs Desai was making about having only 'just heard' because they'd been here, there, everywhere, dashing about the place, what with their son Bubli to see off to Dusseldorf, a conference in Delhi Mr Desai had had to attend and now their daughter's marriage coming off shortly in Bombay, eight hundred guests, a killing expense.

'Can't they just elope?' Tusker asked. Tusker said things like that to Mrs Desai. It was a form of flirtation, although she knew he didn't like the woman. Mrs Desai threw back her disgustingly beautiful head and laughed, and her diminutive husband who had no conversation that wasn't about money actually smiled as if this was an idea he had turned over in his computer-like mind and regretfully rejected. Their daughter was to marry a minister's grandson.

'What a marvellous idea,' Mrs Desai said. 'Ved and Sita would adore to do just that, but his parents are crashingly orthodox and seem to have literally hundreds of relations, apart from all the government people who'll expect to be invited. Thank God it's Bombay and not Delhi, or I suppose we'd have had to have *her* too.'

'Come,' Mr Desai said.

Tusker now sat down. In public he was punctilious about such things. As he settled again he muttered, 'With a crore of her husband's black market money to try and get rid of, what's she complaining about?'

'Oh, Tusker,' she whispered, then – looking at the prices for the first time – thought, Oh God. 'I think the soup of the day, don't you?'

'Not unless you want to kill me off for good. You're looking at Tahble Dhoti, which is the usual load of old rubbish from yesterday's left-overs.'

That's us too, Lucy thought, not quite thinking it in words but getting their resonance. She wished he wouldn't use his private language in public. Tahble Dhoti. People sometimes misunderstood.

'What we're looking at is the Allah Carti. Or the Allah Cart, after all we're all in it up to the neck. Say what you want, Luce and don't look at the rupees.'

She took off her spectacles. First 'old thing' and now 'Luce'. A goose walked over her grave. 'I'll have what you have, Tusker, but I'm honestly not terribly hungry and remember what Dr Mitra said. Please be circumspect.'

Was he going to mention the *mali*? It was strange that he had refused to mention him so far. He had not mentioned the garden once, since the night she found him crying on the loo. Perhaps he was ashamed. She had never seen him cry before. She had half-hoped that Dr Mitra, who had visited one day soon after the *mali* started, would say something, so that Tusker would be forced to take note and say something himself, but Mitra was a man who never noticed domestic arrangements and had hardly listened, probably hadn't taken it *in*, when she confided to him that the state of the garden was getting on Tusker's nerves.

But I'm not going to think about all this today, she told herself. I am here, at the Shiraz, with Tusker. She looked round the room. There were some American tourists at the far end of the room. She guessed they were American because they were all talking to one another, and at least two of the women had their hair done like Jackie Kennedy. Between her and the Americans was a table-load of Japanese with their cameras slung over the backs of their chairs. The Japanese were saying nothing but eating with oriental patience and waiting – waiting for what? For Kohima to fall at last? For the gates of Delhi to crumble? Or for the snow on the peaks of the distant mountains to melt under delayed radiant heat from Hiroshima?

Just then Mrs Bhoolabhoy billowed in, in shocking pink. Wasn't she supposed to be playing bridge? Her companions didn't look like bridge-players, in fact they looked to Lucy like a gang of Mafia-type Indians. One even had a suit with gold-glitter thread woven in it. The party went to a table far down the room, behind a lattice-work screen. Tusker had not seen her. Lucy was relieved. It would have put him off his food and spoiled things for both of them. She could not be sure whether Mrs Bhoolabhoy had seen them. And what did it matter.

'Have you decided, Tusker, dear?' She asked.

At that moment, Lucy could have sworn, Mrs Bhoolabhoy had sat down. The five storeys of the Shiraz seemed to lean a little farther towards the East and a tremor to pass through the whole fabric.

To Sarah Layton

The Lodge,
Smith's Hotel,
Pankot,
(Ranpur).
March 2nd, 1972.

Dear Sarah (Lucy wrote the following day),

It's getting on for 25 years ago that we last saw one another and you'll scarcely remember me, although we were all in Pankot during the last war and of course it was my husband (Tusker) and I who moved into Rose Cottage when you and your family moved down to Commandant House.

A friend of ours, now back in England, and whom you won't know because they were Tea and didn't come to Pankot until 1965, has sent me a cutting from last month's

78

Times about your father's death because she imagined we must all have been acquainted. I felt I must write to say how sorry I am to learn of this, and indeed of your mother's death earlier.

Poor Tusker has been quite ill recently, so although he is now on the mend I've not yet told him for fear of distressing him, but I know he would wish to join me in offering my sympathy to you and to Susan. He always spoke so highly of your work when you were in the WAC(I) and worked in his department at Area Headquarters, and, as I did, he had a great respect for Colonel Layton and indeed the whole family.

I shall not intrude on your grief by going into all the hundred and one things that come to my mind about the Pankot you knew so well and Pankot as it is today, but should you be interested presently it would truly delight me to correspond with you from time to time.

Tusker and I remained at Rose Cottage until early in 1949. You may remember he was invited to stay on for a year or two on contract with the new Indian government. When he finally retired he took a commercial job with Smith Brown & McKintosh in Bombay. The firm sent him home on a short business trip in 1950, and naturally I went with him, but that's the only time I've been in England since first coming out over 40 years ago. It seems so strange to me, put like that. Tusker finally retired about 10 years ago when he was sixty and we've been back in Pankot for most of that time and are now literally the last of the permanent British residents on station. Quite a lot of people pass through from time to time though, young people from home and of course tourists, and we have a number of good friends among the Indian officers and their wives.

Rose Cottage still stands. Colonel Menektara, who commands the depot, and his family live there. Tusker and I dined in the mess a few weeks ago when they celebrated the end of the war with Pakistan. The silver tray your father so kindly presented is still a prized possession, as is the silver donated by Mrs Mabel Layton's first husband. Colonel Menektara will be sorry to hear of your father's death, although of course they would never have known one another. He was originally Punjab regiment and I think only a young Lieutenant in 1947.

We, as you see, are back at Smith's Hotel where we were quartered throughout the war, or rather we're in The Lodge, the adjacent bungalow which was taken over as an annexe. There is now a new and very smart hotel next door called the Shiraz. Unfortunately it does rather loom over our own compound. The bazaar is much the same, although there are some rather smart new shops. Ghulab Singhs and Jalal-ud-Dins you will remember. The New Electric cinema has been smartened up, but is still there and I go quite often because they show English and American pictures. We are really quite cosmopolitan and getting more modern every day.

But there I go rambling on. Please forgive me. I'm addressing the envelope to Miss Sarah Layton at Combe Lodge, the address in the notice, although I doubt you yourself live there or that Miss Layton is correct. I expect you married years ago and that one or more of the grand-children mentioned are your own children. I do hope that you and Susan have had happy and fulfilled lives since you both went home and put India behind you.

There is just one thing I ought to mention. I assume that Teddie may be Edward, Susan's boy by her first marriage to poor Captain Bingham who was killed in Imphal. Teddie must be grown-up now, in fact nearly 30, I suppose. The point is his little ayah, Minnie, now works for the proprietor of this hotel, a Mrs Bhoolabhoy. Little Minnie (hardly little now!) wanted to work for me at Rose Cottage when she and her uncle Mahmoud got back to Pankot after accompanying you all to Bombay to see you off on the boat. She loved the bungalow and its memories, but I already had a woman servant and anyway Mahmoud insisted on their both going to Ranpur to the household your father had kindly recommended them to. Then of course Tusker and I went to Bombay. When we came back we found her working at the hotel, which was then still owned by old

Mr Pillai, although managed by a new man called Bhoolabhoy. When we moved into the annexe she would have
liked to work for me entirely but of course Tusker needed
a male servant and one servant was the most we could afford
and actually needed. A few years ago Mr Pillai died and
this woman bought the place and then surprised us all by
marrying Mr Bhoolabhoy. Anyway, Minnie has secure
employment. Her uncle, your old bearer Mahmoud, died
in his village soon after his retirement, which was why
Minnie came back to Pankot. But I imagine your father
knew this. I remember Minnie saying that Colonel Layton-
Sahib had been very kind, keeping in touch with Mahmoud
and sending him money. She said neither of them had been
happy in Ranpur once the family your father recommended
them to went abroad in some diplomatic post and had to
leave them behind. She spoke very disparagingly of the
new household they found work in. I can believe it because
frankly servants are not often so well treated as they used
to be and those who are old enough to remember how we
treated them do seem very much to regret the change. We
are fortunate in the man we have now. Of course, Minnie
was very young when she was little Edward's ayah and
seems to have adjusted and runs to and fro for Mrs Bhoolabhoy as to the manner born. I shan't say anything to her
about her young charge of all those years ago until I hear
from you that 'Teddie' is one and the same – which I should
so much like to do, Sarah, if ever you have a moment to
spare. Please forgive this absurdly long letter, which was
meant to be no longer than was necessary to convey my
sympathy.

With Love,
Lucy (Smalley)

PS. I hope not but fear that the reference to the Cancer
Research Fund indicates that your father suffered from this
terrible thing, as my own dear father did, whose illness
too was described as short. It was all over in a month.
Tusker and I were then down in Mahwar, in the early

'Thirties and I could scarcely believe it when my mother wrote from home to say he had gone. In those days of course they had none of the drugs that make this disease now a little easier for everyone to bear, easier for those who succumb to it and for those who simply have to watch and wait.

I have had rather a sad life, Lucy told herself, as she sealed the letter.

First the twins had gone, her elder brothers, both killed in a motor accident on the Kingston By-Pass. Then her father. Then Mumsie, no doubt of a broken heart because the men of the house were no longer there and Lucy had never quite counted in that male-oriented household, and was anyway now beyond reach, in India, a place of which her mother had disapproved. 'I'm told the climate is very heating,' Mumsie had said, wrapped in woollies against the persistent chill of the vicarage. Mumsie had disapproved of Tusker, too, although she had tried to disguise it, because he was a soldier serving his King. But anything Lucy did, anyone Lucy chose, anyone who chose Lucy, had to be disapproved of because she was only a girl and Mumsie hadn't wanted another child after the twins, certainly not one of the female sex which was what she'd got.

'Yes, from the beginning I had a sad life,' she repeated. 'A life like a flower that has never really bloomed, but how many do?' She stuck a stamp on the envelope and decided to walk down to the post-box herself rather than entrust the letter to Ibrahim who would read the name and address and gossip like mad to everyone, including Minnie.

Tusker was on the verandah at work on his notes. She had not inquired what these were. He had been a good boy the night before, actually in bed when she got back from the pictures, having made his own cocoa and left hers in the pot to rewarm. The level of the gin in the new bottle suggested restraint, unless Billy-Boy had brought his own bottle with him. She wondered whether the subject of the garden had come up. If so it had passed off amicably enough because Tusker had been in a good mood and was in a good mood this morning.

'I'm going to the bazaar,' she said, 'to get your pills, Tusker dear. Is there anything you want?'

'No thanks, Luce.'

'Then I'll be off. Bloxsaw!'

The animal groaned but obediently got to its feet and padded after her. The *mali* was tending the potted plants that flanked the gravel path.

'Good morning, *mali*,' she said on the spur of the moment. The young man rose and touched his forehead. The dog kept its distance, sheltering behind her. She said, in her terrible Urdu, 'To you, from me, for your work, many thanks are.'

He lowered his eyes, touched his forehead again.

'Come, Bloxsaw. *Chalo.*'

Mali, of course, was as yet too young to be a Toole, she thought. But there is a Toole in him. ('Bloxsaw!'). The neck isn't right, yet, but the eyes are promising. Devotion and challenge. Muni's eyes had been the best eyes. Newman's and McQueen's eyes were different from Muni's and from one another's. But interesting. One needed an identikit to make the perfect Toole.

'Bloxsaw!' She put the dog on the lead and addressed it thus: I must apologize, Mr Allnutt, at having really to insist that we go this way when all too obviously you are determined to go that way, but it is absolutely imperative, just as it is imperative that instead of lifting your leg at every tree we pass, and going off at a tangent, we go as quickly and directly as we can to Ghulab Singh's the chemists so that I may purchase those few commodities essential to my husband's health, I might say survival, do I make myself plain?

'Yes, ma'am,' Bogie/Bloxsaw muttered, and pulled again on the rope (the lead) that dragged the boat in which she sat, shaded by her parasol, through the Afro-Indian swamp.

83

When Lucy had gone Tusker, instead of continuing the notes he was making about the library book ('A Short History of Pankot' by Edgar Maybrick, BA, LRAM. Privately Printed), interpolated the following passage:

'Well, that proves it. The *mali* isn't an hallucination, or if he is then Luce is even more hallucinated because she just spoke to him. Not that I've ever really thought he was an hallucination except for that minute or so when Billy-Boy first brought him into the compound and I wondered whether I'd actually died weeks ago that night on the loo and had since been having a sort of dream-time all to myself. But it's been interesting the way nobody has once mentioned the fellow to me. Originally I didn't dare in case I actually was damn' well seeing things. I mean even Bloxsaw ignored him until that day we came back from our walk and then he barked at him and suddenly turned tail, so I thought well dogs *are* odd, I mean they sometimes see things we don't. And why has Billy-Boy never mentioned him? Obviously though it's been some kind of plot to humour me and they're waiting for me to show gratitude because I grumbled so much about there being no *mali*. I'll be buggered if I say anything first. The young fellow's got the garden up a treat though, unless I'm imagining that too, but I expect the Punjabi bitch will send me a bloody bill in which case she can whistle for it because I can always say, *What* mali? (NB, though, wait and see and say nowt.)'

He resumed his notes on the library book.

'Old Maybrick was always a bit of a fool, but a harmless one, and I must say I admire the way he can write a 78 page monograph on the history of Pankot and refer to the Pankot Rifles only in one paragraph. Stuck up bloody regiment it was in our day. Thought the sun shone from its collective arse. The pinkest young subalterns on station gave themselves airs if they were Pankot Rifles blokes. They even condescended to the Area Commander. There was that one who ducked out of an appointment as *aide* to a general

84

because the general was originally only a Gunner. Bloody fool him. Died in North Africa with the first battalion which old Layton later managed to get put into the bag to a man, or what was left of them. As a Mahwar Regiment chap I didn't begin to rank with them at all, of course, not that I minded a bugger. I was never regiment-minded anyway, especially after it was made plain I'd blotted my copybook by marrying at home without the CO's approval. Approval! Great Scott, I was pushing thirty.

'Never forget his face when I got back from long home leave with Lucy in tow and said, Colonel, I have the honour to present my wife, her name's Lucy. It used to be Lucy Little but it's now Lucy Smalley, which seems a logical sort of progression don't you think, sir? (Ha.)

'Poor old Luce. She didn't help matters when she told the Colonel's lady that she'd been at Pitmans and her speeds were such and such and that the solicitor's office where she worked was where we met. If old Luce's dad had been a bishop it would have been okay, but he was only a vicar, a parish priest. It didn't matter a damn to me. If it had I wouldn't have married her. People used to think of me as a dull conventional sort of chap, but that was their problem, not mine. Mind you, I never did anything to disabuse them of the idea they'd got hold of that young Smalley was "safe", a bit dim, but good with paper if not with people. It suited me well enough. Always did like paper, working things out on it, arranging things with it. The best job at battalion level was adjutant. I was acting adjutant when I went home on long leave that time. I was supposed to be appointed when I got back, and had told Luce as much. I never did work it out whether it was her, or the fact I'd married her without going through that bloody silly rigmarole of having her vetted, that persuaded him I'd be better out of the regiment altogether. Bit of both probably. He got rid of us by putting me up for a temporary job in one of those small princely Indian states which the Political Department was circularizing, and within the month Luce and I were off to Mudpore. I was never regimentally employed again. Didn't care a fig. The Mudpore thing carried extra pay so I spun it out as long as I could. Can't remember what I was called, something like Administrative Adviser to the Commander of the State Forces, but I remember the job clear enough: sorting out the balls-up the previous British attached officer had made and which led to a stampede of the Prince's elephants. The clot had cut down their feed because he thought there was jiggery-pokery going on in the stables.

'What a joke. What a lark. Ought to have written my memoirs. Old Luce adored Mudpore. We had that bloody great bungalow practically in the grounds of the palace, the use of one of the Daimlers with a liveried chauffeur, and when we first met the Maharajah he had on all his paraphernalia and looked a regular bobby-dazzler, coat of silver thread, pearls festooned in his turban; and Luce said, This is the *real* India, Tusker. Only she didn't call me Tusker because nobody did until later, when I'd got the elephants behaving properly again. Of course the Mahwars have always been nicknamed the Tuskers because of the insignia but I'm the only chap the nickname stuck to personally and permanently. A young punk of a subaltern once said I must be called Tusker because it took me as long to work out a problem as it took a pregnant cow-elephant to drop its calf, that's to say twice as long as a member of the human race needs. Must say I gave him full marks for that one.

'He fancied Luce. You could see him working out how and when he could have it off with her. Joke was she seemed to have no idea what was in his mind. Bit dim about things of that sort, old Luce. This was in Ramnagar where we were after Mudpore and where she was the only white woman for miles around. He used to come in from the *mofussil* every Friday night, so regular that I called him Amami. He followed us to Lahore where we went next but went off her because Lahore was crammed with what he couldn't get his mind off. In 1935 he blew his brains out in Quetta after being found in bed with a senior officer's grass-widow. He blew them out at 2 o'clock one morning. An hour later the earthquake reduced the bungalow he

86

blew them out in to rubble, so he could have saved himself the bother.

'We were in Quetta the year after the 'quake. Whenever we packed up to go to another station Luce used to describe it as setting out again on our little wanderings. People called her Little Me because she had this ridiculous habit of saying things like "There'll just be the four of us, including Little Me," or, "Oh how nice, is that just for Little Me?" So there we were, Tusker and Little Me. A boring couple, but useful. Luce never seemed to cotton on to the fact that people found us heavy-going. Knowing shorthand she was in demand on every woman's committee that was going. She mistook it for popularity and was chuffed for days if one of the senior bitches complimented her on her minutes or called her Lucy instead of Mrs Smalley. As for me, I deliberately kept what nowadays they call a low profile. I *wanted* to be thought dull. Dull but thoroughly reliable at the desk-work officers usually affected to despise. I worked hard at getting a name as the man who could sort out other people's balls-ups. I liked moving around. My majority came through in '38. We could have gone home on leave next year but put it off and then it was too late because the war started. In 1940 the regiment asked to have me back. Not bloody likely. Knew how to short-circuit *that* sort of thing. Moved round more than ever before, then in September 1941 we came up here to Pankot to Area Headquarters. Took one look at it and I thought, nice scenery, good climate, this is where I'll dig in for the duration or know the reason why. So set about making myself indispensable at the *daftar*, which meant making the job look more complicated that it was even after I'd sorted out the mess the previous fellow had made and could do it standing on my head. I was 40, still only a major. Had to wait another four years for a half-colonelcy, but didn't care. Accommodation was short. Luce and I were billeted at Smith's, a sitting-room and a bedroom, the ones Billy-Boy and that monster of a wife of his now live in. Luce always hankered after a bungalow of our own, but Smith's was fine by me. It helped me merge unobtrusively with the background. My only ambition ever has been to survive as comfortably as possible.

'Old Maybrick doesn't mention Smith's at all. He's got the date of the Church right but is out by a year over the installation of the organ, according to Billy-Boy, but then Maybrick only played the bloody thing. Maybrick was an enthusiast. Enthusiasm is the most ruinous thing I can think of.'

Tusker's birthday was April 10th, Lucy's September 12th. They had fallen into the habit of repaying station hospitality mainly by inviting people to what they called Birthday Buffet suppers. Lucy's birthday buffet was less troublesome than Tusker's because she simply went ahead with the arrangements, writing chits to people to whom they owed, warning Mr Bhoolabhoy and confirming the approximate number of guests expected. The number of guests was always approximate because sometimes people rang at the last moment to announce they had people staying and could they bring them along, or rang to say they'd been ordered to Delhi. This could be tiresome because the cook at Smith's needed several days' notice to arrange the catering, and once the order had been given and a per head price agreed with Mr Bhoolabhoy it was difficult to make changes.

The other difficulty was that of trying to remember or find out who was veg and who was non-veg, how many were fruit-juice only people and how many ranked as what Tusker called certified alcoholics; but at least – now that the whole province was 'wet' the liquor was easy to get, could be drunk in the open, and unused bottles returned to Jalal-ud-Din's. In Pankot there was not even a dry day, although there was one in Ranpur. The anomalies of the Indian drinking laws from province to province had always been too many for Lucy to grasp, but Tusker professed to be an expert, to be able to tell anyone who cared to inquire what obstacles had to be overcome to get a drink in any major Indian city you could name, to know where you could get beer ad lib but needed a permit for hard liquor, where what could be drunk in public or only in a permit room, which states were dry but had capitals as wet as a Sunday afternoon in Wales (as he put it), where your car migh: be stopped in transit from a wet to a dry area and searched, in which places a permit holder could buy his whole month's ration in one go and in which the liquor shops were run by men he described as suffering from a touch of the Morarjidesais and allowed only one bottle a week.

Tusker's obsession with the liquor laws dated from the time he'd been in trouble with the police in Bombay. But Lucy preferred not to think about that because it was all part and parcel of what she called the débâcle and he'd begun to knock it back at half-past ten in the morning.

For the past ten years a bottle of Carew's gin a week and a monthly bottle of Golconda brandy, a dozen bottles of beer had been about all they could afford to have in the house, and a lot of it went on people who dropped in, as Indians tended to, especially if they had an American staying with them who had asked 'Are there any old-style British around here?' and were brought along to see for themselves.

'We should write to Cooks,' Lucy suggested to Tusker after one such visitation (Mrs Desai and a lady from Virginia who called Lucy Honey), 'and ask them to put us on the tourist itinerary. After the Taj Mahal, after the rock temples of Khajarao, after Elephanta, after Fatehpur Sikri, after the beach temple at Mahabalipuram and the Victoria Monument in Calcutta, the Smalleys of Pankot. We could make a packet, Tusker, especially if you wore your old topee and I could be discovered playing Mahjong. A little tableau-vivant. Ibrahim could take the money at the door and guard their shoes.'

Tusker's birthday buffets were more difficult to organize because he invariably said he wasn't going to have one this year and couldn't afford it and people would have to whistle for it and sod the lot of them. His habit of bad language dated from the day of his final retirement from the army in 1949 when he shook her to the core on his return home from the *daftar* for the last time, flung his cap on the floor and said, 'Right that's ******* that,' using a word Lucy could only think of as spelt in asterisks. A few hours later he shook her again by making love to her twice between lights out and reveille.

As a lover Tusker had been something of a disappointment to her. Her mother had warned her that men were insatiable, especially in heating climates. Finding that on their short honeymoon, on the boat out, and on arrival in India, Tusker seemed satisfied by limiting his conjugal performances to Wednesdays and Saturdays (with an occasional matinée performance on the honeymoon) she had thought of her thin rail of a father with new respect since she had to assume that he was her mother's only source of experience. After a while even Wednesdays began to fall off. She awaited the falling off of Saturdays too but this never came about. Tusker seemed to have been wound up in such a way that Saturday night was the night he rang.

But then he was a methodical man. There was a drill for everything, even for this. Saturday nights were usually club nights and they usually got back to their quarters at half-past eleven. At midnight she climbed in under the massive white mosquito net that shrouded the large double bed of those early married days and switched off her light, leaving Tusker's on. Ten minutes later he came out of the bathroom, climbed in on his side, switched the lamp off after ten minutes spent reading something of military significance, and settled. About five minutes later still his hand sought her waist. She breathed out heavily, as if her slumbers were only momentarily disturbed. His hand then moved to the mound of venus. She breathed in. He muttered something and heaved himself up and over on top. He smelt of the Bay Rum which he favoured as a hairdressing. She tried hard to get the erotic sense of this particular smell because often she needed every bit of help she could get. But in regard to Bay Rum the law of diminishing returns had set in long ago. Perhaps part of the trouble was that on their first coition she had been so ripe in anticipation that she may have misled him about the degree of attention he need pay her. She hadn't noticed Bay Rum on that occasion.

Subsequently he scarcely seemed to notice her at all. He went through the motions. Of these motions, so she had worked it out over the months and years, there was an average of thirty. His climax was not so much a climax as a sigh, after which he collapsed as if pole-axed, rolled away and slept.

And so in the pale dark, and the stillness, a dark lightened by the white net, and a stillness punctuated by Tusker's snores and the yelps of distant jackals, she had found herself remembering Toole and re-creating him. She had been doing so ever since.

Now Tusker had conked out.

And was about to be 71.

She would have all the bother of finding out whether he really meant it this time that he wasn't going to have a birthday buffet. She usually allowed two or three weeks before his birthday before opening discussions. And so on Monday March 20th when she came back from the bazaar she was ready with the opening shot. But before she could open her mouth he said, 'Who's Mrs Guy Perron?'

'I have no idea, Tusker. Why?'

'You've got a letter from her, that's all.'

He handed her an airmail envelope.

CHAPTER SEVEN

When she opened the letter she realized that Mrs Guy Perron was Sarah Layton. *Dear Mrs Smalley*, Sarah began. Of this formal opening Lucy approved. Although she had always called Sarah Sarah and Susan Susan, they being so many years her juniors, they had always addressed her properly (in the way she for years had called their mother Mrs Layton and not Mildred. She'd tried the Mildred once and been properly snubbed).

'Dear Mrs Smalley, It was so good of you to write to me about Father's death. He would have been so interested to hear you were still in Pankot. His death was not due to cancer and he was alert and active almost right to the end which came rather suddenly. It was mother who had cancer, I'm afraid.

'You are quite right, Teddie is Susan's son by her first husband Teddie Bingham. Teddie is now a father himself, which is where "Boskie" comes in, a little boy of three which is about the age Teddie was when you last saw him in Pankot. He and his family are in Washington just now, but I've written to Susan telling her of your kind letter and the interesting news about Minnie. She'll no doubt tell Teddie next time she writes to him. She married for the third time a couple of years after we all came home. They live in Scotland. He's a physician. Since their marriage she has been in good health and I think very happy and contented. Teddie has followed in his step-father's footsteps by going into medicine. I'm sure he'll recall Minnie because he has a vivid memory and used to astonish me with the clarity of his recollections of India, although some must have been helped out by the family photographs. There's one taken in the garden of Commandant House at our farewell party in 1947, which includes you and Colonel Smalley. Perhaps you have a copy? If you have and you can still pick me out, the tall fair-haired man in civvies on my left is my husband Guy.

'Guy is an historian and has the chair in modern history at one of the new universities. Presently he's on a sabbatical and we're living at Combe Lodge. Normally we live in Falminster but rented the house there to a visiting American professor and his family last autumn and came down here so that Guy could work on his new book and I could look after father who found it lonely here after Mother died. Lance and Jane, as you imagined, are our children, but both are quite grown-up now and at Universities. We may continue permanently at Combe Lodge if Guy gets an appointment in London that seems to be on the cards. I'm not banking on it though. Academic life is as itinerant as the one we used to live in India, or nearly.

'You probably don't recall Guy at all because you only met on that occasion when father was handing over at Commandant House. Minnie, in fact, probably recalls him as the young Englishman who turned up in Mirat in August '47 just after Susan's second husband, Colonel Merrick, had died. He was in the carriage with us on that awful journey to Ranpur when the train was stopped and people were killed. He had to go on to Delhi but came up to Pankot later to see how we all were before flying home, which is why he was at the farewell party. Actually he'd been in Pankot before, very briefly, in '45, so he's as interested as I am in anything you can tell us about it nowadays.

'I do hope Colonel Smalley is now well on the mend. I was sorry to hear he'd been badly under the weather. I still have the lovely sandalwood box he gave me when I stopped being a WAC(I) and gave up the *daftar*. (Incidentally, I've always thought of you both as Tusker and Lucy, so may I call you that after all these years?)

'Another reason for this letter is to tell you that I've given your address and telephone number to a very pleasant young man called David Turner, who was a student of Guy's. He's going out to India in April to lecture at various universities and collect material for a thesis. Ranpur is on his itinerary so we'd already suggested he should take a few days off and go up to Pankot to get some hill air. He flies to Delhi on April 10th. He doesn't start his main lectures until the universities reassemble in the wet weather but he's keen to see as much as possible and also to go down into Bangladesh (as all young people seem to be). He's been in India before and has friends in Calcutta. He wants to spend a month or so acclimatizing himself again and travelling around. He's also interested in talking to English people who stayed on, and I know he'd love to meet you. He's a very good amateur photographer incidentally and especially interested in old British gravestones which sounds awfully morbid to me, but I told him there are some family gravestones in Pankot (Muirs and Laytons) and he's promised to bring back pictures if they're still identifiable. I'm sure he'll be in touch with you, probably towards the end of April, but knowing how casual young people are nowadays he may just turn up. But don't worry. He's not the kind of person you need to go to the least trouble over. Guy and I are awfully fond of him. I've told him about the new Shiraz and that Smith's still exists. If there's any small thing you'd like him to bring out from home please tell me and I'll get it and give it to him. There's just about time for me to hear from you before he leaves, so please don't hesitate, I'll send something to Minnie via David anyway. Meanwhile my thanks again for your very kind and most welcome letter. Please let us keep in touch. Kindest regards to you both. Sarah.'

From her escritoire Lucy could just see through the window the top of Tusker's head which meant he was still settled and content in his chair. She was glad. She would not have liked to be interrupted and interrogated about the letter. It had both an ebullient and a disturbing effect on her. She read it through once more. Again it both raised her spirits and lowered them. It provoked a variety of emotions and she could not for the moment sort out one clearly from the other: delight in new contact, renewal of contact, envy

94

of a life so free and open, nostalgia for Pankot as it had been.

She put the letter down, took her spectacles off and realized that her heart was going very fast so that she sat still and breathed slowly and deeply and wondered whether she was going to have an attack of the kind Tusker had had.

It came to her then that fundamentally she did not believe in Tusker's recovery, in there being any firm foundation, any foundation at all, for accepting Dr Mitra's assurances that another attack was not inevitable. She had merely been closing her mind to what at a deeper level of consciousness she knew had to be faced. In a year, perhaps sooner, she could be a widow.

She would be alone. She would be alone in Pankot. She would be alone in a foreign country. There would be no one of her own kind, her own colour, no close friend by whom to be comforted or on whom she could rely for help and guidance. The question whether she would be virtually destitute was one that frightened her so much that even her sub-conscious mind had been keeping that fear buried deep. There were areas of Tusker's affairs over which he had always presided like a jealous God and over which he still presided even though he must remember the time when she lost faith in his capacity to preside sensibly over anything.

'What I must do,' she thought, 'is go out to him now, regardless of the consequences, and say, Tusker, what is to happen to me if you die first?'

But just then she heard him say, 'Ha!' which meant he had found another passage to criticize in poor old Mr Maybrick's charming little book on the history of Pankot, and that if she went out to say Tusker what is to happen to me etcetera she wouldn't have the chance to open her mouth because he would start complaining about some tiny little error Mr Maybrick had made. Either that or he would be so absorbed (or pretending to be) that the vital question would be rewarded at best with no answer or at worst by some coarse counter-question such as What the bloody hell are you talking about?

'Tusker and I do not truly communicate with one another any more,' she told the empty living-room. 'His silence is his silence and my loquacity is my loquacity but they amount to the same thing. I can't hear what he is thinking and he does not hear what I'm saying. So we are cut off from one another, living separate lives under the same roof. Perhaps this is how it has always been between us but only become apparent in our old age.'

Life might have been different if they had gone home when he retired from Smith, Brown & McKintosh in 1960. She had been weak and foolish not to insist, not to issue an ultimatum. Bleak though England had seemed during the few weeks they'd spent there in 1950 by 1960 things had vastly improved by all accounts, although at the expense of a huge rise in the cost of living which, as old India hands on pension, priced them – so Tusker insisted – out of the home market.

But that had been an excuse. Slowly it had been borne in on her since that Tusker had never intended to go home. It was as though he bore a grudge against his own country and countrymen, whereas if either of them was entitled to bear a grudge it was she, for the way she'd so often been treated by some of those awful women who had condescended and taken every nasty little advantage of her as a junior wife who was not in a position – no, not in a position – to tell them where they got off but instead, oh yes instead, under an obligation to bear their treatment meekly not just for Tusker's sake but because a hierarchy was a hierarchy and a society without a clear stratification of duties and responsibilities and privileges was no society at all, which the Indians knew as well as anyone, let alone the British who had had the whole burden to bear and without whom India would just have fallen apart and nearly did in 1947 when the British handed over and the Indians started killing each other and would have fallen apart if Dickie Mountbatten hadn't been backed up by men like Nehru who was an aristocrat, an old Harrovian and a thorough gentleman and by an army whose senior officers were mostly Sandhurst men and awfully reliable.

There really wasn't a single aspect of the nice civilized things in India that didn't reflect something of British influence. Colonel Menektara had impeccable English manners, as did his wife who was in many ways as big a bitch as Mildred Layton had been, but this comforted Lucy since it indicated continuity of civilized behaviour, and as the wife of a retired colonel herself she was in a position to give delicately as good as she delicately got which meant that she and Coocoo Menektara understood one another perfectly.

The new Indian army was a credit to the old. The men never failed to get to their feet at the club if you paused to say good evening. With such an army and with such a prime minister as Nehru's daughter at the helm one need never fear a dictatorship of generals, such as they'd been forced to have in Pakistan.

Nor could one anticipate the subversion of the peasantry who remained as they had presumably been from time immemorial: tough, self-reliant, hard-working, astute, shrewd and long-suffering. This was how the British had found them and had the sense to leave them although with access to all the advantages of western technology which upper class Indians were certainly proving themselves keen to understand and adopt for the benefit of the country as a whole.

What filled her with anger, often, was the recollection that because of Tusker's lack of ambition she herself had had to wait until the very end to rise to the position she had aspired to and longed for, the position of Colonel's Lady. No sooner achieved, and the old hierarchy collapsed and the new one, the Indian one, took its place and in this one her position had been marginal and temporary and soon exchanged for that of, to be blunt, yes, to be blunt, box-wallah's wife, mixing with other box-wallahs' wives in a world which had increasingly dismayed her because it was one which had brought her into contact with the emerging Indian middle class of wheelers and dealers who with their chicanery, their corrupt practices, their black money, their utter indifference to the state of the nation, their use of political power for personal gain were ruining the country or if not ruining it making it safe chiefly for themselves: a hierarchy within a hierarchy, with the Mrs Bhoolabhoys at its base and at its peak people like the Desais, who had been nothing, were now as rich as Croesus and marrying their daughter into the family of a minister who himself had become rich by putting a price on his department's favours; or so she understood if she were to believe Tusker. But what of what Tusker said about anything was she to believe?

The answer came as if whispered in her ear by a winged messenger who had been standing patiently for years waiting for the moment to deliver his message. *Nothing.* She could believe nothing Tusker said or did because nothing he said or did revealed continuity of thought, intention or action. He had become devious in spite of that combative forthright manner. This meant that she could no longer believe *in* Tusker. She had begun not to do so on the day the British left India and they had stayed on, on loan. His personality change really dated from then.

She resumed her spectacles and said aloud, 'I shan't think about that today. I'll think about it tomorrow.' But the magic formula for transformation and transmigration was not working today. The Lodge was not Tara. She found her attention divided between the letter from Sarah which needed a quick answer and the problems that Tusker's personality change had encumbered her with.

Dear Sarah, she would begin—

'Ha!' Tusker said again, banging another nail into Mr Maybrick's coffin.

Dear Sarah (she would begin) So many thanks for your letter. *(Without actually saying it's the first time I've heard of a sandalwood box I don't remember Tusker mentioning it or you showing it to me at the time.)* It was so nice to hear from you. This is just a hurried reply to say we shall be delighted to see your young friend David Turner here in Pankot. *(I shan't say anything to Tusker yet, he'll only grumble and say something unkind about young English-*

men who can afford to swan around India no doubt at
someone else's expense probably the taxpayer's, which is
ridiculous when I tell you he's prepared to pass the time
of day with a dirty little English hippie whose begging
is a disgrace to us all.) I'll write more fully in a day or two.
(But then you see I'm afraid Tusker has lost his sense of
proportion and only seems to like English people who have
dropped out.) I do hate to ask for such a silly little thing
and on no account go to any trouble over it *(just for little*
me though why you shouldn't I don't know, it's not much
to ask and you can't rely on people like Mrs Desai who's
always going to and fro between Delhi, Zurich, London,
Paris and New York and comes back loaded with stuff
from the duty free shops and other stuff that if she doesn't
smuggle in must cost her a fortune at the customs not that
she can't afford it but she always seems to forget my little
requests). But if young Mr Turner wouldn't be most
awfully embarrassed to have such an item in his luggage
(he sounds to me as if nothing would embarrass him at
all, I wonder how long he wears his hair?) and if you could
obtain it easily, I mean locally, without going to the bother
of a journey to Selfridges *(which Mrs Blackshaw made such*
a fuss about having had to do) I really should appreciate
enormously two dozen sachets of Martin and Williams's
Belle Madame Special Blue Rinse No. 3, which is the only
thing that suits my stupid old hair and is virtually un-
obtainable here and I'm fast running out of the sachets Mrs
Blackshaw kindly sent last year *(which were held up in the*
customs and cost more in dues really than was worth the
trouble because Tusker grumbled so much although he'd
grumble if I stopped paying attention to my personal ap-
pearance and my hair is my only vanity)—

'Ha!' Tusker said again. Then he called, 'Luce?'

'Coming Tusker.'

'Are you there, Luce?'

'I've just said so.' She went out to the verandah.

'Who was the last person buried at St John's?' he asked.
She thought for a while.

'Mr Maybrick,' she said.

'There you are! He's got that wrong too. He says here it was old Mabel Layton.'

She stared at him.

'But Tusker, dear, I think he was buried after he'd written his little book.'

He stared at her in retaliation. 'Well for God's sake, I'm not such a bloody fool as not to realize that.'

It was a warm morning but wild irritation was bringing her out in goose-pimples. She had the urge to beat him over the head with *A Short History of Pankot* which she now wished she had never found hidden away on a dusty shelf in the club library and brought back for him.

'Then what is your problem, Tusker?'

'I don't have a problem. It's Maybrick's problem. I beg your pardon. *Was* Maybrick's problem. He says here, "With the interment in 1943 of Mabel Layton, the record of burials in this old churchyard ends and this chapter in the history of Pankot as it reveals itself to us through the headstones that mark the graves of British men and women who died far from home is closed." '

'That's wrong,' Lucy said.

'Well that's what I just said.'

'I don't mean that. What I mean is that it was 1944 when Mabel died so she couldn't have been interred in 1943, could she?'

'In Maybrick's book people can be buried any bloody time or not at all. *He's* there, isn't he? But according to his book he can't be.'

'She wasn't supposed to be there either.'

'Who wasn't supposed to be what?'

'Mabel Layton wasn't supposed to be buried at St John's. She wanted to be buried at St Luke's in Ranpur next to her second husband, James Layton, ICS, John Layton's father, but Mildred just shovelled her into the ground so as to be shot of her.'

'What on earth are you talking about? I don't know what you're saying or what it's got to do with old pissy-pants Maybrick.'

'It has quite a lot to do with Pissy-Pants Maybrick, Tusker,' Lucy said levelly, 'because it was Edgar Maybrick who went with Miss Batchelor to the mortuary only he didn't go in to view the body because of his wife who had died, so Miss Batchelor went in alone to convince herself that Mabel was really dead and after that she went off her head and tried to stop Mildred burying Mabel at St John's. She hadn't believed Mabel was dead and had a bad conscience about having left her alone to spend the afternoon repairing Mr Maybrick's Handel.'

'His what?'

'For his organ. It was coming apart. Perhaps it was his Bach.'

'Sometimes you kill me, Luce,' Tusker said, helpless it seemed with mirth and wiping his eyes.

'I am glad that I have some kind of positive effect on you, Tusker. It is at least proof that I am still alive and in possession of certain faculties. Among them for instance the faculty of provoking a response if only a response to me as an absurd person. But naturally I could not expect to be able to jog a memory so deeply buried in deliberate forgetfulness and wilful obfuscation.'

'Obverse-what?'

'Obfuscation. It is a word currently popular among critics of government. This morning I find it pertinent to you, Tusker. You obfuscate. You stupefy me. You bewilder me. I do not know where or what I am when I talk to you.'

She clasped her hands under her chin the better to stop him interrupting. 'And I do not know *why* you obfuscate. Presumably it's because nothing is clear to you any more and you deplore the idea of things being clear to other people. You were born under the sign of Aries, which reminds me we must discuss your birthday, and you do not want to be left out because people born under this sign hate being left out of anything but are utterly selfish always trying to control and order other people about to suit themselves and going on doing it or trying to do it even when they seem to have lost their grip on reality but of course they are probably only pretending half the time to have lost their grip in order to attract sympathy and attention. It is typical of you to pretend to have found one error and at the same time overlook a real error – the fact that it was on June six nineteen forty-four which was the day of the landings in Normandy that Mabel Layton died on the verandah of Rose Cottage when there was no one in the bungalow except Susan because Miss Batchelor was having tea with Mr Maybrick and Susan went into premature labour as a result and after the baby was born she went off her head too and Minnie had to save the baby from being burned to death, which of course they tried to hush up but we all knew because you can never stop Indian servants gossiping. And Mildred never never forgave poor old Miss Batchelor for not being at Rose Cottage on the one day in years when there was some excuse for her being there at all and she told her to vacate and didn't care that Barbie had nowhere to go, all Mildred was interested in was moving into Rose Cottage at last herself with Susan and Sarah, and you're not going to tell me you don't remember, and don't remember Susan being rude to us at the Church and how you said later that her being rude was probably the first real sign that she was off her rocker and hadn't recovered, but of course you were always making excuses for people like them and pretended not ·to notice what *I* had to put up with which I only did because it was my duty to do so although it was a very different matter when they'd all gone home, you were free with your criticisms then, Tusker. Take Rose Cottage. You knew I'd longed and longed to live there but after we'd moved in and the Laytons and all the other people had gone all you did was poke fun and complain about Mildred's bad taste getting rid of the roses and making a tennis court. You poked fun at the Laytons even in front of Indians and were insensitive to the fact that very often the Indians were shocked and that I was embarrassed and am still embarrassed by the way you belittle things and people that belong to a part of your life you have decided is behind you. In Bombay you poked fun at the Indian officers you'd been working with who'd taken over the reins, you poked fun at them to all those box-wallahs. It is not an attractive trait Tusker, and it is too late for you to do anything about it, it seems to be part of your nature to attack, to denigrate and now to obfuscate, and I have lived with it too long to have the strength to do anything but regret it and to observe it as the reason why *I* have no friends, because all our friends are your friends, Tusker, not mine, and – yes, I *will* say it – *they are all black* and I want you to realize that it has been much on my mind recently that if you had not recovered from your attack I would have been alone here, alone, Tusker, and having to rely for human sympathy and moral support upon people who frankly do not care for me, not deeply, and for whom I do not deeply care either.'

A pause.

Tusker said, 'You're pissed, Luce.'

'Which is another thing. I have noticed that you do not use words like that in front of Coocoo Menektara or Mrs Srinivasan, nor even in front of their husbands. You seem to reserve them for me, for Dr Mitra, for Ibrahim and for your bosom-chum Mr Bhoolabhoy. And I am not as you so crudely put it, pissed, but might be before the day is out. You call me to ask who was the last person to be buried at St John's knowing perfectly well that Edgar Maybrick was entirely within his rights to say it was Mabel Layton, and that it would have been highly macabre for him to have nominated himself, even though he *was* the last person, and will ever remain so, because there is no more *room.*'

'Yes there is. There's a nice little space in the southwest corner. Enough for two if they dig deep enough.'

She crossed her arms over her long-unclaimed bosom. Suddenly there was a grunting sound from the mower and then (was it?) a distant shriek of outrage from Mrs Bhoolabhoy. The symbolism did not escape her: two aspects of the grim reaper.

'I am not concerned what you do with me, Tusker, if I predecease you. You can sell me to Tata's for soap, for all I care. But what I do with you if you predecease me is entirely my business. I shall probably float you down the

Ganges on a raft woven of the paper in which you have all your life buried yourself, but not – you understand – so that you may drift out into the Bay of Bengal to become a speck of water and merge with the Absolute, but so that you may merge with the millions of tons of silt that are making the Hooghly river un-navigable and giving concern to the Public Works Department of the city of Calcutta. Have you decided what you want to do about your Birthday Buffet?'

'Yes,' Tusker said. His eyes looked filmed over. His skin was blotchy. Perhaps another attack was imminent.

'Then give me instructions.'

'That's soon done. Bugger the birthday buffet.'

'This is your message to your friends? This is the way in which you wish me to convey letters of non-invitation to, say, Colonel and Mrs Menektara?'

'I'll dictate it if your bloody shorthand's still up to it.'

She nodded, gripped her beads. 'Bugger is not a word Pitman's taught me, but for subtlety of sound and elegance of outline the Pitman method has never been surpassed and I suspect your dictation would not find me at a loss. But it grieves me, Tusker, that in our old age you too should sneer at me for having once had to acquire a skill which I was proud to have acquired and of which I remained proud even when I realized that in India it marked me as a girl who had once had to work for a living. And it came in handy enough, didn't it? Without it, the cost of discovering one had married a man without manly ambition might have proved insupportable. Every hour you spent hiding yourself behind a desk, Tusker, was paid for by me in little humiliations, dogsbodying for the wives of the men who profited from the work that flowed from your desk, your desks, your hundreds of desks, none of which any man who thought as much of his wife as he thought of his own peace of mind and comfort of body would have sat at for a moment once he realized that other men were enjoying the fruits of his work and their wives with them and his own wife suffering. It was you, Tusker, who made *me* a dogsbody because a role of dogsbody for yourself was

104

the one you had chosen to play. But at least you might have gone on playing it and not begun to freak out the moment you left the army. People do not understand when they find an apparently mature man acting in an entirely different way from the one to which they are accustomed and what people do not understand they dislike or fear and they do not easily forgive the person who is the cause of these disagreeable emotions. I shall not raise the subject again and shall not discuss it further. I think I have made my feelings plain and in all the circumstances I should be grateful if you would be so kind as to make plain the position I should be in if you had another attack and did not survive, and instead of making absurd notes about poor Mr Maybrick's inoffensive little book you made plain notes in plain terms about my financial position as it would be were I to find myself alone here and weeping amid the alien corn.'

Tusker's mouth hung open. Her heart was racing, but triumphantly. She had never *stunned* him into silence. His silence now was like the silence she had years ago imagined creating in a darkened theatre, one which would hold until after her exit when it would be shattered by prolonged applause, a deserved ovation: the kind she had dreamed of and might have got back in 'Pindi before the war when they did *The Wind and the Rain*, except that that hard grasping little bitch Dulcie Thompson got the part, not that there'd ever been any doubt that she would nor that she, Lucy, would end up in the prompt-corner as assistant stage manager to the incompetent Captain Starling, and anyway the part had never been auditioned for. Leading parts went automatically to Dulcie and you took your life in your hands if you prompted her during one of her Pauses or alternatively got chewn to a rag if you couldn't tell the difference between a Pause and a Black-Out, which was virtually impossible because Dulcie's addiction to Pauses was matched only by her susceptibility to Black-Outs which she covered by succumbing to her other addiction – business: business with a handkerchief or a handbag, un-rehearsed business that ruined other actors' concentration, even moving props that caused black-out for someone else a few minutes later when he found the prop not in its place.

'I need a prop now,' Lucy thought. 'Something to help me get off while Tusker's mouth is still open.' But there was no prop. She would have to ad lib. 'I don't suppose, Tusker, that you even remember the time when Dulcie Thompson was ill on the fourth night of *The Wind and the Rain* and the GOC was coming and everyone was in despair and Major Grimshaw rang you and said as ASM I was also understudy and obviously knew the part backwards so would I do it and you said, no?'

Tusker closed his mouth but still said nothing.

'If you remember the incident at all no doubt you only remember me saying Oh Tusker thank you for getting me out of it I'd have been terrified but terrified – which I would have been but not of me making a mess of it but of making us conspicuous and putting Dulcie Thompson's nose out of joint and so making things difficult at the *daftar* for you, with Colonel Thompson, because after all you knew of my interest in amateur dramatics before we were married and listened apparently so sympathetically to what I told you of my hopes, then, of doing a part, so what you said to Major Grimshaw was a lie, but in my silly little way I thought of it almost as a compliment because I thought you were worried that I'd act Dulcie Thompson into the ground, but I'm afraid it was simply another example of the way you have always deprived me, yes, deprived me, of the fullness of my life in order to support and sustain the smallness of your own. And there is no need to remind me, Tusker, that at the last moment Dulcie Thompson arrived anyway and without actually giving the performance of her carefully modulated, calculated, controlled and disgusting life created a sufficient enough impression to cause her husband to be elevated two months later to the rank of brigadier and to be posted abroad, during which time no doubt the GOC had it off with her in Ootacumund.'

'Naini Thal,' Tusker said.

'Ootacumund, or Naini Thal, it is neither here nor there.'

'Don't agree. It was definitely Naini Thal. And it wasn't the GOC but that other general, old Trumpers. Ootacumund was the place she had it off with young Bobbie Beamish. Old Thompson divorced her and she became the Marchioness of Peacehaven and was last seen in Cairo at a party given by Henry Kissinger for Golda Meir.'

'Don't be ridiculous, Tusker. You're making all this up. Dulcie Thompson died years ago.'

'Luce, love, people like Dulcie Thompson never die.'

'Which means you remember her.'

'Oh, I remember Dulcie Thompson. Biggest knockers in 'Pindi.'

He had deprived her of her scene.

'I shall go for a walk,' she said.

'You've been for a walk.'

'Then I shall go for another. Is there anything you want from the bazaar?'

'Nothing you can buy,' Tusker said.

It was better not to inquire further into this.

CHAPTER EIGHT

Before going out she rummaged in the bottom drawer of the chest in the bedroom among the old snapshots and photographs.

They should, of course, be assembled properly in an album, Mr Turner, she thought, opening the first of her imaginary conversations with this as yet unknown young man who might turn out to be a sympathetic listener, *but my husband caught me at it one day and said sticking snaps of one's past life into albums is onanistic. I didn't know what that meant but looked it up, so you'll understand my reluctance to continue the good work. Ah, here's the one Sarah mentioned. The Laytons' farewell party at Commandant House.*

She took the photograph over to the escritoire where she had left her spectacles.

'Memsahib?'

Ibrahim startled her.

'What is it now?'

'It is Monday, Memsahib.'

'I know that. After all, yesterday was Sunday.'

'I book a seat at the movie?'

'No. I don't know. I'm busy at the moment.'

'Bhoolabhoy Sahib not coming this evening?'

'I have no idea.'

'Memsahib ordering trays for lunch or going to the dining-room?'

'I don't know that either. Kindly stop interrogating me, Ibrahim. I don't know what I shall be doing at lunch time or come to that for the rest of the day. I'm going out and I may stay out but if I elect to come back it doesn't necessarily follow that I must be driven out again to see a picture I may not want to see simply because Colonel Sahib and Mr Bhoolabhoy propose to spend the evening knocking it back and gossiping like a couple of old women.'

The mower started up again.

'And will you be so good as to tell your *mali* to stop that infernal noise? Mrs Bhoolabhoy is not the only one entitled to have nerves. I never said he should work every day. It seems to me he's finding jobs for himself at my expense.'

'Memsahib is no longer satisfied with Joseph?'

'At the moment I'm not satisfied with anything or anybody. Tell him to *stop*. If things go on like this I shall have to start keeping a time-sheet, or rather you will have to start keeping one, showing the hours he's worked and the work done, so that I can decide what is necessary and what is sheer exploitation.'

'Exploitation, Memsahib?'

'Exploitation! Of me!' Her voice had risen. Instinctively they both glanced at the window. 'Of *me*,' she continued, *sotto voce*. 'But I'm not a fool. I'm not to be exploited. I'm not to be led by the nose. Tell him to stop. *Now*.'

Ibrahim went.

She put her glasses on and considered the picture. She smiled. 'Well, that's gallant of you, Mr Turner, to recognize me. I scarcely recognize myself. But it's a quarter of a century ago. If you recognize me you must know who this is. Yes, of course, Sarah. That's Tusker. He's lost a lot of weight since. And a lot of hair. A lot of everything, including today what I'd call most of what is left of his credibility. This, I think, must be Sarah's husband, Mr Perron, or should I say Professor Perron?'

The sound of mowing stopped.

Peering closer at Mr Perron certain resonances came through, weakly at first, then strongly. 'Yes, I do remember him, Mr Turner. He followed me home and for a night or two haunted our bedroom at Rose Cottage, I mean Tusker's and mine, standing there in a corner in the dark, waiting for a snore from Tusker and a sign from me. He was the right height and the right breadth, perhaps a bit too tall, but his hair was fair and his eyes blue-grey. But he smiled too often. Look at him grinning here. He did not have the smouldering quality that is necessary in Toole and when he opened his mouth he talked himself right out of the part except physically, because Toole is rough of speech and hardly articulate. I remember Mr Perron being a disappointment to me, Mr Turner, because the back of his neck was the first thing I noticed, it was like the back of Toole's neck, and I said to Sarah's Aunt Fenny – that's her, the rather stout woman, seated, with her arm round little Teddie – I said, Who is that young man? And she said oh, that's Mr Perron (she must have said), who was with us in the carriage when the Hindus stopped the train and dragged Muslims out, he's come up to see how we all are before flying home, come and meet him. Susan isn't in the picture, Mr Turner, because she was in the nursing home again, getting over the shock of her second husband's death and the shock of what happened on the train. And I confess that when I met your Mr Perron I thought: Are you going to be Susan's *third* husband? She did rather run through them. I oughtn't to tell tales out of school but it's a long time ago now and I'm glad Sarah has found happiness, but in those days it was well-known in Pankot that Susan was always pinching her elder sister's young men, but then she was a pretty vivacious little thing, though perhaps the vivacity was an early sign of hysteria. Sarah in those days was to put it plainly a bit dull from young men's point of view, although a veritable brick so far as pulling her weight in the family was concerned. The mother drank, you know, I don't mean embarrassingly, but she did have this tendency to start before anyone else and still be at it when they'd finished. But of course for a woman she was in the prime of life and had been without her husband for years. I expect you knew he'd been a prisoner of war in Germany. So one took that into consideration. There was never any unpleasantness and she was tireless in the work she had to do for the soldiers' families. Her father was a Muir. GOC, Ranpur, early in the 20s. In a way the Laytons and the Muirs *were* Pankot. I'll show you the graves of some of the forebears. Well, well, so it was Sarah Mr Perron had his eye on. I'm glad of that. There was a time when some of us became a bit worried about her. She sometimes gave this odd impression of not taking things seriously, I mean India, us in India, and I think that's what put the young men off. There was even a moment when one wondered whether she was unsound in that respect. Sometimes she seemed to be laughing at us, and it suddenly occurs to me that this may have been why she got on well with Tusker when she worked for him at Area head-quarters because if you listen to Tusker now you begin to suspect that he was laughing too because really he hasn't a good word to say nowadays about anything connected with the past and this sometimes makes me feel, Mr Turner, that my whole life has been a lie, mere play-acting, and I am not at all sure, Mr Turner, if when you turn up and turn out to be self-reliant and young and buoyant and English and light-hearted and enthusiastic about your researches but look as if you will go home laughing at us like a drain that I shall be able to stand you, even though I yearn for you because simply by being here in this house you will be the catalyst I need to bring me back into my own white skin which day by day, week by week, month by month, year after year, I have felt to be increasingly in-capable of containing me, let alone of acting as defensive armour. You don't understand what I'm saying so let us pay our little visit to the cemetery where you can take your photographs and after that we could go up to Rose Cottage, or 12 Upper Club Road, as it's really called, and ask Mrs Menektara for permission to take snaps of the old place as it is now, not changed much outside, but inside, oh dear dear me, a world of difference. She burns incense, you know, and the place is crammed with priceless carvings and statuettes that make it look as if they've raided a Hindu temple. It's lit like a museum and it's not easy to find a comfortable place to sit except on the verandah and in the dining-room, but sometimes when I lunch there I find some of the guests eating with their fingers which I know is traditional but I'm sure some of them do it because it's now thought smart by the younger people, but oh it does put me off, and seems such a waste of all that lovely cutlery which has come from Liberty's and is so incongruous when you

111

know the chairs and tables have come from Heal's and all the pictures on the walls are terribly modern, and lit, even in daytime.'

A shadow fell.

'What is it now, Ibrahim?'

'*Mali* has stopped.'

'Actually I'm not deaf. If you have nothing else to do this morning except *hover* you can go and fetch me a tonga to the side entrance.'

'Memsahib is going to the club?'

'Memsahib may indeed be going to the club.'

'And having lunch there?'

'Possibly. Just go, Ibrahim. Just bring the tonga. What is wrong with you this morning?'

He put his hands behind his back.

'Yesterday all was sunshine. Today all is gloomy. Memsahib much preoccupied, sorting out drawers. Sahib is now in a bad temper. Sahib and Memsahib not pulling on well together. This morning the house is not well settled on its feet. Cook reporting same applying at Bhoolabhoys. Ibrahim not knowing whether coming or going. *Mali* very dejected because grass grows and he is told to stop mowing, and make self scarce.'

'What you say may be so. I don't know what you expect me to do about it.'

'It is a very funny picture,' he said after a moment. 'Repeat showing, *How To Murder Your Wife*, starring Jack Lemmon. Memsahib much enjoyed last time round. Very popular film. Indian officers especially are liking it. Manager-sahib at cinema expecting full bookings. I bring tonga then go down to cinema and book memsahib's ticket?'

'Perhaps you'd better book two, Ibrahim. One for Burra Sahib and the other for Mr Bhoolabhoy. *How To Murder Your Wife* sounds more their sort of thing. Are you drunk?'

'Memsahib must know that for Ibrahim alcohol is forbidden.'

'The tonga, Ibrahim.'

It was a shamefully long time since either she or Tusker had been to church although her reasons were different from his. Tusker was not a believer. She had never grown out of the habit of belief acquired in childhood and at the major Christian festivals she had managed to overcome the disquiet she had begun to feel worshipping in a place where her pale face seemed to put her at a disadvantage.

She felt conspicuous. She felt like someone who had never sought but had nevertheless achieved notoriety. She did not, she was sure, mind at all being preached to or blessed by a dark-skinned brother-in-Christ, nor kneeling in the presence of other such brethren, but at the level at which awareness of ambiguities and ambivalences existed she was conscious of them. It was like – as Phoebe Blackshaw had said after going to church with her once – being a black sheep in reverse exposure. Since the Blackshaws went home her own attendances had fallen off, and she had not gone to communion for years. As the tonga turned into Church road, going past the old rectory, now not a rectory but the home of Mr Thomas, the cinema manager, who had six children, she tried to work out precisely how long it had been since she last entered the little churchyard which in the days of the *raj* had each Sunday morning been such a social focal point, with all the tongas gathered outside waiting to take people home afterwards to their luncheon parties or to the club for cocktails and curry.

'Wait here,' she told the tonga-wallah. When she went in through the old lychgate she paused under the arch. The recollections the gate aroused were not of her father's gaunt suburban church but of the church in the village of Piers Cooney where long before she was born her father had had his first curacy, where later she and the twins, Mark and David, staying at Piers Cooney Hall for a fortnight three glorious summers in a row, had been driven to attend Sunday matins.

'I must tell you about that, Mr Turner,' she said, sitting on the bench which she was sure she had never done before and was surprised to find herself doing now. She could not recall making the decision to sit but here she was doing so.

113

'Forgive me, Mr Turner, this morning I am a little disorganized, a little disoriented. My mother's name was Large. She was a poor relation of the people at the Hall. They employed her to look after their sickly son. She was a great woman for games in the open air. Her first name was Emily. Emily Large. My father's names were Mathew Mark Luke Little. People's names, like their lives, should not be targets for mockery, but I forgive you for smiling because you have connected Little and Large and Little to Smalley. I grant you it is funny. But it is not funny here under the arch of the lychgate with a view to the pathway through the green pastures of our dead who passed under this gate. Have you ever noticed, Mr Turner, that the grain in wood – as witness this seat – looks much the same wherever you find it? That a pebble is always a pebble, a blade of grass not to be mistaken for anything else, and that granted different intensities and degrees, depending where in the world you are, light falls here, there, indifferently, even with a kind of monotony, causing you no surprise other than the mild one of realizing that nature is not as inventive as you had supposed. The sound of the sea washing the beach of Juhu, north of Bombay, is the sound of the sea at Worthing or wherever. If you close your eyes, Mr Turner, there is no telling where you are.'

She closed her eyes and bent her head. Some distance away the tonga wallah hawked and spat. Crows protested her occupation of the gateway. A wind sprang up, chilled by its journey from a source in the distant mountains, and then was gone, leaving a profound silence, interrupted (she realized) by the rhythmic sound of the coppersmith bird beating out its endless saucepans in the smithy of the great pine-clad hills in which Pankot rested two thousand feet or more above sea level.

Snick-snick

How strange, Mr Turner. What is that sound? It's not the coppersmith. It reminds me of Saturdays in the summer at home, the sound that father made, cutting the hedge to the accompaniment of that other sound, click-cluck, which was the sound the twins made playing cricket on the vicarage lawn with their sleeves rolled up and smelling odd when you got close to them with the tray of lemonade mother made me squeeze and strain and take out to them. The only difference between them was that David had more freckles than Mark, otherwise they were identical twins and strangers got terribly confused. I'm afraid they often took advantage of that. They weren't generous-natured boys. Sometimes they were very unkind to me but I didn't dare complain – not after the time they poured green paint over my head and swore it was an accident which mother was inclined to believe, but not father who liked my pretty light brown hair and was so cross that for once he gave them each a terrible thrashing, or thought that was what he was giving them but I heard them sniggering afterwards, which they never did if mother used the strap on them. They punished me though, by sending me to coventry for almost the rest of the summer holiday and if they referred to me at all it was as Tell-Tale or Baldy, because most of my hair had to be cut off, which mother did herself in a way that made me feel I deserved it and that it gave her pleasure to see me looking more like a boy than a girl. So most of those weeks I spent indoors, or hiding in the orchard, what we called the orchard, but it was only a few diseased old apple trees at the back of the vicarage garden, but I used to sit there listening to father clipping the hedges on a Saturday afternoon which was when he practised his sermon. Snick-Snick. Then click-cluck, the sound of the boys playing cricket and mother's voice egging them on. She kept wicket. She had very large hands. But then she would wouldn't she, with a name like that?

Snick-Snick

She left the lychgate and set out on the path through the churchyard but suddenly stood arrested – not by the sound which, coming again, was clearly that made by a pair of shears, but by the appearance of the graves. A lot of grass had been trimmed and many of the headstones cleaned.

Whoever was responsible for this was obviously even now at work, but invisible, presumably on the other side of the church, in the part of the yard where Mabel Layton was buried. Mabel herself had been a great gardener. Her crazy old companion, Miss Batchelor, had always said Mabel would never rest while she remained buried in the wrong place, in Pankot instead of down in Ranpur. But Mabel had remained buried. Or had she?

Well let us not be silly, Lucy told herself, and set off again, taking the path that ran along the south side. Just as she reached the south door it opened and a figure emerged causing her nearly to jump out of her skin. She uttered a cry.

Then: 'Oh, what a fright you gave me, Mr Bhoolabhoy.'

Mr Bhoolabhoy was himself in no condition for such a shock, particularly the shock of seeing Mrs Smalley, of whom he had just been thinking. Her sudden manifestation made him go weak at the knees for the second time that morning. Had he conjured her? But no. There she was, smiling at him now in her dignified ladylike way.

There was a special corner in Mr Bhoolabhoy's heart reserved for Lucy. His regard for her was of longstanding. It saddened him that she was no longer a regular member of the congregation. The sight of her upright and neatly dressed figure, her modest demeanour, the manner in which she attended and followed every phase of the service (as to the manner born, as indeed she had been) had always reassured him about the fitness and decency and meaning of what they were all gathered together to do. When she and Tusker had first come to Pankot, in retirement, she had sometimes brought Tusker along and they had sat in the front pew. After Tusker stopped coming she, year by year, had sat farther and farther back, as if fading away. It had hurt him a bit, early on, but dimly he had begun to understand her reasons without being able quite to name them, and in any case self-effacement fitted so well the

116

image he had of her as a real English lady of the old school, a lady who seldom raised her voice because she seldom had need. She had the gift of quietly commanding obedience from those who owed it to her. This did not of course include Tusker, whose manner with his wife sometimes puzzled Mr Bhoolabhoy but also interested him as an example of old English custom.

It was always a pleasure to see her in the dining-room at Smith's. Her presence made the place look less seedy. The same, at a different level of sameness, could also be said of his friend Tusker. It was pleasant to watch them dining on a night when there were no other guests, saying virtually nothing to one another in that reserved British way. Tusker of course was free with his criticism of the food, the service, the state of the table-cloth, but his complaints were the kind a man made who also saw the funny side of there being need to complain and of the fact that it was he who was complaining.

Mr Bhoolabhoy had often heard it said that one of the troubles with the British in the days of the *raj* was that they had taken themselves far too seriously. He was not quite old enough to have formed a firm personal judgment in the matter but he had formed an interim one to the effect that if it was true about the British in those days it was equally true of the Indians now; which would mean that it was being responsible for running things that shortened the temper and destroyed the sense of humour.

Whenever Tusker and Lucy dined at Smith's and other tables were occupied by Indian guests it was from the Smalley table that a glow of mildness and pleasure emanated. On such occasions they spoke more often to one another, exchanged cross-table chat with other diners if they knew them but devoted their attention to their plates if an altercation took place between another table and the waiter or Mr Bhoolabhoy, or on one or two dreadful occasions Mrs Bhoolabhoy who was convinced that the customer was not only always wrong but had to be proven wrong. It was the sense of responsibility that caused these altercations.

Why was it then that his responsibility as manager hadn't shortened his own temper? One answer was all too clear. He didn't run things. It was Lila who ran them. He sat metaphorically in the crook of her great arm like a ventriloquist's dummy, merely mouthing her complaints and orders. The other answer perhaps was that although he had a *sense* of responsibility he had never had a very strong inclination to take it.

He had been content to be dominated, first of all by Mr Pillai, now by Lila. He knew he would continue to be dominated. This morning he had been regretting this. Coming face to face with Mrs Smalley who was in her way as strong-willed a woman as Lila, but not domineering, he wished that he had been blessed with greater strength of character.

'Please forgive me, Mrs Smalley. As you see, I was also startled. You may not believe me but I had just been thinking about you.'

His morning had begun in a peculiar way. He woke to find himself in bed with Lila, stark naked, his mouth and nose half-smothered in her immense breasts, his shoulders clamped in the iron embrace of her arms and his legs pinioned between hers. She seemed to be blowing playfully on the top of his head.

What puzzled him was to find himself in bed with her at all. He could not actually recall being summoned. He wondered whether while he slept she had crept into his room and carried him over her shoulder to her own bed, stripped him of his pyjamas and then lowered him on top of her. Since he had daily waking evidence that he probably spent most of his sleeping hours in a state of readiness, he supposed it would have been quite possible for her thus to have availed herself of the opportunity to enjoy what otherwise went to waste without his having to wake up and consciously co-operate. After all, she had the strength.

It was amazing how strong even smaller-built women

118

than Lila could be, and how determined. Their sudden inexplicable whims and preferences in what seemed to him sometimes irrelevant matters (for example y-fronted underpants instead of the looser cooler boxer-style trunks) were equally astonishing. It was all part of their charm, of course, not knowing what they'd say or do next, not knowing where you stood with them. Or lay. On the one night he had succeeded in catching Hot Chichanya's eye in Ranpur and been admitted to her room she had laughed at his underpants. She had also insisted first on their standing, and then on their lying, and then on adopting a position she had to show him in an illustrated book before he believed it possible. 'Thin men are so supple,' she said, turning him out into the night to go home to his own hotel. 'Come back tomorrow but with proper underpants and we'll do the Koshak Dance.'

But into the delights and mysteries of the Koshak Dance he had not been initiated. Next evening she greeted him in full Koshak Dance uniform which apart from the whip which he eyed unhappily would have been interesting to divest her of but it seemed for the moment that she intended to remain fully clothed while Mr Bhoolabhoy 'and these two other nice boys' danced round her in a circle. The two other boys wore nothing but red leather boots and red y-fronted briefs. There were several pairs of boots he could try on, she said. 'You have the pants?'

'Oh, yes,' he said. 'But they are the wrong colour. I will go and change them.'

He beat a retreat. Ever since when he had been viewing the prospect of a return engagement for Hot Chichanya at the Shiraz with dismay and delicious apprehension. Even while performing with her what she called double-lotus an area of his imagination had been occupied by the picture of being locked, so, with Mrs Bhoolabhoy, and had continued to be occupied, so that now and again he smiled, then giggled and had to call himself very sternly to order to avoid having to absent himself from Lila's company and succumb to a fit of hysteria. Lila in the double-lotus position would be even more of a sight to see than Lila stuck all over with Dr Battacharya's accupuncture needles.

Except, he himself would not survive to see the sight long. On the count of weight and gravity alone she would break every bone in his back and legs before the connection had been achieved. Either that or she would be unable to control the arc of the rocking movement and break him at the pelvis or fall on top and smother him.

Brought fully awake by these images he realized he was being smothered now. He unstuck his perspiring face from her bosom and squinted upward.

She was fast asleep. The playful blowing on the top of his head was no such thing. Oblivious, she was puffing at dreamtime dandelion clocks. Her slack lips quivered with each expulsion of breath. The brows were contracted: storm signals of another migraine, another bad morning. When she woke life would be difficult. It would be wise to extricate himself before she did so. He had a technique for this which he used occasionally in the middle of the night to return to his own room without waking her. Mostly she chucked him out with no ceremony. She preferred to sleep alone and he had learned from experience that the morning glory of Mrs Bhoolabhoy's conjugal contentment (a rare bloom) withered rapidly if she did not find herself alone, even if she had not personally dismissed him because incapable of doing so (pole-axed, he liked to think, by a particularly passionate five star performance on his part).

He could not remember ever having to leave surreptitiously with the morning light already filtering through the curtains and illuminating the fine hairs on her upper lip; but the technique would have to be the same, thus: nuzzle up to a nipple if you could find one and give an amorous little groan. This usually brought in response a groan of a different kind. Next, find a free hand of one's own, which wasn't as easy as it sounded, what with cramp and pins and needles already set in, and place it on the back of a thigh or whatever part it could reach, or, if already in contact, move it suggestively to another part. Before doing this it was best to tense the muscles slightly to withstand the convulsion this combination of loving approach and fond leavetaking usually provoked.

It was provoked now. Mrs Bhoolabhoy moaned loudly, heaved and turned herself over and away, predictably taking Mr Bhoolabhoy's head with her in a kind of wrestler's half-nelson. It could be painful and was this morning; but the rest of the drill was comparatively easy because the two of them were well lubricated with perspiration. One just slipped the head away from the grappling hold inch by inch.

Free of Mrs Bhoolabhoy, Mr Bhoolabhoy slid backward out of the bed and knelt, automatically groping on the floor for the place where he must have left his pyjamas. Finding none he came finally and fully awake and stood up. His head was throbbing. He went weak at the knees so dropped to them again, quietly. Was he imagining the whole thing? Was he dreaming? No. Looking round the half-lit bedroom the memory of the night before came clearly back to him.

There were no pyjamas because he had never got into pyjamas. Before he went to bed with Lila he had been in this room in his clothes, the same clothes he had worn for Sunday Evensong: clerical grey lightweight suit, white shirt, dark blue tie, black shoes, black socks, white aertex undervest, white aertex boxer-pants. They were there – cast away with utter abandon, unbrushed, unhung, victims of scandalous neglect; dying of it, by the look of them, having been all night out in the open with no one to care for them, gather them up and take them to a place where they would have felt comfortable and wanted.

Yes, there they were: thrown by him across the settee, Lila's day bed. He approached them, knee by knee, and collected them item by item, careful not to jog the coffee-table on which was set out further evidence of the previous night's carousal – an empty gin bottle, two glasses, one of them one-third full of stale gin and tonic; an icebucket, a revoltingly full ashtray, two trays of the remains of huge dishes of curried chicken, pilaf rice, papadoms, assorted congealed chutneys; a jug one quarter full of water and air bubbles; curled slices of lemon, three bottles of beer (one opened but scarcely used, the others empty), an empty packet of India King cigarettes and a three-quarter empty box of marrons glacés.

Still on his knees, Mr Bhoolabhoy, clutching his clothes, an awkward task, made for the door to his own bedroom, feeling like the actor who played Toulouse Lautrec in that film, one of the few he had ever seen. (Mr Thomas had recommended it for the can-can.) He dropped a shoe, and froze, but Mrs Bhoolabhoy simply snored. He had to stand to open his door but once inside unaccountably dropped to his knees again, placed his clothes carefully on a nearby chair, shut the communicating door, bolted it, then hobbled over to his bed and climbed up and lay upon it in the embryo position. He closed his eyes to open his aching mind to the light of yesterday.

It had been a good day to start with; Sunday, his day off. It had also been the Reverend Stephen Ambedkar's day. The Reverend Stephen was a very fussy fellow. Mr Bhoolabhoy was a bit afraid of him. His predecessor, the Reverend Thomas Narayan, had always stayed at Smith's on his monthly visit to minister to the spiritual needs of Pankot's Christian community. The Reverend Stephen Ambedkar had done so only once, since when he had stayed mostly with the Menektaras, who weren't Christians but one of whose friends, the Inspector-General of Police in Ranpur, was. Mr Bhoolabhoy wondered whether after his first parochial visit the Reverend Stephen had said something unkind to the Inspector-General about the accommodation his predecessor had had to put up with.

Spiritually joyful though the monthly visitations were they were also a source of administrative tension and slight anxiety. This had never been the case in the days of old Mr Narayan who had come up on the Saturday night train which got into Pankot on Sunday morning, deposited his meagre bag in Room 5, joined Mr Bhoolabhoy for breakfast and then walked with him up to the Church at about 9.30. Mr Bhoolabhoy had been up at the church earlier, to let Susy in and by the time he returned with Mr Narayan she had done the flowers. Over a cup of coffee from Susy's flask and seated round the table in the vestry Mr Narayan had told them the hymns he would like sung and the lessons he would like read. While Susy went to mark the places in the bible on the lectern and insert the hymn numbers in the frames, he and Mr Bhoolabhoy would go over the month's accounts and discuss parish affairs. At 10.25, while Mr Narayan put on his vestments, Mr Bhoolabhoy would climb up to the chamber and toll the bell six times.

The bell was to summon communicants. The Reverend Thomas Narayan never failed to celebrate communion before Matins however few people turned up, and he had no strong opinions about the need for abstinence prior to the mass. Mr Bhoolabhoy took care to eat nothing and merely sip his coffee. Sometimes he and Susy were the only two communicants to approach the Lord's table. After communion, and after the morning service that followed and was better attended, Mr Narayan would wander among his flock in the churchyard and sometimes accept an invitation to lunch with one of them. At other times a group of them would go back with him and Mr Bhoolabhoy to Smith's. In the afternoons he visited the sick or the unhappy or Susy's Sunday school which she held in the bungalow that had been her mother's but where she now lived alone. After evensong, more thinly attended than matins, Mr Thomas Narayan might dine with her or with the other Thomas, Mr Thomas who managed the cinema, or with Mr Bhoolabhoy. On Monday he went back to Ranpur on the midday train but had been known to delay his departure if a death seemed imminent. It was not so much a case of his having a nose for death but one for saving church funds: the cost of a sudden trip to Pankot to conduct a funeral service either in the church or in the little chapel attached to the crematorium at the General Hospital which the British had built. In the case of sudden death he could be telephoned in Ranpur at any time of the day or night and had been known more than once to hitch a ride in a military truck coming up on army business. Marriages and christenings, of which there seemed these days to be fewer than there were funerals, were fitted in with his weekends.

They had been good days.

By contrast the days since the death of the Reverend Thomas Narayan and the advent of the Reverend Stephen Ambedkar had been in one sense better, in another worse. Mr Bhoolabhoy couldn't say just what the better and worse arose from or amounted to but he was aware of Mr Ambedkar as a man who caused him both to cherish expectations and condition himself to sustain disappointments.

'We must do something about this ancient instrument,' Mr Ambedkar said, during his first visitation, meaning the organ; and when Mr Bhoolabhoy pointed out that the cost of even marginally maintaining the fabric of the church itself was already greater than funds could bear Mr Ambedkar smiled in a worldly way and left Mr Bhoolabhoy with an impression that the right man could always find money for the right thing if sufficiently convinced of its necessity and if he happened to be endowed with the right kind of connections. But Susy was still having to hammer out the hymns on the piano and tune it herself; and the congregation had to be content to celebrate Holy Communion when it suited the Reverend Stephen to officiate, which wasn't often because unlike old Tom Narayan he insisted on doing so no later than eight o'clock in the morning, on an empty stomach, which meant that he could usually conduct the service only at those weekends which brought him up to Pankot on Fridays or Saturdays, weekends which seemed difficult not to connect with the weekends when the Inspector-General of Police in Ranpur came up to play golf; arriving in his official car with the identifying flag fluttering and Mr Ambedkar sitting next to him wearing dark glasses and looking forward to some golf too and to a weekend not at the Menektaras but at the old Flagstaff House where they would both be fellow guests of General Krippalani, the senior officer in the Ranpur area.

There was just one other possibility of holding communion apart from on golfing weekends. Mr Ambedkar was persona grata with the director of the Indian Airlines

office in Ranpur and occasionally got a free air passage to
Nansera, which meant that he arrived in Pankot on the
airport bus late on a Saturday afternoon but then usually
had to return to Ranpur on Sunday evening. Sometimes
Mr Bhoolabhoy had very short notice of Mr Ambedkar's
intended arrival by this method and was hard put to it
to spread the news to intending communicants to be at
St John's by eight o'clock on Sunday morning if they wished
to avail themselves of the opportunity offered. Mr Ambedkar always expressed his understanding of this difficulty but you could see he was a little put out if less than
half-a-dozen turned up to kneel at the rail. Before beckon-
ing them forward he rather ostentatiously counted them and
then consecrated the requisite number of wafers, and the
wine. Mr Bhoolabhoy noticed that his accuracy in regard
to the wafers did not extend to accuracy over the amount
of wine, of which there was usually a fair swig left at the
bottom of the chalice which Mr Ambedkar drained and
then wiped with a sigh of resignation.

On an ordinary monthly visit, though, and yesterday had
been one of them, Mr Bhoolabhoy did not expect Mr
Ambedkar to put in an appearance at the church until
approximately a quarter to eleven, when he would arrive
in the Menektaras' car. At about 10.40, then, Mr Bhoolabhoy would go down the lychgate to wait for him. But
yesterday Mr Ambedkar had turned up at a quarter past
ten and surprised Mr Bhoolabhoy, Susy and Mr Thomas
drinking coffee in the vestry, all preliminary work done,
flowers arranged, hymn and prayer books set out, collection bag taken from its cupboard.

And he had not arrived alone. With him was a young
priest of such dense blackness of skin it showed purple.
Irradiating this blackness was a set of teeth so white they
looked like an advertisement for a miraculous new tooth-
paste not yet on the market but being sample tested and
already offering proof of the happiness and confidence to
be inspired by its regular use.

'Francis,' the Reverend Stephen Ambedkar said to Mr
Bhoolabhoy, 'this is Father Sebastian.'

125

'Hello, Francis,' Father Sebastian said, offering his firm and confident hand. 'And this must be Susy. Hello. And Mister Thomas. Stephen has told me about you all and how you've helped him keep the church up. What a fine example it is of British hill station church architecture. 1885 or so?'

'1883,' Mr Bhoolabhoy said.

'Not far out, then. Good. By the way, who looks after the churchyard? So many of these other old places look run down."

For a moment Mr Ambedkar looked perplexed, but kept his own smile going and offered it to Mr Bhoolabhoy without quite turning it away from Father Sebastian. Mr Ambedkar had not noticed the improvement in the churchyard. If he had he hadn't mentioned it.

'It is a boy called Joseph,' Mr Bhoolabhoy said. 'He works as a *mali* at the hotel. In his spare time he comes here.'

'I should like to meet him. May I see inside?'

The Reverend Stephen guided him out of the vestry and into the body of the church and shut the door. Mr Bhoolabhoy, Miss Williams and Mr Thomas remained. For a while none of them spoke.

Then Susy said, *'Father* Sebastian.'

'Anglo, it must be,' Mr Bhoolabhoy murmured, 'not Roman. He is South Indian. Anglo-Catholics very strong there nowadays.'

'I was born chapel,' Susy declared, pushing her coffee cup away. 'At least that's what Ma said Dad was. Sergeant Taffy Williams, Welch Regiment. Attached Pankot Rifles 1928-1930. Small arms instructor, killed North-West Frontier, 1934. I don't remember him. But I remember chapel. That old corrugated iron roof place we used to go to on West Hill every Sunday regular as clockwork. We never came here. Ma said it was because Dad was chapel and wouldn't have liked us to. But chapel was nothing to do with it. Ma was brought up C of E. Chapel was where we went because most people like us went there. If we'd come here we'd have had to sit at the back because Ma wouldn't have liked to embarrass the English ladies whose hair she did. Even to have sat at the back would have embarrassed her. She might have come if I'd looked like Lucille but I didn't and I don't but I'll be damned if I'm going to go on playing the piano for a minister who wants to be called Father and is as black as two hats, especially in a Church Ma wouldn't bring me to.'

'Susy, love,' Mr Bhoolabhoy said, putting an arm round her. 'You're talking nonsense. And he's only a visitor.'

'No he's not. I'm sure he's not. I hear things. I hear things in the Seraglio room at the Shiraz just as I used to hear things in my own salon before I was run out of business by the bloody Punjabis.'

'Watch your language in church,' Mr Thomas said.

'What things do you hear, Susy?'

'That any day now Mr Ambedkar will be promoted and that he will probably end up as Bishop of Calcutta.'

'You are telling me that Hindu and Parsee and Muslim ladies gossip about such things while having their hair done? Be honest now. It is purely your own imagination.'

'What if it is? Anyway, I bet I'm right. I bet Father Sebastian isn't just any old visitor.'

The vestry door opened and Mr Ambedkar looked in. 'Francis, may I have a word?'

Calling him Francis was new. Having shut the door behind them the Reverend Stephen murmured, 'I should explain about Father Sebastian while he is outside looking again at the churchyard. Who pays this boy Joseph?'

'Sometimes I used to give him a few paise out of my own pocket. But now he is employed at the hotel he is all right. It is a labour of love for him. He is a Christian boy.'

'Good. Good. Father Sebastian is very impressed with the way we have kept things up inside and outside. I had prepared him to expect it of course.'

Mr Bhoolabhoy looked at his feet. A hand fell heavily on his shoulder, causing him to look up into the Reverend Stephen Ambedkar's rather bloodshot eyes.

'Something troubles you, Francis. OK OK I know what it is. *Father* Sebastian. What are you thinking, that we are going over to Rome and planning already a lady-chapel?'

127

'No, no.'

'I too could call myself Father. It is a matter of personal choice. It does not mean Rome necessarily.'

Mr Bhoolabhoy grinned as brilliantly as he could in the circumstances. Was Susy right? Were they to have Father Sebastian instead of the Reverend Stephen?

The Reverend Stephen let go of his shoulder, put both hands behind his back and led the way down the south aisle, pacing slowly. Mr Bhoolabhoy put his behind his and followed.

'It is necessary finally,' he said, 'to think what life is all about.'

'Exactly,' Mr Bhoolabhoy said, suddenly having a vision of Mrs Bhoolabhoy who – at this very moment – would be checking Management's accounts.

'Like myself, Father Sebastian is much concerned in the ecumenical movement in India. If we are to *advance*—' and here he glanced round as if to check that there were no lurkers who would go back to report to Government that there was a plot afoot in the Christian Church to go for growth in India by stepping up the conversion business – '—if we are to advance we can only do so together. Now, Francis, let me take you into my confidence. You, you alone. I know I can rely on you not to gossip.'

They halted. Mr Ambedkar looked down at him.

'In two or three months I think I shall be going – Elsewhere.'

'Ah,' Mr Bhoolabhoy said. Then added, 'Oh,' wondering whether the poor Reverend Stephen was mortally ill.

'Do not misunderstand, Father Sebastian is not my successor-to-be, but he may be in the area for quite some time and may fill in for a while if there is any difficulty about filling the living at Ranpur. One may call him in the meanwhile a supernumerary with a roving commission, very advantageous to us. I propose to send him up to you at Easter, in two weeks' time. It may well work out that you will have a visit every fortnight instead of monthly. I think you can look forward to a happy year on that score. And perhaps, one day, to a permanent incumbent.'

'Ah.'

'I may tell you, again in confidence, that Pankot may in the not too distant future benefit from certain plans already afoot down in Nansera. The Nansera Valley Development Scheme. You have heard of this?'

Mr Bhoolabhoy didn't think he had. Only Mrs Bhoolabhoy heard of things like that. But the airfield in Nansera had itself brought greater prosperity and – at the time it was being built – an influx of engineers, technical experts and advisers: British, Indian, American, Eurasian, the men, their wives and families sometimes, some of them Christian. The Nansera Development Scheme, whatever it was, could hardly fail to do the same, and better. The hotel would benefit. The church would benefit. A rosy prospect opened before Mr Bhoolaboy and some of its glow seemed to surround Mr Ambedkar like an aura.

'We shall miss you greatly, sir, when the time comes,' he said, and was rewarded by a manly grip on his shoulder which happened to coincide with the reappearance of Father Sebastian who looked pleased by this evidence of comradeship between priest and lay preacher, and joined the fraternity, placing his left hand on Mr Ambedkar's right shoulder and his right on Mr Bhoolabhoy's left.

'What a beautiful church. Tell me, Francis, how quickly could you let me have photographs of the interior and the exterior? I should like them to illustrate an article I am doing for a magazine in Madras which finds its way all over the world.'

Father Sebastian had preached beautifully, taking as his text verses 17 and 18 and part of 19 from chapter two of Ecclesiastes: 'Therefore I hated life, because the work that is wrought under the sun *is* grievous unto me: for all is vanity and vexation of spirit. Yea, I hated all my labour which I had taken under the sun: because I should leave it unto the man that shall be after me. And who knoweth whether he shall be a wise *man* or a fool?'

Even Susy Williams looked mollified. The congregation, although at first almost visibly shaken by the contrast between Father Sebastian's blue-black skin and the lily-whiteness of his laced surplice and none too happy when he sank to his knees during the creed when reference was made to the mother of Jesus, was not just mollified but positively hooked.

The sermon was very funny. For the first time in his life Mr Bhoolabhoy heard little titters of barely suppressed laughter from the congregation. But it was happy laughter. The Reverend Stephen seated in the choirstall gave it both cue and countenance by smiling broadly at Father Sebastian's opening sally: 'I have always felt, you know, that the fellow who wrote Ecclesiastes suffered either from constipation or acute indigestion.'

Mr Bhoolabhoy was entranced. The spirit of God moved across the still waters of his soul. And when Father Sebastian, judging the length of his first sermon perfectly, ended ten minutes later, sketching a Popish blessing while he spoke the words, Now God the Father, God the Son and God the Holy Ghost, Mr Bhoolabhoy's hand moved as if mesmerized across his breast.

An immense peace settled in him. Mr Ambedkar came forward and said, 'I asked Father Sebastian what last hymn we should sing and after consultation with Miss Williams he chose Hymn Number 391 in Hymns Ancient and Modern.'

The congregation, already alerted to this rousing old favourite by the number on the board, rose happily: Mr Bhoolabhoy, clutching the collection bag, rose too. Mr Ambedkar had never liked *Onward, Christian Soldiers*. He had once described it as vulgar. He looked happy enough about it today though. And no one was happier than Susy whose favourite hymn it was, the one she had always played best of all, either on the organ or the piano. The opening chords crashed out. She had not lost her touch in spite of having been discouraged from playing it at services, although today she tended to ignore the *p* and the *cr* and the *f* and play everything *ff*, but this suited the mood of the congregation too, to the advantage of the collection bag

130

that got heavier and heavier and crisper and crisper and was taking longer to pass from hand to hand than usual, so that Mr Bhoolabhoy had scarcely finished going the rounds by the time Susy reached the penultimate verse:

(ff)   Crowns and thrones may perish
            Kingdoms rise and wane,
            But the church of Jesus
              Constant will remain;
            Gates of Hell can never
              'Gainst the Church prevail;
            We have Christ's own promise,
              And that cannot fail.

(ff)   Onward, Christian soldiers,
             Marching as to war,
            With the Cross of Jesus,
            Going on before.

The two ministers had arrived that morning by train but were returning to Ranpur the same evening by air; so there was to be no evensong. It had been such an exciting happy day that Mr Bhoolabhoy thought this just as well. Another service would have been an anticlimax.

Parting from the Reverend Stephen after morning service Father Sebastian had spent the rest of the day in Mr Bhoolabhoy's company. They had lunch with Mr Thomas and tea at Susy's. At six they went to Smith's where Father Sebastian accepted a drink; two in fact (tall whisky-sodas; Mr Bhoolabhoy stuck to gin and tonics). To drink these they sat on the verandah of the hut that had once been the airline office. Mr Bhoolabhoy was glad that Father Sebastian showed no curiosity about the inside of the hotel. Lila would still be doing the accounts and the new minister had a penetrating voice. Perhaps Mr Ambedkar had warned Father Sebastian that Mrs Bhoolabhoy was not someone it was necessarily rewarding to go out of one's way to meet.

At seven o'clock they walked round to the Shiraz where

131

Father Sebastian and Mr Ambedkar were to catch the Indian Airlines bus. Both bus and Mr Ambedkar were waiting.

'Don't forget the photographs, Francis,' Father Sebastian said as he climbed aboard. Mr Bhoolabhoy said he would start making the necessary arrangements first thing in the morning and post the results to him before the end of the week. When the 'bus had gone he walked down the road to the place where the spire of St John's could be seen in silhouette against the evening sky. Then, content, he went slowly home.

Reaching there he again settled on the verandah of the hut. There was a light in Lila's room and in the lounge, but no other sign of life. Next year, or perhaps before this present one was out, the place might again be as it was in its heyday. They would have to decorate and get new furniture, restore the former air of quiet distinction and homely comfort. Not every visitor cared for the flamboyance of places like the Shiraz.

When it had turned 7.30 he went over to the hotel, switched on the verandah light, plumped up the cushions in the lounge. In his cubicle he checked the register which Lila must have finished with because it was back in place. No one had booked in. There were no dining-room bookings either, which wasn't to say no one would turn up, so he went into the dining-room to inspect the tables. As usual places were laid only sketchily. He collected missing knives and forks and spoons and cruets and napkins from the dumb-waiter.

As he was doing this Lila's door opened and a man came out. Mr Bhoolabhoy was so startled that it took him a second or two to recognize Mr Pandey, the lawyer's clerk. Mr Pandey looked exhausted. He barely acknowledged Mr Bhoolabhoy's surprised greeting, but murmured something and went to his own room. According to the register Mr Pandey wasn't supposed to be in the hotel, not that the register was much to go by because often Mr Pandey failed to sign in, but Mr Bhoolabhoy invariably had a few days' notice of his arrival.

While Mr Bhoolabhoy was standing there wondering

and entertaining vague suspicions about Mr Pandey's
relationship with Lila, Lila's door opened again and she
emerged with her hair down her back and across her massive shoulders wearing her shocking pink nylon negligee
– a see-through outer robe and underneath it, also see-
through but rendered opaque, a nightdress of the same
colour and material. Her feet were stuffed into pink mules
with pink nylon-fur trimmings.

'Ah, it's you,' she shrieked. 'Good. Poor old Mr Pandey.
He wasn't up to it any longer. What are you doing? Leave
all that and wait for me in my room.'

She billowed past him shrieking to the cook which was
to say using her normal speaking voice, which Mr Bhoolabhoy often thought must be a contributory cause of her
splitting headache. To get to the kitchen you went out of
the dining-room along a passage and then down another
at right-angles to it and eventually reached the place where
the food was prepared. She was audible to Mr Bhoolabhoy throughout this journey. At some point on her return
journey she stopped talking to cook and started talking
again to Mr Bhoolabhoy.

She was, he realized, in a good mood, a pleasant surprise
after a day spent checking the accounts.

'Pour me a drink, Franky,' she was saying. 'I am dying
of thirst from all this question, answer, checking, checking
and so much rigmarole with wheretofores and wheresoases
and as beforesaids. I feel worn to a shadow. I ordered a
tandoori and a chicken curry. It will be ready soon. We
will have it in my room. Come, come, come.'

He followed her in and shut the door. The bed was
rumpled, but it was also littered with papers of the kind
Mr Pandey brought up from his law firm. Moreover the
room was full of cigarette smoke and Lila only smoked
during the day when she had business to attend to. She
normally attended to it stretched out on the day bed, the
settee, which she collapsed on to now as if resuming a
position only momentarily abandoned. And Sunday *was*
hairwashing day even if by this time of night she had
usually put it up. Sunday was also deshabille day. So he

must not harbour these dark thoughts. And as if certifying the innocence of the hours Mr Pandey may have spent with her, there was his briefcase, propped against the legs of the upright chair he must have been sitting on, a half emptied glass of orange juice on the table by its side. On the table in front of the settee there was a tray of drinks, Lila's ashtray, a legal-looking document and a magnifying glass. The drinks were untouched as yet. Smoke she might, but drink never, until business was over.

Mr Bhoolabhoy poured her a large Carews gin and tonic. Taking it she smiled fondly at him from under her moustache.

'Have one yourself, Franky.'

The 'Franky' was an indication that he was in favour.

'Cheers,' she said, had a good swig, put her head against the high arm of the settee. She was still smiling.

'Did you have a nice day?' she asked.

'Oh, yes. Very nice. And you, Lila?'

'I had a nice day too. But, oh, quite exhausting. Only poor Mr Pandey has had a rotten day. Because of flying up this afternoon. He has never been in an aeroplane before.'

'Flying up? Mr Pandey?'

'You fly when you have to fly to be quick off the mark, whether you like it or not.' She drained her glass and held it out. Mr Bhoolabhoy replenished it. 'Tomorrow he can go back by the midday train because the train gets in even earlier than the evening flight and anyway now everything is settled, signed and witnessed.'

'What does this mean, Lila, my love? Settled signed and witnessed?'

'It means, Franky, that at last I am going to make some real money. Come, sit with me. Tell me you still love me. What is money if one is not loved?'

Tears sprang to her eyes and spilled down her cheeks. 'What is the life of a woman if she is not loved?' she said. He could not bear to see a woman cry. He sank on to the settee and began to kiss the tears away.

'Ah!' she cried, clasping him. 'My little Franky.'

Realizing he was getting an erection he thought: I am

seriously oversexed. I have only to touch or be touched by Lila and I am in this state. Perhaps I should have a word with Father Sebastian about it.

'Ah,' she was saying again. 'Oh, my Franky.'

'What do you mean, my love, real money?' he murmured into her throat.

'Real money is real money, but what is money? No – No!' she pushed him away, laughing, the tears drying. 'Later, later – for now just give me that drink. Real money you ask? Real money is when you start thinking not in thousands of rupees but in lakhs of rupees because then you can also start thinking in crores.'

'How are you going to make this real money, my love?' he asked, handing her the glass again and then refilling his own.

'It is a secret. No one must know.' She sipped. 'But I will tell *you*. Can you not guess? You who were down in Ranpur for me and making a good impression?' She smacked a kiss on his forehead. One spectacular episode apart the main things he could remember about Ranpur were taking a locked briefcase to the lawyers, then calling every day from his hotel to see if he was wanted – although wanted for what he could not tell because he seldom had been wanted and then only to answer questions about the Smith's accounts. Eventually he had returned with the same locked briefcase, slightly heavier, none the wiser except in regard to something called double-lotus.

'I cannot guess,' he said.

'Truly? Honestly?' She clasped her hands. 'Then I will tell you, but not a word to be breathed. Completion date is not until a month from now.'

'Completion date?'

'For the contract.' She paused. Her mouth quivered. 'I am buying into the consortium. You know what this means? It means I shall now profit from all the enterprises. Shiraz Hotel Pankot, Shiraz Hotel Ranpur, Shiraz Hotel Mayapore, Mirat Lake Palace Hotel, and all the Go-Go-Inns. Part of these profits of course will be ploughed back into the consortium so that we can expand our enterprises, particularly down in Nansera which is to be developed. Only that is very very confidential, my Franky.'

'But Lila, all this buying in must be costing you a great deal of money.'

She raised her hands in mock horror. 'Oh, don't speak of it. Dear God! It makes me quite ill to think what it is costing.'

Mr Bhoolabhoy sipped his drink. It made him feel rather faint to be married to a woman rich enough to buy her way into consortiums. It also made him wonder whether as her husband he had in some way been illegally deprived of his rights. She had sometimes, too, asked him to sign papers and he had done so without demanding to read them, being a man for a quiet life. Perhaps, without knowing it, he was a member of this consortium too; and, also without knowing it, for some years one of what he occasionally heard Lila and Mr Pandey referring to as nominees. If Lila suddenly dropped dead (his eyes on the open half-eaten box of marrons glacés) what kind of mess would he find himself in? Mess, somehow it would be sure to be, not clover. 'You're a loser, Billy-Boy,' Tusker had told him once, 'Lila's a winner.' He had always imagined that if Lila died before he did he might, just, with luck, find himself the proprietor of Smith's, which she had bought before their marriage and which she'd sworn had cost her every penny she owned in the world plus what she'd had to borrow from the bank at extortionate interest.

'Lila, my love, my love,' he said, sitting next to her again, 'wherever did you get this money?'

'What money, Franky?'

'To buy into the consortium.'

She smiled. To Mr Bhoolabhoy the settee they were on suddenly felt as though it were stuffed with blackmarket rupees. Most of Lila's business friends looked like people who owned such settees, come to think of it. Perhaps he should have thought of it before. He *had* thought of it before but the thought had so thoroughly frightened him that he had stopped thinking it ages ago. Government was very hot on catching people dealing in black money. The Prime Minister herself took a personal interest in putting a stop to it. Tusker was always saying that the Prime Minister was the one person in India capable of ending corruption. Mr Bhoolabhoy, although a Christian, was also a patriot. He had now a terrifying vision of Mrs Gandhi walking into the room in that aristocratic way of hers and demanding that he and Lila stand up while she personally investigated the settee to find out what it was stuffed with.

'What is wrong, Franky, my love?'

Actually, he realized, there were two things wrong: the thought that Lila had bought her way into the consortium with black money (a deal to which he may unwittingly have been a party, down in Ranpur particularly, signing this and signing that and thinking of nothing so much as Hot Chichanya) and the thought that if Lila hadn't used black money she must have sold her only apparent asset: the hotel. Apart from St John's his managership of the hotel was the only thing he had in the world. Well, no. He had Lila. But what was Lila? A cross or a blessing?

'There is nothing wrong, Lila, my love.'

'You look so sad. Let us have another drink. Then we will eat a lovely Tandoori, and chicken curry, and perhaps some mutton-do-piaza and some lovely saffron rice. After that we will make love.'

He poured more drinks, and tried to ignore the twinge of anticipation in his traitor-loins. He did not want to make love but knew he was going to. He went heavy on the gin and light on the tonic. The first swig of this richer mixture gave him the courage to say:

'Lila, have you sold the hotel?'

'Sell, buy? You cannot make this distinction. I buy my way into the consortium. The hotel therefore becomes part of the consortium's assets. But the consortium's assets are also my assets, so how can you say I have sold the hotel when it remains among my assets? All one can say is that when I bought it I made a sound investment after all, which they tried to do me out of by building the Shiraz. Now they know the value of this place. They cannot do without me. Achchha. So now we make something out of it and of it. In this you will help me, my Franky. We shall become rich together. But what is rich? What is rich if alone?'

She was crying again, or about to be.

'We make something of Smith's?' he asked, trying to concentrate.

'Why not? Why else would I buy into the consortium?'

'We redecorate? Refurnish? Advertise? I have heard about Nansera, Lila. It could be a great opportunity for us.'

'This is what I am saying just now. I am very hungry, Franky. Ring the bell.'

He did so. Having done so he began to pace the room. His imagination was on fire. The future looked promising after all. The hotel would flourish, side by side with the Shiraz. St John's would flourish too. And if they were going to make real money he could perhaps persuade Lila to employ an under-manager. That would give him more time to devote to St John's.

'Lila,' he said, pouring more gin. 'What a clever Lila it is. What a lovely Lila.' He kissed her. Her tears flowed over his nose.

'Franky, Franky. Later, later.'

Old Prabhu came in with the tandoori. While they ate Mr Bhoolabhoy began to describe the various things that ought to be done to bring Smith's back up to scratch. Lila, occupied with her chicken leg which she ate with her fingers, as he did his, nodded, nodded, said nothing, burped, drank, attacked the chicken curry and rice and occasionally murmured, 'All such things will have to be gone into,' an apposite phrase that registered in Mr Bhoolabhoy's mind in a somewhat different context as he anticipated a reconnaissance of that vast territory of her flesh.

At what hour precisely the reconnaissance had begun he could not recall when he woke in the morning and returned on penitential knees to his own room, there to curl up in the embryonic position. He could not remember the end of the meal, the beginning of conjugal rites, or how many times they had been celebrated.

But he slept for only a few minutes in his own bed before being woken by the recollection of Lila whispering at some stage of their gigantic couplings, 'Bombay, Calcutta, New Delhi, London, Rome, Paris, Cairo, New York, Warsaw, Prague, Washington – oh in those places to be like this Franky, my tireless lover. Ah! What happiness you will give me world-wide. What is Pankot but a beginning? What do we know of Pankot if we only know Pankot? Ah! Ah!'

He sat up, stabbed by spears of revelation, blunt last night, razor sharp now. He groaned and, driven by a demon, got out of bed, half-fell to his knees as if these were the only supports he had left, then got to his feet and, naked, opened his door in to Lila's room and surprised Minnie in the act of stealthily clearing up the ruins of last night's feast. She placed a hand over her mouth to stifle a shriek of laughter and fled, foolishly forgetting to close the door quietly so that Lila shrieked and sat up and stared at Mr Bhoolabhoy, then shrank back because he was coming at her. He grabbed her shoulders.

He wanted to shout, the occasion called for it, but his voice came out cracked and hoarse. 'What did you say, Lila? Bombay, Calcutta, Delhi, Cairo? What are you up to, Lila? What are you hiding from me? I will know. I *must* know. You must tell me. You will tell me. You have sold the hotel. You did not consult me. Am I not your husband? Am I not entitled to give an opinion? Are my wishes of no account? You will make what you call this real money. You intend to go to all these places. You imagine I will go to them with you. But only I want to stay in Pankot. Only I want an improvement here, an improvement there, decorators, new furnishings, new tablecloths, new cutlery, pukka fittings in all bathrooms, telephones in all bedrooms, new typewriter, new letter-heading. Aren't these modest wants, Lila?'

'Modest?' she shrieked. 'Who is talking of modesty? Look at you! Stark-bollock, isn't it? Frightening me out of my wits!' She broke free, grabbed a pillow and smote him with it smack in the genitals.

He groaned but grabbed the pillow – an instrument of punishment translated in a moment into a comforter – and held it to his numbed parts.

'Lila,' he pleaded, eyes closed. 'Lila, my love. All I want is to stay on here and manage the hotel for you, for you, my Lila.'

'Liar!' she shouted. 'You do not love me! All you want me for is one thing.'

In the passage between dining-room and kitchen, Minnie covered her mouth again and then said to her fellow listener, Prabhu, 'Management wanting it. Ownership not giving it.' They went to spread the news among the other servants that there had been an intended rape in Room 1.

'All you want,' Mrs Bhoolabhoy said, but now instinctively lowering her voice to a hiss, 'is hotel and church, church, hotel, what difference? There is nothing to be had from either. The hotel is fit for nothing. Only the site is worth anything. So stay on by all means why not? Like in the old days, perhaps we could brick you up alive when the new building starts, to give place an auspicious start. Not that that would work. Only fine strong handsome Punjabi boys were worth bricking up. If we bricked you up the whole building would collapse even if we aren't cheated by the man supplying the concrete. Now go to your room. I do not want to see you again until you have come back to your senses, then I will deal with you. What have I married? A fool? What was I when I married you? Also a fool? Dear God, what a beginning to the day!'

She groaned and turned over and kept on groaning.

'What new building, my love?'

The iron had entered his soul. Only temporarily he supposed but it had entered. Be my guest, he said to it, stay as long as you like.

'I am talking to you, Lila my love. I ask, what new building?'

She lay doggo. But he knew she was listening. He was also listening – to the still quiet voice not of his conscience but of his commonsense which his passionate nature and wish for an easy life had kept under restraint ever since his marriage.

'If you will not tell me what building, Lila, then I will tell you. It is the building you hoped to put up when you bought the hotel from old Mr Pillai's executors, but which you found you could not put up because the people who would give planning and development permission and permission to pull down the old place and people who would have lent you the money were already in the pockets of the consortium, is that not it? And the members of the consortium did not like you Lila because you had stepped in and bought the site before they had quite made up their minds. You knew what was in their minds and hoped to profit by it, instead of which they buggered you up by ignoring this site and building the Shiraz opposite. But now they find they wish to expand because of the Nansera Development project and heaven knows what else, so in the end you have been very clever, Lila my love, because you have what they now want and they will give you what you want to get their hands on it. The site is worth several times at least what you paid for it and hanging on to it has cost you little. To you, Lila my love, it has always been a site, not an hotel. It has always been the rupees you were thinking of, never the guests. The guests have been left to me, and what am I?

'I will tell you what I am. I am the man who has maintained, what is it you call it, the goodwill of the business, what is left of it. Single-handed I have maintained it Lila with no help from you but more with hindrance. In Ranpur people say, So you are going to Pankot. Shiraz is most modern, ring Shiraz, if you can't get in there ring old Frank Bhoolabhoy at Smith's, he will see you are all right. It is true, Lila, my love. I grant you it does not amount to much but that is not my fault. All the time I have been thinking I am maintaining goodwill of the business to carry us through a bad time by being a good manager I have only been a caretaker of a development site. Now bulldozers come in. New monstrosity goes up. But the good name of Frank Bhoolabhoy of Smith's Hotel, Pankot, my Lila, will take a little longer to ruin. I do not know whether goodwill has been considered in all your figurings and workings and manipulations because all that sort of thing is beyond me. I am not an intelligent man, and proof of this is that I do not want to go to Bombay, Calcutta, Delhi, London, Paris, Cairo, New York, Warsaw, Prague or Moscow. What would a man like me do in places like that?'

He waited.

'What indeed?' she murmured. 'You are a fool.'

'I know, Lila, my love.'

She heaved herself up and round and looked at him.

'And fools are sometimes wise without knowing it which doesn't make them less of fools. The crooks! Perhaps they get away with too much! Tell Mr Pandey to be here in ten minutes. Tell Minnie to come at once. Go and get dressed. I shall want you later.'

'I shall not be here, Lila. I shall bathe. I shall get dressed. I shall have a modest breakfast. Then I have things to do. I shall not be available for the rest of the morning.'

'It is Monday!' she cried. 'You *will* be here!'

'Sunday, Monday, what is the difference when all one has to manage is a site? I really cannot stand here any longer with my sex in your pillow.'

He placed the pillow gently on the bed, turned, then turned back again to face her amazed glance.

'What of the Lodge?' he asked.

'What of it?'

'People are living there.'

'Here also at least one person is living,' she said. 'And she asks herself why? She asks herself for how long? She asks what is the point? She asks why she has to live at all if she is always to be surrounded by fools and crooks! Call Minnie.'

'Call her yourself, Lila my love. You are in better voice than I am.'

'You will pay for this, Frank Bhoolabhoy,' she shouted at his bare bottom.

'I know,' he murmured, 'oh yes, I know.'

By the time he closed the door between them he was already beginning to because the iron had melted and the prospects ahead were almost too atrocious to contemplate.

142

CHAPTER NINE

When he slipped out of the hotel half-an-hour later it was in a spirit more of desperation than of lingering rebellion. Used though he was to bad Monday mornings there was usually the pleasure to look forward to of Lila's midday departure for bridge at the club and a convivial evening with Tusker. But today, even if Lila managed to despatch her business with Mr Pandey in time for him to catch the midday train and for her to recover sufficiently to welcome the idea of expending the rest of her temper over cards, he did not think he could face an evening chatting amiably to a man whose days themselves might be numbered and whose days at The Lodge certainly looked like being. He would not dare tell him. And, who knew, perhaps what he had said to Lila that caused her to refer to her prospective partners as crooks would spur her to actions that would delay completion of the contract or even lead to its cancellation.

Wishful thinking, no doubt; but any thought that gave a glimmer of hope had to be cherished. He cycled to the bazaar and spoke to his old friend, Mr Mohan Lal the photographer (Weddings, Home Portrait Specialists, Passport Photographs) and did a deal with him to take a couple of time exposures of the interior of the church and a series of exteriors. The deal was for a cut rate if Mr Mohan Lal was credited in Father Sebastian's magazine article, and for the shots to be taken today when the Sunday flowers on the altar would still be fresh.

'I will send young Ashok right away,' Mr Lal promised, which Mr Bhoolabhoy knew meant in about an hour. As for 'young' Ashok, he must be well over thirty years old. Ashok was an untouchable, although you were supposed nowadays to call him a member of the Scheduled Castes. He had been an orphan and a ragamuffin who as a kid ran wild in Pankot picking up jobs here and there including jobs running errands for Mr Allah Din the previous owner of the Paramount Photo Studio (motto: Time passes, a photograph Remains) who had packed up in 1947 and gone to Pakistan. Mr Lal (coming the other way and leaving *his* studio behind) had been accosted by young Ashok on the first day he opened for business, had let the boy make himself useful and, as he grew, begun to teach him the trade and the art, until now, as Mr Lal's Outside Man, he was a familiar face behind his camera at weddings, christenings, coming of age parties and at grander occasions accompanying Mr Lal to regimental sports days, receptions at the Shiraz and speech days at the Chakravarti College. As an untouchable he was potentially a convert and Mr Bhoolabhoy wondered whether he ought not to do more to urge him into the fold. Perhaps today a seed could be sown because Ashok had never been inside the church.

Reaching Church road, Mr Bhoolabhoy dismounted and pushed his bicycle up the incline. Once inside he inspected the vases of flowers. They were still in good fettle. It was a lovely sunny morning. The church was full of light. It looked beautiful. The personal pride he took in keeping it so was a sin Jesus would surely forgive him. He sat in the front pew and gazed with love at the altar. As a youth he had wanted to take Holy Orders, but his father, although a devout Christian himself, insisted on him following in his footsteps and learning the hotel business.

Mr Bhoolabhoy Sr said that short of eternal life in Jesus's arms he could want nothing better for Francis than the managership, even ownership of a seemly and decent hotel such as he himself worked at as assistant manager. That was at the old Swiss Hotel in Muttipore. Mr Bhoolabhoy Sr's career had suffered from ill-health and lack of ambition perhaps. Francis hadn't inherited the ill-health but often felt he'd inherited the lack of ambition to the extent that it seemed to have been fulfilled the moment old Mr Pillai appointed him manager at Smith's, just in time for his father to know and write him a letter of congratulation from what turned out to be his death bed.

Mr Bhoolabhoy knelt to pray for the repose of his father's and mother's souls and for peace to ease his own troubled mind.

But the harder he prayed the more troubled his mind became. Ah, so many sins! Not least adultery in Ranpur, and occasions of fornication before marriage. Also the deadly sin of lewd and lustful thought – once committed even here in St John's when observing Susy Williams's neat little bottom as she raised her arms and stood on tiptoe to arrange some flowers better. Then there were the sins of suspicion, of jealousy, greed and envy, and also of cowardice which perhaps was the worst of the lot. Oh Lord, he muttered, when it comes to sin you name it I've done it.

You can say that again, a Voice said in his head.

He looked up wildly and stared round the church. But for the first time in his recollection the place seemed devoid of a Presence. He felt abandoned so completely that another sinful desire sparked in him. He wanted to confess aloud, unburden himself not to God directly but through the comfort of an intermediary, another human being. He wanted to kneel before Father Sebastian or someone looking in his imagination remarkably like Father Sebastian.

Father I have sinned (he would say). I have spent the night in debauchery and enjoying sexual congress for the hell of it procreation being out of the question what with the coil which probably isn't necessary because it's unlikely a woman could have so many husbands and all of them turn out sterile so it must be her and she's probably long past it anyway and all the business of the coil and complaining about periods is just to kid me she's as young as she said she was. And after spending the night in debauchery I have used angry words and laid hands on her with violent intent. Moreover I have appeared naked in front of her handmaiden. Where I could have offered wise and sober counsel I have offered only provocation and have parted from her in anger and dare not show my face. I am guilty of the sin of adultery with a lady in Ranpur and of the sin of lascivious expectation, item, the purchase of an unseemly garment for Koshak Dance, not having been content to call it a day with double-lotus, but then chickening out and so committing the sin of failing to keep a promise and disappointing a fellow human being and causing her bosom to swell if that is further possible with anger or contempt or both which means I have been the instrument by which she added yet another sin to her sum of sins which I should have tried to talk her out of and not let her talk me into. But mostly, Father—

(pp) Snick-snick

—I have committed the sin of turning a blind eye and not speaking up like a Christian and a man and where does my salary come from, pocket money you could call it, but still where does it come from except Ownership? So wasn't it my duty to start speaking long ago in a calm Christian manner and ask, What are we doing, Lila my wife, what are we up to? What is the future? So that I could fulfil my obligations as a husband and as a manager and as a Christian to see all those things in which I am concerned directed to good ends and not to bad? But oh no, for me anything for a quiet life, until the moment comes and the quiet life looks about to end—

(pp) Snick-snick

—not only for me but for other people trusting in me because I am Management which means I am responsible not only for welfare and happiness of those who serve but also for that of Colonel and Mrs Smalley who are aged and one of them ailing and what will happen to them if the bull-dozers come?

(p) Snick-snick

The sound, so soft, scarcely a sound but just audible in this place that seemed this morning no more than an echoing chamber for noises of temporal activity outside, suddenly impinged on Mr Bhoolabhoy's outer ear. The hairs on the back of his neck stirred, thousands of tiny antennae programmed to tune in to signals of approaching disaster.

(cr) Snick-snick

Mr Bhoolabhoy stumbled to his feet. The demolition gang had already arrived and begun work on the churchyard. He staggered along the pew making for the south door and reaching it opened and thrust himself forward and out almost into the arms of Mrs Smalley who uttered a little cry like that of a ghost on its way to a haunting.

'Oh, what a fright you gave me, Mr Bhoolabhoy.'

She had given him a fright too, to judge from the way his mouth hung open and his eyes popped. He looked at her, then round her, then back at the church door which he shut with a clang as if he had been up to something in there and was discouraging her from going in.

Prior to his marriage Mr Bhoolabhoy had had something of a reputation as a quiet little man with an eye for the girls and although Lucy thought the reputation probably exaggerated, since it was chiefly from Tusker she came to hear of it, and unlikely in the extreme that he would have been living up to it inside the church, she couldn't help recalling that little Susy Williams and he were often there together on church business and that people had once imagined, and Lucy had rather hoped for poor Susy's sake, that the two would one day make a match of it.

'You gave me a fright too,' he said, almost wringing his hands and heightening by a degree or two the temperature of her suspicion. 'You see I was only just now thinking about you.'

'Really, Mr Bhoolabhoy?'

It always fascinated her to see an Indian blush. She sometimes thought she could detect it even in an Indian with a darker skin than Mr Bhoolabhoy's, which was only a delicate brown. He looked at his feet, at her feet, anywhere but at her. She felt a little tingle of apprehension which wasn't altogether unpleasant. Usually neatly dressed, the sort of man who nearly always wore a jacket and collar and tie, he had, she noticed now, either dressed in a hurry or become disarrayed since. He had no jacket on (was it inside the church?) and although his shirt sleeves were buttoned at the wrist the collar was open. She must have seen him bare throated before but had not noticed that for a man so meagrely built the throat was rather a good one. Not at all scrawny.

'It is nice to be thought about, Mr Bhoolabhoy, unless of course the context of the thought is disagreeable. It happens that I was thinking about you too. I was thinking how nicely you are keeping the churchyard.'

Snick-snick-snick-snick

This time the sound was near at hand. Both turned their attention to its likely source which was now revealed. Round the bend of the path came Joseph, making slow but steady progress, sideways, and on his hunkers, rather like a Russian dancer in slow motion, but also because of the sharp claws of the shears that seemed an essential probing part of him, like a large landcrab, foraging.

He was cutting the edges of the grass.

'Why, *mali*! It's you!' Lucy said.

The young man glanced up and then unwinding himself came to a standing position. Holding the shears to his side in one hand he gave a grave salutation with the other. Mr Bhoolabhoy was already making for him; making *at* him it looked, and shouting at him in Hindi. The *mali* stood his ground but cast his eyes down.

'What are you saying to him, Mr Bhoolabhoy? You're surely not scolding him?'

'I am asking him what he is doing and why isn't he working in your garden. Only in his time off is he supposed to do all this.'

'You mean he works here too?'

'Only in his spare time. It is a labour of love. You did not know?'

'I may have done.' She had shut her mind to *mali* as *mali*. 'But you really mustn't scold him. He's doing nothing wrong. I told Ibrahim this morning to stop him cutting the grass. I had such a headache and Colonel Smalley wasn't feeling up to much either. Is he a Christian?'

'You did not know?'

Again she said, 'I may have done. I'd forgotten. Tell me, *mali*, you speak English? If you are a Christian I suppose you speak some English. Well I mean, there are prayers.'

148

Joseph nodded his head from side to side then said, 'Speaking some English, Memsahib. Not yet reading. Reading very little.'

'But you speak very well! And what do you read, *mali*?' After a moment he indicated the nearest gravestone.

'Gravestones? You read gravestones? How charming. Why do you read gravestones?'

Joseph looked at Mr Bhoolabhoy. Mr Bhoolabhoy spoke again in Hindi, presumably repeating the question. When Mr Bhoolabhoy had stopped gabbling the boy looked at his feet again and then everywhere except at either of them and began to gabble too and use his arms, indicating this, that. Then he stopped as abruptly as he'd begun and looked at his feet again.

'He is a simple boy, Mrs Smalley. He tries to read the names on the stones because when he tidies a grave he says a prayer for the soul of the departed and it troubles him when he cannot understand what the stone says because then he thinks God will not hear properly and get the souls mixed up.'

'Oh,' Lucy said. She was touched. *Mali* was such a strong manly looking boy. It always moved her when such boys proved to be sensitive too; to have spiritual as well as physical attributes. 'Well, now, *mali*,' she said, speaking very slowly and distinctly, and approaching him, sketching a gesture that almost was but wasn't quite a touching of his arm, 'show me a gravestone you *cannot* read. *Malum*?'

How straight his gaze was! How devoted and grateful his look. How gallant the gesture he made, tucking the shears behind him so that they did not constitute a threat or source of danger to her. How lithely he moved, going with no nonsense and yet chivalrous awareness of her presence, towards one of the graves. How touching the way he stopped and stood to one side of it, giving her precedence but yet indicating his wish to know whose grave it was.

'Well, now, *mali*. No, I must call you Joseph.' She peered at the stone. 'It says, Here Lies. Here Lies, *malum*?' He nodded. 'Here lies Rosemary. Beloved daughter of John and Gwendoline Fairfax-Owen. Well you really don't need

149

to bother with the Fairfax-Owen. Five December, Eighteen ninety-one to Twelve April Eighteen Ninety-six. That makes her five years old. Oh dear. *Malum?* Chokri. Little Miss Sahib. Then it says, Suffer Little Children to come Unto Me. Who said that, Joseph?'

'Lord Jesus.'

'That's right. Show me where it says Suffer little children. Can you?'

As Joseph bent down she caught the pungent smell of his body. He pointed at the inscription, ran his finger along each of the words.

'There you are, Joseph. You can read very well. It's just the funny names that worry you. But all you need to know about this grave is that it is Rosemary's, aged five. *Malum?*'

'Ros merry. Age five.'

'Good. But I'm sure little Rosemary went straight to heaven. Not, of course, that prayers for her will not be heard. But now, show me a gravestone that you *can* read.'

They followed *mali* to the south-west corner.

'This, Memsahib,' he said, stopping. It was old Mabel Layton's grave. Like the others in this section the stone had been cleaned and the grass over the hummock newly shorn. There were marigolds in a tin vase which looked as if it had been painted recently. Joseph knelt and pointed at the name Mabel.

'Mah-Bel,' he said.

'Very nearly. Mabel.'

'May bll,' Joseph repeated, then rearranged the flowers. *Click.*

She glanced round. An Indian with a camera held in front of his face was taking photographs. *Click, click.*

'Oh, Ashok,' Mr Bhoolabhoy was saying. 'You are here then.'

'Just a moment,' the man said. 'Memsahib, please stand just behind and to one side of the headstone?' She did so. *Click, click.* He said something in Hindi to *mali* who placed a hand on the vase and stared at the flowers. Click, click; click, click. 'Good,' the photographer said, 'It is a good composition. Okay, Bhoolabhoy Sahib. What next?'

'You mean they might be published, Mr Bhoolabhoy?' she exclaimed. He had accompanied her to the gate to make sure her tonga was still waiting. The photographer having click clicked his way round the churchyard was now setting up more formidable equipment in the church itself.

The tonga was there, the driver obviously impatient, but Mr Bhoolabhoy seemed determined to detain her. He was acting very oddly, hovering, darting, almost dancing round her as if she were a bonfire, to be fanned at one moment and dowsed the next so variable were his responses to the responses it struck her he was trying to get from her. It was almost like being flirted with.

'Published yes. Some will be published.' He spoke as if it was necessary to raise his voice above something like the sound of the wind or the sound of the sea. 'One or two anyway. But I will give you prints of all. Tomorrow. Not later than tomorrow. A complete set. Then you will tell me just how many copies you would like. As many as you wish. Ashok is an excellent photographer. All his pictures come out very well. Every detail shows.'

She touched her lined cheek and smiled, uncertainly.

'Won't they be very expensive?'

'No charge! No charge!' he shouted, and put his hands behind his back, like Ibrahim, yet unlike Ibrahim, more like a man who put them there to forestall an intention to put them on her.

Well, well.

'That is very generous of you, Mr Bhoolabhoy. I shan't presume on your generosity to more than a modest extent, though. A print or two, particularly of the one of *mali* and me at the graveside, to send to – to send home. Oh you'd be surprised how welcome they'll be and how nostalgic people are. Old Pankot friends. People before your time, of course. They like one to keep up. Pictures of the church and the churchyard will be looked and looked at and sighed and sighed over, I assure you.'

They were standing now under the arch of the lychgate. She looked at her watch. It was half past midday. The tonga wallah again hawked and spat. She thought of going

151

home. She was no longer cross with Tusker. But it would be no bad thing to remind him that she was not to be taken for granted. And indeed she wasn't to be. Here, after all, was Tusker's friend almost making a pass at her. Had she been younger it would not have amused her. But it did. Lunch alone at the club struck her as a satisfactory way of bringing an unusual morning to a suitable climax.

'Well, I must be off,' she said.

'Wait!' (Whatever next?) 'Wait, Mrs Smalley! I will send Joseph back with you. Some of these tonga drivers are very reckless. Joseph can sit with him and restrain him from excitement.'

'I really can't think what could excite the tonga wallah, Mr Bhoolabhoy. Actually he's a slow old coach. He's driven me often enough before. There'll be no need of Joseph. And in fact I'm not going home. I'm going to the Club, which will be far too long a way for Joseph to walk back.'

He looked crestfallen, then suddenly alarmed. 'It is Monday!' he cried.

'Yes, it is Monday.'

'Monday is not a good day for the club. In fact it is a very bad day.'

'A bad day?'

'A very bad day. The worst day of the week.'

'But whatever can be wrong with it? Surely Mrs Bhoolabhoy spends most of Monday at the club?'

'But this is the point, Mrs Smalley! It is a bad day for you to be there precisely because Lila will be there. She will disobey my advice not to go today. If you see her do not approach her. Keep away. She has fever. Fever of some kind. She does not know what she is saying or doing. She should stay all day in bed.'

'Well perhaps that's what she's decided to do. It would certainly be unwise of me to expose myself to infection, so I'll take your advice and try to keep away. But the fact that today she has fever doesn't surely explain why all Mondays are bad days?'

'But the bridge! The bridge! That is a fever in itself. All day they play. Rubber after rubber after rubber and losing

152

money and getting cross with one another and ordering the servants hither and thither. One moment coffee, next moment sandwiches, more coffee, tea, drinks. People in the dining-room complain because the servants are running to and fro between the kitchen and the card room hour after hour. People who are not playing bridge get no service. They are calling it Black Monday and no longer bothering to go.'

'Well, I have never heard that. How interesting. All the same I'm determined to go to the Club. I shall risk the poor service. A sandwich would do me very well, too. My appetite is not large.'

'If you must you must,' he said (despairingly?). 'But please do not approach Mrs Bhoolabhoy. Please also tell Colonel Sahib that tonight he and I should not be convivial. I too perhaps have fever.' He took a few startled paces back. 'Forgive me, forgive me. Thoughtlessly I may have infected you already. What have I been thinking of? God grant it is not cholera. Get near no one. Speak to no one.'

He was wringing his hands again.

'Mr Bhoolabhoy, as Doctor Mitra can probably confirm, the last case of cholera in Pankot was years and years and years ago when there was a mild and very swiftly dealt with minor epidemic down in Ranpur. If your poor wife has a fever it is almost certainly no more than the result of having eaten something that disagrees with her.'

She turned, walked slowly enough to the waiting tonga to convey that she welcomed Mr Bhoolabhoy's company as far as there. Just before she climbed in she said, 'I shall probably ring Colonel Smalley from the club. Shall I tell him you think it unwise to meet this evening or shall you send him a chit to that effect? Or do you think the fever will have abated by then?'

'Please tell him. Perhaps I also shall send a note.'

He now stood with shoulders adroop. She smiled down at him and then holding the strut of the canopy with her left hand she extended the other in a gesture of farewell.

153

When the tonga moved off Mr Bhoolabhoy remained where he was; just as in her fantasies of Toole, Toole had often stood to watch her go, poor inarticulate passionate man, his unquenchable desire endlessly torturing and endangering him. It was not safe for him to be seen near her. The consequences of being seen would be terrible. But he did not care. And whatever they did to him he would be back again eventually, risking all for just a glimpse of her.

'When I get to the club,' she told herself, 'I shall have lunch right away. Or perhaps a gin fizz first at that little table tucked away at the far end of the terrace where one need not be bothered by people. But if I see Mrs Menektara I shall ask whether she has a snapshot of Rose Cottage as it is now. Afterwards I shall write to Sarah and say we'll be delighted to meet Mr Turner. I shall say that in a day or two I'll send by separate post some photographs I have, snaps taken quite recently, one of which shows Mabel's grave with myself and *mali* tending it. Is it dishonest not to explain how this happened to come about? No. Anyway it must be a short note. It must be posted today so that it's sure to reach her before Mr Turner leaves for India. I'll leave the matter of the blue rinse for a postscript.'

The tonga horse began to plod slowly up East Hill. She changed her mind about the order in which things should be done. She would ring Ibrahim first and tell him she would not be home for lunch and that she would go to the pictures that evening after all. Then she would definitely have a drink. Two perhaps. After lunch she would write to Sarah and post the letter in the club box. At tea time she might walk up to Rose Cottage on the off-chance of finding Mrs Menektara in if she hadn't shown up at the club.

'Rose Cottage is such a beautiful bungalow, Mr Turner. The oldest in Pankot. I was very happy there. We moved in when the Laytons moved out. Tusker had been asked to stay on for a year or two and we decided that would be the right thing because he wasn't near retiring age and the Indians were keen to retain the services of senior English officers to help them during the period of transition, particularly in the army. You'll find it's in the army where the clearest evidence of our influence for good is found, but then of course many of the senior Indians in 1947 were Sandhurst trained. Some of them became generals overnight.

'It's ironic and perhaps sad don't you think, Mr Turner, that in the wars between India and Pakistan, the one just over, for instance, the opposing generals are often old classmates, some of them even once subalterns together in the same regiment. I've heard that described as a good thing because if one general knows another well he knows how his mind works but I think that cuts two ways and might almost be a guarantee of stalemate, although it didn't work out that way last December. It seems to have been an absolute walk over. The army people here in Pankot are quite understandably still pretty chuffed about it.'

The tonga lurched as the plodding horse slipped.

'It's wise to hang on to a strut, Mr Turner. After all these years I still do it automatically. I hope you don't mind coming to the club in one of these contraptions. We no longer have a little car. Actually although it can take an age uphill particularly with two of us aboard a tonga is a good way of getting around in Pankot what with all the slopes and curves and twists and the fact that the roads were not really built for motor-traffic, although heaven knows there's enough of it around these days with all the military transport and the cars that go with people's jobs. In the very old days, before Tusker's and mine even, only very senior officers were allowed motor cars and even when *we* first came people still mostly got around in this way. More people rode then too.

'Anyway I thought this was better than a taxi, quite the best way to bring you to the club because sitting like we are with our backs to the driver and looking back at what we're leaving behind you get this gradually unfolding and expanding view of the Pankot valley.

'We're coming up what we call East Hill, which was always the British side. That's the golf course on our left. There's St John's spire down to our right. I'll take you there tomorrow. I hope Sarah liked the photographs I sent her. But your own will be better.

'Ah, now, Mr Turner. This is where you begin to see right down into the valley and the bazaar. Down there to the left, all those old buildings amid the trees, that's the old area headquarters where Tusker worked during the war. That's the Shiraz of course. It really is rather dreadful, isn't it? You used to be able to see Smith's from here but the Shiraz blocks it out. For the same reason you can hardly see the General Hospital, it's that group of white buildings snuggling into the trees about half a mile beyond. Over to your right you get a good view of West Hill which is where the rich Indians always built their summer villas and still do. And from here you get the best view of the bazaar. It reminds me a bit of the bazaar in Gulmarg. On a misty morning the upper storeys of those old wooden buildings sort of peep out as if from the cloud. Some people think it looks Swiss or Tyrolean. But sometimes I'm reminded mostly of home, the hills beyond are so gentle.

'What we call South Hill, that is. Although of course it's several. There beyond the bazaar. That's where the Pankot Rifles are. Boys and young men still come in from the hill villages to the recruiting *daftar*. It's part of Pankot's tradition. That isolated grey building is Commandant House, quite the draughtiest one in Pankot. The Menektaras simply wouldn't live there. If you direct your gaze an inch or so to the left that's the mess. I must ask Colonel Menektara to let you see it. It's kept up just as in the old days, which I find very encouraging.

'No, you can't see Rose Cottage from here. That's behind us and above us quite a long way yet, the very last bungalow at the top of Club road and we haven't come to the bungalows yet, they all lie beyond the club in what's called Upper Club road that takes you up and round the peak so that you're facing north, and that gives you the loveliest view of all. At the back of the garden at Rose Cottage you can stand almost virtually on the edge of a very steep and wild and lovely descent and the nearest hill must be five miles away, and beyond there's another hill and then another and then many, many more rising higher and higher until they become distant mountains with snow on them even in summer, and on the hottest day the air comes on your cheek with a bite in it and the smell of resin.

'But you'll have caught a glimpse of the mountains when you arrived, as you came through the little pass at the top of South Hill, the only road into Pankot from the station. I remember so clearly the morning Tusker and I first arrived, years and years ago, over thirty. It was a day like this, Mr Turner. They'd sent a car from Area Headquarters to meet us and when we got to the pass and we saw the valley below and the mountains beyond I thought, well, perhaps Pankot won't be so bad after all, even though I was tired of all our wanderings and never having a home for longer than a year or two and often less and hadn't wanted to come. Not at all the sort of life I'd expect when I first came out.

'Before Pankot, I'd only been really happy once in India, Mr Turner, and that was in a little princely state called Mudpore, India in the way I'd more or less imagined it when typing those letters dictated by Mr Smith of Coyne, Coyne, Smith and Coyne to Lieutenant, then Captain, T. U. Smalley of the Mahwar Regiment which all had to be filed under F. J. Smalley Decd. The carbons I mean. The letters themselves went to the bank in Bombay and Bombay sounded so glamorous.

'I used to think how marvellous it was that a letter typed in the office and posted in Chancery Lane just by me would actually find its way to a bank in Bombay and then to wherever Tusker was which wasn't always clear because the postmarks were sometimes smudged and although he used regimental notepaper there was no address on it except the one Tusker filled in himself which was always the bank. I got to know the insignia of the Mahwar Regiment

157

so well that I could have drawn it by heart – the elephant with the huge tusks and the howdah on its back and the palm tree sprouting from the howdah. I didn't know it was called a howdah and I didn't know how to pronounce Mahwar properly, neither did Mr Smith. But not knowing only added to the glamour. Amid all those dusty boring files and boxes and deeds which were nearly all about dead people it was this unknown young officer serving in India who provided the single element of mystery and romance in my life, Mr Turner.

'The girls in Litigation had much more fun, but Litigation was young Mr Coyne and I hated it if I ever had to take dictation from him which I sometimes had to if Mabel Temple was ill. He referred to me once as the Virgin from the Vicarage. Not to my face, but I heard him, and I heard Mabel Temple laugh. She did her hair like Clara Bow and smoked what she called gaspers. She wore black for weeks after Valentino died, and sometimes broke down and cried when taking dictation and had to be comforted by young Mr Coyne. And welcome she was to that. He was over six feet tall but very thin and I swear his nails were polished. I once said to Martha Price that his height had gone to his head and that he made my flesh creep. After that she started inviting me out. I was in digs, then, Mr Turner, because my twin brothers had been killed in a motor accident the year before and the awful atmosphere in the house, mother's hysteria, what we'd call her psychosomatic illnesses, her continual demands on *me*, were affecting my work at Coyne, Coyne, Smith and Coyne, and not only that but putting my job at *risk*, because I was always having to stay at home to look after her and making excuses to Mr Smith. And one night Daddy found me crying because Mr Smith had suggested that perhaps I ought to look for another job nearer home. It was forty minutes there and forty minutes back on the Southern Electric and the 'bus, every day, including Saturday mornings. Coyne, Coyne, Smith and Coyne represented the only freedom I'd ever had as a person in my own right, if you understand. Daddy understood, when he found me crying. He called me Mops,

the name he'd used when I was a child and my hair began
to grow again. I was twenty-five now. I'd been at Coyne,
Coyne since I was twenty. It was my first job and only job
and I really was happy there in spite of not getting on all
that well with the other girls. Of course I realize I must
have looked a perfect little goose to them when I first went
there, which would have been 1925.

'Being a vicar's daughter I automatically dressed like one,
skirts always below the knee – and my hair! Heavens, Mr
Turner, do you know I had it in earphones? Oh, dear, what
a sight. I never had it bobbed or shingled, mostly I expect
because I hated the thought of losing any of it again. In
fact I didn't have it cut at all until the year I was in digs.
Daddy said I mustn't leave Coyne, Coyne, so he got me into
the Y. I went home at weekends, although not always then.
I was awfully nervous and shy being on my own, but I was
away from that awful atmosphere of Mother's cease-
less mourning for the twins, and after a while Mr Smith
said my work hadn't only regained its original high stan-
dard but had even improved and he gave me another seven
and six a week. I used to get in early and never minded
staying late because there was no train to catch, and
gradually I came out of my shell and got on better with
the others. They were a nice lot really.

'I didn't stay long at the Y because Martha Price who
was *old* Mr Coyne's secretary got me a bedsitter in a very
strictly run house just round the corner from the flat where
she lived with her mother. That was in Bloomsbury. She
was older than me of course and took me under her wing
rather. The other girls thought her a frump and I'd always
been scared of her so it was a terrific surprise that she
loved dancing and was mad about the cinema. We never
went dancing but she taught me in her home, dancing to
a little portable, she taking the man's part. As for the pictures, I was mad about them too or rather I'd loved them
whenever I was allowed to go but became mad about
them now. We started going once or twice a week and
sometimes sat through the whole thing twice. It was a bit
of a scramble getting from the office to the cheap Saturday

matinees they had in West End cinemas, but we used to dash into Lyons and have something like patty and chips and a cup of tea, then off we'd go. I liked it best in the evenings though, coming out aching in every limb, dazed and dazzled by all the lights and advertisement signs but happy, so happy, clutching on to one another to protect ourselves from being accosted. We felt tremendously daring walking home through the West End, I assure you.

'Since then I've wondered about Martha. Perhaps her feelings for me were not entirely natural, but I knew nothing about such things in those days. But she was very hurt when Tusker suddenly came into my life.

'He'd come home on long leave and walked into the office one day without an appointment and Mr Smith was engaged with a client. He said he'd wait, so I made him a cup of tea and sat him down in my own little cubby-hole. My officer from India! Heavens, how thrilled I was. Oddly I was only a little bit nervous. He wasn't really at all as I'd imagined him but at the same time he wasn't a disappointment, and he was so kind and somehow open with me, but reserved. He asked me a few things about F. J. Smalley Decd, just by way of explaining what he wanted to talk to Mr Smith about so that I could get the necessary papers because he didn't want to waste Mr Smith's time. He seemed impressed by my knowledge of the estate and of the changes the trustees had made in the investment of the capital sum Tusker had a life interest in. He said, "Well, Miss Little, I scarcely seem to need to take up Mr Smith's time at all now." But of course it was only a joke.

'I'm afraid when he dies the interest on the capital sum dies with him – so far as *we're* concerned. It's never yielded much, but as a little cushion it's always been helpful to him. The money was his grandfather's. His own father and mother died young and left nothing. He was brought up by an Uncle, and his grandfather old F. J. Smalley willed him this life interest. It helped to educate him, and it helped him in the army. It's been particularly useful to us in retirement, if only helping to defray the cost of what he has to pay into the Indian Military Widows and Orphans fund to make sure I have some income if I'm left alone. His army pension stops at his death, you know, and heaven knows it's little enough. In England it would put us on the poverty line. Whatever I get from IMWOF as we call it will probably have to be supplemented by a Royal Warrant pension. I know he's never carried much life insurance and I know he's never saved. Furthermore, Mr Turner, I know that the one decent bit of capital we ever got our hands on, his compensation from the Indian Government when he finally had to retire from the army in 1949 when he was only forty-eight, has all gone.

'Yes, all gone. In what I call the débâcle. But I mustn't talk to you about that. And I forgave him long ago. And at least he didn't do what one man did, and that was stop contributing to the IMWOF directly he retired, when contributions were no longer compulsory. But this man also compounded the premiums already paid in and when his wife found out she had a fit because if he'd dropped dead the next day she'd have been left with nothing except charity from the Royal Warrant. She had to spend virtually the whole of her own little capital paying the capital sum back into the fund and then beg, borrow and scratch to go on paying the annual contributions herself.

'So you see how a woman can be placed after years of following the drum in India? If you're a colonel's wife people look at you and think, ah yes, they plead poverty but they've had a good time and quite apart from the nice pension they must have, they must always have had something behind them, a cosy bit put away or inherited.

'People always assume, certainly they did in my day, that officers and their wives are comfortably off whereas of course service jobs are among the worst paid in the world. Tusker couldn't have *afforded* to be in a decent regiment at home, or a swanky one out here. That bit of private income was a godsend to him. But I remember when I told Martha Price that Tusker had proposed to me and I'd accepted and that in a few weeks we'd be off to India and would she be a bridesmaid at the wedding, all she said was,

Well congratulations, you've done well for yourself haven't you?

'No, she didn't come to the wedding. It was the other girls who came, and I'm afraid, yes afraid, and ashamed even to remember it, that when I saw them at the reception I thought, oh dear, has it been a mistake? They look so common. What will Tusker's relations think? Not that there were many of those. An aunt who lived in Bayswater, Tusker's old guardian Uncle George who'd come up from Dorset and his cousin Cyril who inherited the bulk of the F. J. Smalley estate and whose son Clarence will get his hands on the capital sum Tusker's had the income from directly Tusker dies.

'But the girls from the office were just about the only young friends I had, and there they were, getting tiddly on the champers and standing for protection all in a group, all so obviously dressed, so obviously overdressed because it was a wedding. And a bit overwhelmed by the vicarage because it was old and large, a gentleman's residence, but also noticing it was shabby, with pictures on the walls and no chromium anywhere which made it terribly unfashionable. And then, Mr Turner, they were disappointed because I think they'd expected Tusker to be in uniform, even though none of us had ever seen him in uniform, except in a photograph he gave me and which I showed them. I think they expected the two of us to come out of the church with all his fellow officers standing making a little roof of crossed swords over our heads. For all I know they might have expected to meet a Maharajah too, with pearls looped round his neck and the Star of India in his turban. And oh, I suppose in a way that is how I'd imagined it too.

'I've always had this tendency to imagine, to fantasize, to *project*. Like many young girls in those days I was stagestruck but much too shy and nervous to do anything about it except work for the local amateur dramatic society, which I more or less had to because it raised money for the Church Hall. I used to help with coffee at the intervals. Then I graduated to doing props and assisting the stage manager. It was a long time before they let me prompt because I had such a quiet way of speaking they didn't think my voice would carry even that short distance. There's nothing worse than a group of amateurs. They're all so egotistical and self-regarding and there's always a little clique of older members who are jealous of the young ones and won't give them a chance. It was just the same here in India. We did *The Housemaster* once in Rawalpindi and I longed to play the quieter sister, Rosemary, but of course it went to a woman of nearly forty.

'At our Church amateur group only the daughters of the members of the clique got a look in, so not many young people joined. But I knew every line of every play and the first time they let me prompt they realized my voice was just right for that. And one day at rehearsals when a woman hadn't turned up I had to speak her part which I knew by heart already while the others were still reading theirs, and I did, yes, forgive me for boasting, but I did surprise some of them and the man who was producing said that next year I ought to audition if the play they chose had a suitable part for me.

'But the next year was the year I met Tusker and the year I was in digs. Some of the group came to the wedding. The producer, for example. And he said, Lucy I'm not going to forgive you getting married and going off to India just when we've decided to be really daring this November and do *The Letter* if we can and I'd been thinking what a perfect Leslie Crosbie you'd make.

'He said it in front of Tusker. Moreover, Mr Turner, he said it *to* Tusker. "You're taking away a very promising little leading lady, but then she'll have her chance in India, won't she, and she's leading lady today anyway."

'So why, why, when my chance came did he deny it to me? I mean in *The Wind and The Rain*. It can't have been all my fault. Even if you tell a man you adore the theatre but would be terribly scared to go on, isn't he capable of realizing that that is only really an act and that being scared is one way of giving a good performance? And hadn't he heard, hadn't he listened, hadn't he taken in that producer's opinion?

'You may think no, he hadn't heard, hadn't listened, hadn't taken in anything, but you've only seen him as he is now, after what I call his personality change. When he talks nowadays he seems to talk inconsequentially. He doesn't seem interested in listening to any voice but his own or weighing any opinion but his own. But he takes things in. Oh yes. He hears. He listens. But doesn't let on. And he rejects and obfuscates. He rejects anything he hears which it doesn't suit him to hear.

'Of course you've only seen him with what I call his visitor's face on, talking nineteen to the dozen. It's different when we're alone. Sometimes hours go by without him saying a word. Even so he talks more than he used to. One seldom heard his opinion about anything in those days. But his behaviour was impeccable. Never flamboyant. The very image of reliability. The first view I had of him was his back view, standing at the window of the waiting-room, looking out. I said, "Captain Smalley?" and he turned round. I'd always imagined him lean and brown, a soldier in uniform, instead of which there he was, not over tall, thickset rather than lean, in civilian clothes, really quite ordinary. But in spite of that he was not, no, not at all a disappointment. He had such a pleasant, *open* look, and when I explained that Mr Smith was engaged and that I was his secretary he said, "Are you LL? You must be."

'I was so touched. Touched that he had noticed such a little thing. The GJS/LL at the bottom of the firm's letters. From the beginning then, you see, I had reason to think of him as an observant person.

'This was the summer of 1930. His first long home leave. He was going back to India in early November. The girls in the office guessed what was in the wind long before I woke up to the fact that he wasn't just being decent to his solicitor's secretary, ready to pass the time of day with her if he arrived early for an appointment. Arriving early became a habit.

'Then one day, Mr Turner, he was late for once. It was the last appointment of the day. When he came out from

164

seeing Mr Smith he found me with my hat and coat on and the typewriter covered. He realized he'd kept me late and asked if he could drop me off anywhere on his way to Bayswater.

'He got a cab in Chancery Lane and on the way to Bloomsbury I thought suddenly, poor Captain Smalley. He's a bit shy like me, and also finds London dull after all those years in the gorgeous East. He's probably longing to get back there, where all his friends are. And then it struck me that he had been ringing and visiting the office rather more often than was absolutely essential for someone whose affairs were comparatively simple and easily conducted even when he was thousands of miles away. It's that of course which the other girls had noticed.

'So after that lift home in the cab I let my mind open to this possibility that perhaps he came because he had few friends in London and quite liked talking to me not only because he was lonely, but perhaps for myself—

'Myself as myself, myself as a woman who although working as a secretary and *having* to work was all the same what we used to call (Heavens, Mr Turner, how old-fashioned it sounds) a gentlewoman, whose father was in the Church and whose mother although only a poor relation nevertheless was related to the late Sir Perceval Large of Piers Cooney Hall, Piers Cooney, in Somerset, where my father had had his first curacy. Tusker knew about Piers Cooney because he'd asked if I knew Dorset and I'd said no but I knew a bit of Somerset and explained how for three glorious summers just after the war the twins and I had spent a fortnight there and why this was and what the connections were. I told him as much as I did because I didn't want to pass myself off as someone with connections better than they actually were.

'A few days after that cab drive he rang again. And what he said confirmed my thoughts about him being a lonely man. He said he had two stalls for a show that night and would I care to go with him, and that if so he'd pick me up at my digs in time to fit in a bite to eat somewhere first, just a bite because we could have supper afterwards.

'I had no lunch that day, because after I'd put the phone down I remembered he'd said stalls and in those days one dressed for stalls and dress circle, or did if one cared about doing things properly, and I thought that if Captain Smalley had misjudged me and turned up in day clothes I could always change back in five minutes but at least he'd know he needn't worry about inviting me out again to a place where it would embarrass him *not* to be dressed.

'So I spent the whole lunch hour in Oxford Street. I almost broke the bank. Not on a dress. I had a long dress, a black chiffon. And I had a stole. Rabbit, dyed as black as sable. It was my only evening rig. I'd brought it up from home in the Spring of that year when I felt myself coming out of my shell and anticipated a need to have it by me in town. And here was the need. What I broke the bank on was a pair of good shoes and a pair of good gloves. Black shoes and black gloves. Oh, I paid the earth. But one had to on things like that.

'And then I bought a bag. How well I remember the bag. An evening bag. Dark green moiré silk, and a chiffon hand-kerchief to match. Just this one statement of colour, Mr Turner. I have always had to be careful about colour. My eyes never seem to have quite made up their minds about being grey, blue, green or violet. In those days the faint green tinge could be picked up by a green accessory. Later, by wearing deep red. Then the green faded from my eyes forever. But this is woman's talk. It couldn't interest you.

'The black stole, the black chiffon dress, the shoes and gloves, and then the bag. A lovely July evening. I was going to the ball, Mr Turner, and the coach called promptly.

'And he was dressed. He complimented me on the room. I always kept it neat and tidy. I've called it a bed-sitter but there were two little rooms, the sitter and the bed, with connecting doors. I'd bought some sherry. After we'd had a drink I went to fetch my stole and bag. When I came out he was gazing out of the window just as I'd seen him that first day at the office. And then he turned round.

'He didn't say anything and I couldn't see his face clearly. The sun was shining in. I was in its glare. But I felt that its

166

warmth and light were coming from him as well. I remember the whole of the rest of the summer like that. Sun, sun, endless sun. Women need the sun. There's plenty of it in India but that's not the kind of sun I mean. The kind I mean is the kind that if it's absent makes you feel your heart is undernourished and eventually that you are dying, very slowly. Of neglect.

'And it was strange but for me the sun started to go behind a cloud very soon after we got to India. So much sun otherwise. Days and days, weeks and weeks of sun. Not a cloud in the sky. Only this other cloud, so small at first. The cloud of feeling that as Tusker's wife I didn't please people much. That Tusker didn't please them either. That I no longer really pleased Tusker. The cloud grew bigger then.

'It vanished when we went to Mudpore, although in Mudpore it rained and rained, week after week. Most people loved the rains at first and were happy for a week or two after the monsoon broke. Then they got irritable. But I was happy all the time. Tusker thought I was happy because of the prince and the palaces and the elephants, happy in Mudpore because Mudpore was India as I'd imagined it. And partly that was why. Partly it was because I wasn't beset, yes, that's the word, beset by women who in Mahwar were cruel to me in order to be kind. But mostly I loved Mudpore because Tusker was happy there too, and I realized that like me he was something of a solitary person but that this might be a solitariness we could share. There were no other English people in that little state. The Political Agent seldom visited. Tusker liked working alone and he liked working with Indians. And because he was happy he was good to me.

'I wanted never, never to leave Mudpore. But we left Mudpore and there was no other Mudpore ever again, only a succession of places like Mahwar, where cards had to be left and ps and qs minded, and the army lists studied to be sure you knew who was who and who was senior to whom. I didn't object in principle. I never rebelled. Neither did Tusker. But strangely, Mr Turner, so very strangely, I think

167

we rebelled against one another. The rains were over when we left Mudpore, and the sky hadn't a cloud in it except that little one again, coming up over the horizon as if it had been waiting for me to come back to reality, the cloud of Tusker's never explained withdrawal which I'd first felt the chill of in Mahwar and which grew and grew and for years now has largely filled my sky. I expect my own cloud has filled his.

'I ought not to be telling you this. But Sarah said you'd be interested to talk to people who had stayed on and that can only mean you want to know what it has been like, but of course it has not been *like* anything because it has been different for everybody, just as it has been different for me and different again for Tusker, only I don't know just in what way different because we do not communicate. At the deepest level we do not know what the other one is thinking or feeling and you might think that after forty years of marriage we could have got around to that, and I really don't think it's been anything to do with our not having had children, which is one thing he has never *blamed* me for, nor I him, and I don't think that it's been anything in particular to do with India, although that must have helped, because when I look back on it, when I sit back and concentrate on it, I feel that India brought out all my very worst qualities. I don't mean *this* India, though Heaven help me I sometimes don't see a great deal of difference between theirs and the one in which *I* was a memsahib, but our India, British India, which kept me in my place, bottled up and bottled in, and brain-washed me into believing that nothing was more important than to do everything my place required me to do to be a perfectly complementary image of Tusker and *his* position. Do no less, certainly no more, except to the extent that one might judge doing an allowable bit more might help him.

'And you might think that actually I was ideal material, malleable clay. I was. I'd been brought up to know my place. But I thought when I married Tusker and came out that all that was over. I thought Tusker was rescuing me from it. But he was only taking me back to the Vicarage.

168

Father went into his study or off to Church or on his rounds of the parish. Tusker went off to the *daftar*. And little Mrs Smalley went off to a sort of Coyne, Coyne, Smith and Coyne run entirely by women. "You mean you can actually write shorthand, Mrs Smalley?" And up went the eyebrows. You could see them thinking, "We'll have to make the best of her." Which meant making use of me, so that although I was always on this committee and that committee I was on it but not of it.

'And there were these rigid levels of the hierarchy. Put it this way, Mr Turner, if you were a Captain's wife there were always other Captains' wives whose husbands were senior. Even a day or two's seniority mattered. You were supposed to know, you were supposed to find out, and if you didn't know they made it plain you'd made a gaffe. And above them were the Majors' wives. And when Tusker became a major then there were senior Mrs Majors not to mention Mrs Colonels and Mrs Brigadiers and Mrs Generals all living in that heady atmosphere of the upper air. Necessary, necessary, yes, but oh so often not easy to bear. I remember the little thrill I felt when a senior colonel's lady called me Lucy when Tusker was only quite a new major. How petty, to feel a thrill. How petty to get one's own back for little humiliations suffered. But I remember when he was quite a senior major how I sometimes treated junior Mrs Majors.

'I'd learned the rules, Mr Turner. The rules of the club. I'd learned them for Tusker's sake and when they made him a Lieutenant-Colonel at the end of Nineteen forty-five I thought: Perhaps the sun will come out again. But it didn't. We didn't even move out of Smith's hotel. We'd been billeted there from the day we arrived early in the war, two rooms, en-suite, the same ones the Bhoolabhoys now occupy as bedrooms. We used one as a living-room and the smaller as a bedroom. We didn't move because Tusker wouldn't. We could have moved into a bungalow of our own several times, but Tusker wouldn't. He said the hotel was convenient for the *daftar*, which it was. He said it was cheaper living there than running your own establishment

– in those days he was very tight-fisted. In a way I respected this. I'd been brought up to know the value of money, too. Now he's tight-fisted again but that's because there's no alternative. He spent money like water, lost money, gambled money, made a fool of himself directly he left the army for commerce and we lived in Bombay. But that's another story. I mustn't talk to you about it.

'We didn't leave Smith's until the whole British–India thing was coming to an end and Tusker had agreed to stay on for a year or two. Rose Cottage was becoming vacant because Mildred had gone home and Colonel Layton and Sarah and Susan were moving down to Commandant House. We were offered it. For once I insisted. If we were going to stay after practically every other British family had gone then I wanted for once in my life a proper setting, Mr Turner. And for once Tusker didn't resist. He only grumbled a bit. I thought that was a good sign. I thought perhaps after all the sun would come out again, between us. But it didn't. Not really. Except once – and that paradoxically was after sunset.

'I remember the ceremony we had here in Pankot on Independence eve very clearly still, the evening of August fourteen, Nineteen forty-seven, down there on the parade ground of the Pankot Rifles. At sundown, they beat the retreat. After that we dined at Flagstaff House. Then we went back to the parade ground. It was quite chilly. We sat on stands put up for the occasion. The whole place was floodlit. There was still one small British contingent on station, a mixed bunch. They marched on last after all the Indian troops had marched on. There was a band. That was a pretty scratch affair too, but they seemed inspired by the occasion. They played all the traditional martial British music. Then there were some Indian pipers, and a Scottish pipe-major. They played "The Flowers of the Forest". One by one all the floodlights were put out leaving just the flagpole lit with the Union Jack flying from it. Colonel Layton and the new Indian colonel stood at attention side by side. Then the band played "Abide With Me". They still play that, Mr Turner, when they beat the retreat in Delhi on the eve of Republic Day.

'It was so moving that I began to cry. And Tusker put his hand in mine and kept it there, all through the hymn and when we were standing all through God Save the King, and all through that terrible, lovely moment when the Jack was hauled down inch by inch in utter, utter silence. The only sounds you could hear were the jackals hunting in the hills and the strange little rustles when a gust of wind sent papers and programmes scattering. There was no sound otherwise until on the stroke of midnight the Indian flag began to go up, again very slowly, and then the band began to play the new Indian national anthem and all the crowds out there in the dark began to sing the words and when the flag was up there flying and the anthem was finished you never heard such cheering and clapping. I couldn't clap because Tusker still had hold of my hand and didn't let go until all the floodlights came on again and the troops marched off to the sound of the band.'

CHAPTER ELEVEN

Before Easter there was Holi, the Spring fertility festival
of the Hindus whose lower classes spent the day roaming
the bazaar and throwing coloured powder over one another.
Sometimes they squirted coloured water although this was
supposed to be illegal because it ruined their clothes and
they were poor people.

At Holi, the well-off usually stayed indoors to avoid getting spattered by gangs of merrymakers. Some of them had
friends in and played token Holi in their gardens, like the
Menektaras who each year held a Holi party in the garden
of Rose Cottage. According to Tusker this was no different
from any other Menektara party except that as you arrived
Coocoo Menektara lightly smeared the men's foreheads and
dabbed the women's wrists with magenta-coloured powder.
After that, while the Menektara children played Holi with
greater enthusiasm under the supervision of their ayah in
a corner of the garden well out of reach of the grown-ups
in their nylon sarees and smart suits, it was – again according to Tusker – the usual question of elbows bend at the
bar and then round the mulberry bush of the buffets, of
which there were the necessary two (veg and non-veg).

The Menektaras' Holi party was one Lucy looked forward to because it was in the open air and she was able to
wander in daylight round a garden once briefly hers and
now restored by the removal of Mildred Layton's tennis
court to a likeness of what it had been in old Mabel Layton's day, with beds stocked with the English hybrid tea
roses which Colonel 'Tiny' Menektara (he was six feet tall)
was so knowledgeable about.

Tiny Menektara was kind and attentive to her always,
and between herself and Coocoo there was this understanding which might be summed up as their mutual recog-
nition of the fact that while all colonels' ladies (active or

retired) were more or less equal some were less or more equal than others. It depended upon which side you were looking at it from. Coocoo's flirtatious manner with Tusker caused Lucy no qualms. She saw behind it more clearly than she could see behind Tusker's flirtatious manner with Mrs Desai. When Coocoo embraced Tusker it was obvious to Lucy that Coocoo was thinking: 'Yes, you're nice, you can be fun, you make us laugh, you're always welcome, but you're an Englishman so you represent the defeated enemy.

It was different, she supposed, for the new generations of English and Indians who met and made friends with one another; but however friendly you were with Indians of your own generation, the generation that had experienced all the passions and prejudices, there was somehow in that relationship a distant and diminishing but not yet dead echo of the sound of the tocsin.

Coocoo Menektara's Holi invitations came in the form of printed cards with a blank for the date. The print said: 'Coocoo and Tiny are playing Holi on .... at 12 Upper Club Road. Please Come. RSVP.' This year Lucy left the card on Tusker's table, having added in pencil an ? to it. It came back to her escritoire with a note: 'Good-o!'

He was more generally amenable these days and had been since the day she went to the club and had too many gin fizzes and hadn't got home until six, expecting a scene. There had been no scene. He'd merely asked, rather plaintively, if she'd had a good day. After her bath she found him in the living-room reading *The Times of India*, drinking a glass of beer.

'I've ordered trays,' he said. 'Billy-Boy sent a note over. He thinks he's sickening for something. Thought we shouldn't risk the dining-room.'

'Very wise.'

She sat at her escritoire with a gin and lime juice and entered the day's alarming expenditure in her housekeeping book, and added a rupee or so to the actual cost; against the cost of *mali*'s next month's wage. Dishonesty. Wretched dishonesty.

'Are you going to the flicks?' he asked when Ibrahim

brought the trays and set the food out on the table.
'Yes.'

'Anything worth seeing?'

She glanced at him. She wondered if he was about to suggest going with her. Her behaviour today had shaken him. Before she could begin to feel properly contrite she said firmly, 'No. It's a woman's picture called *How to Murder your Wife.*'

A sense of other people's humour had never been one of his strong points. In the days before his personality change he'd had little sense of humour himself – at least none that he shared with other people. It had developed subsequently, but in almost knockabout pantomimic form. Other people's jokes, if subtle, still failed to amuse him. He could be deliberately obtuse about seeing their point but scathing if he made a subtle joke himself and it took anyone time to appreciate it. In the main he had become a man roused most to laughter by ribaldry, and by other people's discomfiture, a man for whom perhaps the supreme comedy of life would be the sight of someone actually slipping on a banana skin. She thanked God he had never quite descended to the level of the practical joke. As it was, Tusker being deliberately funny was invariably an embarrassment to her, particularly when he seemed to be being funny at his own expense – making an exhibition of himself.

He did this at the Menektaras' Holi party by leaving the adults and joining the children, submitting first to their shyly thrown little handfuls of powder, then egging them on by shying back, so that presently they showered him with blue, purple and crimson powder and he returned to the adults covered from head to foot, his clothes caked, his eyes and teeth gleaming through the mask of coloured dust like a miner coming up from a pit where the devil's rainbow had its source. And in this state he had threatened to embrace first Coocoo and then Mrs Mitra.

'Well, he's all right again,' Dr Mitra said, guiding Lucy to the non-veg table. Having guided her he stood back waiting until it was the men's turn to follow the women and fill their plates.

Long used to the demarcation of eating zones as between male and female at parties such as this, Lucy still found it onerous, especially when everyone was sat on chairs formed into a large circle – or rather two large circles, one for the men and one for the women – and you were stuck with just two women to talk to, one on each side of you. Coocoo Menektara spared her guests the boredom of the imprisoning circles but there were chairs dotted here and there on the lawn for those who wanted them and these, random though they were, were the focal point towards which the women were drawn – as much, Lucy thought, by the tradition of segregation as by the wish to take the weight off their feet – and few of the younger ones were ever capable of resistance, of invading the closed ranks of the standing men. Indeed, the men's apparent determination to eat by themselves was itself a powerful dissuader.

Today, feeling her age, Lucy had sat down and then wished she hadn't because the chair she'd chosen and which she now couldn't move from because Mrs Mitra and Mrs Srinivasan joined her immediately she was settled, gave her an uninterrupted view of Tusker.

It was one she would have preferred to be spared. There he was, in the garden of the oldest and most beautiful bungalow in Pankot, a gesticulating clown, coloured from head to foot and giving a performance that was not so much attracting attention as forcing laughter from the immaculately dressed and well-behaved Indians whom he was haranguing, or telling some unseemly story to. Those on the fringe of the group were paying little attention but watching for the moment when the last of the women left the buffets; then they strolled to the tables and presently only Tiny Menektara remained, one hand behind his elegant upright back, the other holding his merely sipped-at glass, his head sometimes nodding, at other times thrown back in soundless laughter, while Tusker went on and on; about what Lucy could not imagine but she hoped it was not about the recent war; she hoped he was not being funny about the *war*; there was scarcely anyone in the garden who did not know of someone whose son or husband had been killed in the fight with Pakistan over Bangladesh.

Tiny was now prompting Tusker to get some food and Tusker went with him but paused on the way to put his empty glass on the bearer's tray and take a full one.

Mrs Srinivasan and Mrs Mitra were talking about Mr Bhutto, the new prime minister of Pakistan. 'He's only a grocer's son,' Mrs Srinivasan was saying, 'so what can you expect? And what is Mujhib? Anyway I am tired of Bengal. It has never been anything but a trouble to us. Like Ireland to the English, isn't it, Lucy?'

But Lucy had no chance to reply because there was a crash and then a commotion on the verandah. People looked round. Some stood up. Lucy stayed seated. She did not need to stand up and peer in order to know what had happened. Tusker had upset something. The final disgrace. There was a hush. She noticed now that the men were gathered looking down at something or someone and the only thing they could be looking down at was Tusker, and that meant that Tusker was no longer upright which in turn meant that he had had another attack; perhaps the fatal one. She hardened her heart again, to withstand the immediate alarm that must presently soften into grief and terror. And here was Coocoo flowing gracefully across the lawn in her lovely saree, a gorgeous bearer of bad news.

'Tusker seems to have had a bit of a fall.'

'Oh, dear. Silly Tusker. I'd better come across and see.' She moved slowly, putting her plate on the grass, gathering her things. At the end of one's life all that was left was dignity and one was damned lucky to have the chance to show it. She left her bag on the chair. It had been a good bag. The treacherous sunlight showed how old it was. She went with Coocoo towards the verandah. The men were gathered round the steps but made way for them. One of them righted the wicker table Tusker must have fallen against or grabbed as he fell. There had been things on the table. The verandah was spattered with broken glass. He lay spread-eagled in his clown's clothes. His eyes were shut. The eyelids were startlingly white against the coloured powder that caked his face and head. The clown's mouth

176

was open. Through it, unconscious or conscious, he was gulping in the pine-scented air. Dr Mitra was kneeling beside him, fingers on the pulse of his left wrist. Tusker's right hand was bloody, still gripping the stem of a glass.

Mitra said, 'I think he just missed his footing and knocked himself out.'

'Will he be all right?'

'Yes, I think so.'

Tusker muttered something.

'Can't hear you old chap.'

'Home,' he said more clearly. 'Not hospital. Bugger hospital.'

'Who said anything about hospital? You'll be right as rain.'

Tusker opened his miner's eyes. 'Luce? You there, Luce?'

'Yes, Tusker.'

'Home. Not hospital.' He began to raise himself into a sitting position. Dr Mitra tried to restrain him but in the end had to help him into the sitting position he was insisting on. 'Sorry about that,' he said. 'One too many, that's all. Slipped on some bloody thing. Bad business. Damned bad form, eh? Ladies present. Get drummed out. Ha!'

The group round the verandah began to disperse. Presently only Tusker and Lucy, Mitra, Tiny and Coocoo and some of the Menektara servants remained. Tusker shut his eyes and bowed his head, concentrating on the ousiness of recovering strength. Then he opened one eye, now the other, as if aware for the first time of the state of his clothes. He rubbed his trouser leg and inspected the palm of his hand.

'Well it's what the card said. Tiny and Coocoo are playing Holi.' He glanced at them. 'Why haven't you played then? It wasn't us who invented it. From the look of me you'd think it was. Keep away old man,' he said to Dr Mitra, shrugging Mitra's hand off his shoulder. 'You'll ruin that lovely suit.'

'You don't believe in things like Holi, do you, old man?'
he said an hour later when Dr Mitra drove them both back
to The Lodge. 'Load of guff. Excuse for a piss-up, like
Christmas for us. More like Easter though. Eh, Luce?
Fertility rites. D'you know Mitra old chap when I first came
out six hundred million years ago or whatever it bloody
well was I was fool enough to ask the colonel's lady what
Holi was in aid of. She told me. Told me the whole thing.
No flies on her, Mitra old fruit. But when Luce here asked
me, when she came out, I was such a bloody gentleman I
just hummed and hawed and said, Spring festival, y'know,
so the poor little thing piped up at a dinner table one night
in one of those awful sodding silences we used to have to
endure because the memsahib at the head of the table had
got her knickers in a twist and anyone who knew a thing
about what you said or didn't say in a situation like that
just naturally kept quiet. I've lost the thread, Luce. What
was I saying?'

'You were telling Dr Mitra about the awful gaffe I made,
Tusker, but perhaps he's not interested.'

'Of course he's interested. He'll dine out on it for weeks,
won't you Mitra old boy old man old boy?'

'Perhaps. Who knows, Smalley old fellow?'

A pause.

'You taking the piss by any chance?' Tusker asked.
'If you are, sod you. Sod you anyway. Sod us one and all.'
He leant back.

It was intolerable. In the driving mirror her glance slid
off Dr Mitra's. She felt as outraged by his composure as
by Tusker's abominable behaviour and disgusting language. She felt outraged too by this reminder of the gaffe,
years and years ago, back there in horrid Mahwar, 'piping'
up in that somehow transient silence which she arrested
by saying – because Holi was the last thing that had been
mentioned – 'Why do they use *those* colours? One had
always thought of Spring as green.' He could have saved
her from that. He could. Yes he could have saved her from
that by telling her the truth when she'd asked him. The

silence at the table then was echoed in the silence in Dr Mitra's car; her eventual realization of the significance of the colours here exemplified by the sight of Tusker caked in reds and purples (ruining Dr Mitra's car seat covers) – the colours that symbolized both the menstrual flow and the blood a groom drew from a virgin bride.

Intolerable too was the homecoming which was so early it caught Ibrahim unawares, taking his ease on the front verandah with Minnie (who fled) and with Bloxsaw whose hackles rose when Tusker in his harlequin disguise emerged from the car. The creature bared its teeth and growled and would have fled too if Tusker had gone near it.

'You must tell me the truth, Dr Mitra,' she said half-an-hour later when she saw him back to his motor. 'Did he fall because he'd drunk too much or because he's had another slight attack?'

'If I were worried about him would I leave him here? Don't worry. Keep him off the booze, that's all. Ring me any time. I'll look in tomorrow.'

'You haven't answered my question, Dr Mitra.'

'I thought I had. The hospital is only a stone's throw, but I've left him with you. Isn't that an answer? It's the best thing. He likes his own home.'

'Yes, I see.'

'I'll give him a new prescription probably. Let's see tomorrow.'

She wanted to ask, How long? A year? Less, more? Any time? But she had lived long enough to know that you did not ask questions to which there were no answers and which you didn't want answered. When she went back into the bedroom Tusker was asleep. His face and hands and arms although washed still bore traces of the Holi powders. The ruined clothes were in the dhobi basket. She thought, her distress giving way to irritation, 'And he was quite right. It's their festival not ours. *They* who should have looked like clowns.'

Between Holi and Easter he regained his resilience. On the Monday after Palm Sunday (March 27th) he announced that he and Billy-Boy would be convivial that evening. She and Ibrahim went to the pictures. She went because any departure from the norm might have alerted him to her concern although this was lessening day by day. He was drinking nothing stronger than beer, and little of that. He had seen the writing on the wall. Nevertheless she couldn't afterwards remember what picture she had see because for her the screen had been filled with images of her arrival home to a house of death, the empty place at the end of a journey, or the dark at the bend of the stairs in her father's house.

So that, arriving home and finding the place locked she panicked. She gave Ibrahim the key and made him go in first. The light was on in the living-room. There was a note on the escritoire. From Mitra?

It was a note from Tusker. 'Gone to the cabaret at the Shiraz with Billy-Boy. Back at midnight.'

'It's all right, Ibrahim. I shall go to bed. Perhaps you'd stay up until he gets back.'

Later, hearing the sound of singing she switched off her light. The singing was Tusker's and Billy-Boy's. The dog in its basket in the garage began to bark. The singing stopped at once. Billy-Boy must have scooted home. She heard Tusker locking up. She'd left his bedside lamp on and when he came in she watched him from under lowered lids. 'Luce?' he said. He wasn't drunk. 'Luce, you awake?' She heaved over on to her other side and covered her head.

'They rush you for the beer in that place,' he said next morning. 'Beer, Luce, that's all I had. It was Billy-Boy who was on the booze. I bet he's copping it this morning from Madam.'

'What on earth made you decide to go to the Shiraz?'

'He was being a bore, that's why. A proper misery. He perked up when he got there, though.'

'How nice.'

180

'Good picture, was it?'

'I don't remember the picture. It went out of my mind when I got home and found you nowhere in sight, Tusker.'

He drank his orange juice and then banged the top of his egg.

'It's Easter this coming weekend,' he said.

'I thought you'd given up noticing things like Easter.'

He cut his buttered bread into soldiers to dip into the yolk.

'There's a new bloke. Black as your hat, according to Billy-Boy. Likes to be called Father. He's coming up at Easter.'

'You're spilling egg on your shirt.'

'Thought we might go on Sunday. What about it old thing?'

She finished her own egg. An egg was symbolic too.

'You're suggesting we should go to church together on Easter Sunday?'

'Good a time as any. Have a shufty.'

'You'll find the churchyard much improved.'

'Wasn't thinking of the churchyard. A shufty at his new reverence is what I meant. Who knows, Luce, it might fall to him to ash us both to ash and dust us both to dust. We might as well have a look at the bugger.'

'Really, Tusker.'

'You think that morbid?'

'I was saying really to the language. But I'll say it to the idea, too. *Really.*'

'Ha!'

They went to morning service on Sunday April 2nd. The church was fuller than she had seen it for years. She stared in dismay and fascination at Father Sebastian. She was glad Tusker hadn't insisted on eight o'clock communion. But when the new priest began to intone the sentences of the scriptures prescribed for opening the order of morning prayer in a loud ringing voice she was struck first by their beauty and then by the recollection of her father mumbling them and then by the resonance of Father Sebastian's voice and the curious appropriateness of the Indian lilt to the lilt and rhythm of the words. She opened her eyes and saw that his were shut and that he was speaking words known by heart.

'I will arise and go to my Father, and will say unto him, Father, I have sinned against heaven, and before thee, and am no more worthy to be called thy son.'

'Dearly beloved brethren, the Scripture moveth us in sundry places to acknowledge and confess our manifold sins and wickednesses,' Father Sebastian continued, without a break, and the service was away, flowing through the church and through Lucy's mind and heart and soul. Standing for the first hymn she glanced at Tusker whose presence comforted her. His forehead was ridged in concentration. He had never been able to hit a note accurately but she was less conscious this morning of that slightly painful effect than of the surprise and pleasure of hearing him giving voice instead of droning.

During Father Sebastian's sermon, the text for which he took from one of the anthems prescribed to be said or sung on Easter Day instead of a psalm ('Christ, our passover is sacrificed for us: therefore let us keep the feast; not with the old leaven, nor with the leaven of malice and wickedness: but with the unleavened bread of sincerity and truth') she thought his attention was drawn to her rather frequently as if she were someone he felt he had seen before, which of course he had done if he'd yet studied the photographs Mr Bhoolabhoy must have sent him days ago. Mr Bhoolabhoy had kept his promise to let her have copies and she had posted two or three, including the one showing herself and *mali* at Mabel's grave, to Sarah. She hadn't shown them to Tusker, nor yet said anything to Tusker about Sarah or Mr Turner who would probably be arriving just about now, in Delhi, with – she hoped – her new packets

182

of blue rinse. Directly he made contact and announced the day he expected to be in Pankot she would make an appointment with Susy and splash out by letting her use the whole of the one packet she had left. She had said nothing to Tusker because she didn't want him to grumble about coping with a stranger. Grumbling was bad for him. It was some days since he had grumbled, and look at him now: so much better and actually in church with her and paying attention.

'Ha!' he exclaimed, bringing her back with a start from her own thoughts to the sermon. Not in church! But then she realized that laughter was the order of the day. The preacher himself was smiling, and Tusker's Ha! was nothing to be embarrassed by. The sermon was funny. She now concentrated on it and found herself smiling. But she was glad when towards the end Father Sebastian stopped making little jokes and became serious, even solemn. She could not wholly approve of laughter in church. Nor, during the creed, although it was her custom to sketch a little curtsy to acknowledge the reference to the Virgin Mary, could she quite approve of the way Father Sebastian virtually prostrated himself and did not rise or raise his voice from a troubled murmur until he came to the line: The Third day he rose again from the dead. He had the whole congregation muttering and bobbing. And then, looking back on the hymns when they got to the last one, All Things Bright and Beautiful, she realized that jolly and rousing and nostalgic as they had all been they were leaving in her mind a sense of naïvety. They had been children's hymns, rather than grown-up hymns. A strange mixture, the whole thing: a sophisticated sermon, naïve hymns, and popishness in the ritual. As the service ended and the congregation broke up she saw that everyone was smiling as if they had just seen a very amusing picture. Tusker was smiling too.

When they were outside he said, 'Hang on.' Other people were hanging on too. 'What for?' she asked. 'Meet the fellow, of course.'

Amazing! First coming to church, now hanging on to

183

meet the minister. She moved from his side to speak to Captain and Mrs Singh whom she scarcely knew because they were new on station. They had met briefly, once at the Ladies' Night in the mess, once at Coocoo and Tiny's Holi party. She had not known they were Christians, and wondered whether they were convert or cradle, and whether Singh meant a Sikh or Rajput origin.

When Father Sebastian came out he was in conversation with Susy. Mr Bhoolabhoy was nowhere to be seen. In fact she hadn't noticed him in the church at all. Mr Thomas had handed the collecting bag round. She did not want to meet Father Sebastian in case he mentioned the photographs. She saw Susy introducing him to Tusker and turned away to continue her conversation with Captain and Mrs Singh but then heard Tusker calling her over, 'Luce.'

She had no option.

'This is my wife,' Tusker said. 'Just been telling him how much we enjoyed the service. Bit of life to it. Don't come often. Thought I would. Next time might not be able to have a word.'

'There's always time for a word,' Father Sebastian said, smiling.

'Not in the circumstances I'm thinking of,' Tusker said. 'Staying with the Menektaras are you?'

'No, Miss Williams is putting me up until tomorrow.'

'Ah, back to Ranpur on the old midday, then. Coming up next week by any chance? Gather you're going to be more frequent than old Ambedkar.'

'Next week I'm in Nansera, I'm afraid.'

'Pity. My birthday next week. Monday the 10th. Usually give a sort of party in the evening. You could have come along. When are you up next?'

Susy said, 'Father Sebastian can't minister to us again until Sunday the 23rd, but you have a very full programme then, don't you, Father?'

'You've got to eat, though,' Tusker butted in. 'Come and have a bite. If you can't on the Sunday, stay over till Monday.'

'I am already doing that because of such a full programme, but it is very kind of you.' He glanced at Lucy. 'I should love to fix something, some time.'

'No, fix it now. Have lunch on the Monday, that's the 24th.'

'I'm afraid I'm committed for lunch.'

'Dinner then. We're down at Smith's. Billy-Boy knows where. Bhoolabhoy. Always call him Billy-Boy.'

Father Sebastian hesitated, again looked at Lucy. She had no alternative. 'Whenever is convenient to you, Mr Sebastian.'

'Thank you, Mrs Smalley. Colonel Smalley. Dinner would be very nice.'

'Good, good. That's fixed then. Come along Luce, we're holding up other people.'

'Old Billy-Boy's pretty pissed off I reckon,' Tusker said as they walked home side by side. 'He said little Susy went all chapel on them when his new Reverence turned up but now Billy can't get an oar in. She won't let him out of her sight. Where was Billy-Boy this morning? Sulking in the vestry, sodding furious because old Sebastian's shacking up with Susy and not at Smith's.'

'Tusker!'

'What? What's wrong? Shacking up? Figure of speech. One presumes. Ha! Priests, though, never know what the buggers are up to.'

Lucy came to a halt. For a few paces Tusker stalked on banging his stick into the road, then realizing he was alone turned round and said, 'Come on, then, what are you waiting for? I'm damned hungry after all that *tamasha.*'

She breathed in deeply and out slowly.

'If you can call it all that *tamasha*, what in God's name made you pester the poor man to come to dinner on the Twenty-fourth? You went on, Tusker. You went on and on and on, you left him no excuse. Now you talk about him like this. But *I've* got to arrange dinner for him. And he didn't want to come, not on that day. But you pestered him so much he thought you needed help of some kind. I could see it. The way his expression changed. The way he suddenly stopped thinking you were just being polite but tiresome and a bit of an old bore and started thinking, This Man Needs Me.'

'Well I do, don't I?'

He turned away and stumped on down the road leaving her to follow. The view from the back was that of an old man, thin, frail, intolerable to live with, intolerable to think of as one day not being there because then she would have nothing to live for herself. Where Church road intersected with Club road, and there was traffic, he paused, waited for her to catch up, so that they could cross the road safely together.

And after Easter there was Tusker's birthday. It fell on the Monday. He was 71. Not a great age at home. He'd sent no invitations, but there were cards from the Menektaras, the Srinivasans, the Mitras, and from Billy-Boy. These arrived by hand. When Ibrahim brought their tea that morning he hung a wet and ripely scented garland of flowers round Tusker's neck, and a smaller one round hers.

Lucy gave him a card too and a Parker ballpoint to go with his Parker pen. She'd ordered it weeks ago from Gulab Singh's, who did clocks, watches and jewellery as well as medicines and toiletries.

They had a birthday peck. When he went out to the verandah to have breakfast Minnie was there and gave him a garland too. He went back inside again. His egg got cold. She wondered whether he was crying in the loo again, so did not go near but jollied Minnie and Ibrahim along by handing out baksheesh to distribute to the servants at Smith's and between himself and Minnie – and *mali*. She supected that the bunch of marigolds on the breakfast table were put there on his behalf.

Eating her own egg she thought of his first birthday in Mudpore, which fell just before they were leaving. The Maharajah had sent a bowl of fruit, hidden within which

186

was a gold watch for him and a gold bracelet for her, both of which had to be sent back to the *dewan* with apologies.

While Tusker was still in the loo the *dak* came. There were one or two more cards for Tusker, a batch of bills, and one letter. The letter was for her. She went into the kitchen to read it. It came from Delhi and was dated four days earlier.

'Dear Mrs Smalley, Mrs Perron kindly gave me your address and telephone number and told me that you and Colonel Smalley had been kind enough to offer me some of your time if I come up to Pankot. I arrived in Delhi a few days ago and fly to Ranpur on the 24th. I have a commitment there on the 25th and then a short break until the 30th when I have to be in Calcutta, so I could fit in a visit between those dates. I'll ring you from Ranpur to let you know which day I could come up. I hope to spend a day or two and have the pleasure of meeting you both. Sarah said that there are two hotels and that if I have any trouble about booking from Ranpur you might be so kind as to help me, since you are at Smith's, which I must say sounds more appealing than the Shiraz. Meanwhile I much look forward to meeting you both. I have with me some packages Sarah asked me to bring for you. Yours sincerely, David Turner.'

'Anything in the *dak* other than these cards?' Tusker asked.

She hesitated. 'Only bills, Tusker.'

'Bugger the bills.'

'Bugger the bills indeed. Especially on your birthday.'

'Luce?'

'Yes, Tusker, dear?'

'Mountain View Room? For lunch? Just you and me?'

Her silly old heart could still turn over when he talked to her like that.

'Oh, Tusker, what a treat. But what if there are people there who wonder why they've not been invited to a buffet?'

'They'll have to lump it. What's on tonight?'

187

'On?'

'At the flicks. It's Monday. You always go on Monday. Thought I'd come.'

'What about Billy-Boy?'

'He'll have to lump it too.'

'But don't pictures bore you? I don't want you to be bored. We could have a quiet lunch here and go to the Mountain View Room tonight.'

'I don't want a quiet lunch. And I want to go to the flicks.'

'Then that's what we'll do. After all it's your day.'

She got Ibrahim to cycle down to the cinema and book two seats for whatever was on. She took Bloxsaw for a walk. She booked a corner table at the Mountain View Room. When she got back Tusker was on his knees using a little fork on the bed of canna lilies. *Mali* was cutting edges in another part of the garden. How strange. He looked up at her. 'Hello, Luce. Had a good day?'

'It's not lunch time yet,' she said fondly.

'Well, I know that, I meant a nice day so far.'

'It's been lovely so far. Has yours?'

'This fork's no bloody good.'

'Where did you get it?'

'From the kitchen.'

'I didn't know there was a fork in the kitchen.'

'It's the one I used to have when I did the pots. It used to be all right. It's no bloody good now.'

'Don't overdo it. It's very hot in the sun. Come inside and I'll pour you a nice glass of beer.'

In the living-room she paused, holding her throat with both hands.

At the cinema that night he fell asleep but woke up now and again and said Ha! because the audience was saying Ha! Ha! Ha! as if trying to persuade her he was enjoying himself. She was glad it was a comic film. She had seen it before. Doris Day and James Garner. The one where

Doris Day makes a career in advertising against her husband's wishes and the sponsors show their appreciation by digging up their garden and building a swimming pool in about eight hours flat as a surprise present, but James Garner is the one that gets the surprise when he drives in at night into what he thinks is his driveway and drives straight into the pool and sinks, very slowly, looking more surprised than any man you've ever seen. Tusker loved that bit. He chuckled all the way home. He said he must persuade Billy-Boy to build a pool in the hotel compound one day when old Ma Bhoolabhoy was out playing bridge so that when her tonga brought her back at night the whole thing would tip in with a bloody great splash.

The next day he was his grumpy old self again.

And after Tusker's birthday there was Monday April 17th, an ordinary Monday with Mr Bhoolabhoy and Tusker being convivial while Lucy went to the pictures and saw *Hello Dolly* for the umpteenth time and for the rest of the week couldn't get the tune out of her head and went round singing it.

'Oh, *goodbye*, Dolly,' Tusker growled because she was humming it as she got ready to go to church on Sunday April 23rd. 'Don't forget to remind Father Sebastian about dinner tomorrow night.'

'Yes, Tusker. What time shall I say?'

'7.30's usual.'

'7.30 here, for a drink. Then what? Perhaps he doesn't drink.'

'Not known a priest yet who didn't drink like a fish. What d'you mean, then what?'

'Do we eat here or take him over to Smith's?'

'I'll think about that.'

'When you've thought about it you'll remember to tell me, won't you? Today, preferably. I shan't be available most of tomorrow morning.'

'Why?'

189

'I told you yesterday. I'm having my hair done.'

'What for? Father Sebastian?'

She smiled. 'Not just for Father Sebastian, Tusker. Have a nice morning.'

CHAPTER TWELVE

Sunday April 23rd was a disastrous day for Mr Bhoolabhoy and Saturday had been hell. On Saturday Lila had
laid hands on him. She pushed him and shouted at him, in
front of Prabhu and Cook and Minnie.

There had been a call from the lawyer in Ranpur. Mr
Bhoolabhoy answered it because there was only one telephone at Smith's and it was in the Manager's cubby-hole.
Not even Lila's room had an extension. She hated the telephone. When she had to use it she shouted as though the
call had come through from the North Pole. Wedged into
the space available she shouted into it to the lawyer, while
Mr Bhoolabhoy waited outside. All the lawyer had told
him was that Mr Pandey would be coming up on the afternoon flight with urgent documents that had to be dealt
with over the weekend. He had then asked to speak personally to Lila.

Whatever the lawyer was saying to her was arousing her
to a terrifying pitch of fury. Her jowls shook. Her moustache bristled. 'Crooks!' she kept shouting. Otherwise she
shouted in Punjabi. Then she banged the phone down,
forced her immense body out of the cubby-hole and
shouted, 'Fool! Fool!'

And pushed him.

Pushed him.

In full view of the servants.

The physical shock was great. The humiliation unbear-
able. 'Why do you push me?' he shouted at her as she
waddled her way back to her room.

'Because you are a fool!' she shouted back. She banged
the door. From within she yelled for Minnie who ran in,
hand clapped to mouth as usual in that ridiculous common
way. Mr Bhoolabhoy went into his cubby-hole and banged
its door. The glass-panes shook. Minnie came out. She

stood in front of the cubby-hole. He raised the window.

'Yes?'

'Ownership wanting.'

He banged the window down and pretended to busy himself. He took his time. But no amount of time would heal his shame and fury. She had never pushed him. Never. When he at last went into her room her found her sitting on the edge of the bed, knees wide apart to accommodate her belly. Her head was bowed. Her elbows, resting on her knees, supported the weight. Slowly she looked up at him.

'Goodwill,' she said. 'Goodwill! Goodwill you were saying!'

'What of goodwill?'

'You might ask! What indeed of goodwill? Whose idea was this goodwill? I ask this. Whose idea was it? Who raised the question of this being called goodwill? And what is the result? Instead of better terms, worse terms. That is the result of your meddling. Fool! Fool!'

'You call your husband a fool?'

'I call him a fool. He is a fool.'

'If I am a fool, then you too are a fool. All I asked was whether goodwill had been taken into consideration in arranging terms. It is quite clear. You did not take it into consideration. And they were laughing at you. Then because you are greedy you tried to renegotiate. And they laugh louder. You did not sign the contract, you sent it back for revision. So now there is a new contract, isn't it? Not such a good contract. Why do you blame me? You are a greedy woman. I will not accept blame. When have you ever consulted me? Your greed only is to blame. In the consortium you will be in good company. You are all greedy people. You enjoy trying to do each other down. But what do I care? I will have nothing to do with it. I am only Management. It is my misfortune to be married to a greedy woman who is Ownership and who humiliates her husband in front of servants by pushing him. I will not be pushed.'

'I am pushing you now. Okay? I am giving you notice. One month's notice according to contract.'

192

'You cannot give your husband notice, Lila.'

'This is true. To husbands only divorce can be given. To managers giving notice is as easy as falling off a log.'

'This I should like to see,' he cried. 'And what do I care? In a month or two there will be nothing to manage. You are getting rid of it. So I care as little for job as that English hippie who was here a few weeks ago sleeping rough in the bazaar. Only he was a fool too. He was thinking of India as a spiritual place. From all over the world they come, ringing their bells and smoking pot and getting into Hinduism. But then they have never seen a man pushed by his fat greedy wife who is going to pull everything down and put up concrete just like in the West.'

He was nearly at fainting point. He turned to go.

'Come here.'

'I have things to do.'

'This is what I mean. You are still Management even if Management under notice. So you have things to do. You will write for instance to the Smalley man warning to quit. You will write saying that it will be impossible to grant a further year's tenancy of Lodge when current letter agreement expires. You will advise him to look for other accommodation. You will say that from July 1st tenancy can only be on weekly basis with one week's notice because ownership is developing the site.'

'Pulling it down.'

'When I say developing I mean developing. During process of development they can always move into Shiraz.'

'You are joking of course. How can they afford Shiraz?'

'What they can afford or not afford does not interest me. It is no concern of mine. When *they* ruled the roost *our* concerns did not enter their heads. It is tit for tat.' She slapped her bosom, in emphasis.

'I will not send such a letter to my old friend.'

'I am ordering Management to send it. I am ordering Management to write it. I will sign it. I will see that it is sent.'

'Such a letter will give him another attack.'

'Am I responsible for the state of his health?' she

193

shouted. 'He is a fool too. Only a fool could have failed to see the point of the letter last year. He has had time to make different arrangements. I can give him no more time. I cannot sign the new contract until such a letter has been sent to the Smalley man. The new contract guarantees no encumbrances in regard to tenants.' That is your fault, not mine. They would have had to go anyway but it is your fault such a letter must be sent now.'

'What is to happen, Lila?' Mr Bhoolabhoy asked, quietly. He saw that he was in an impossible position. 'What are your plans for The Lodge?'

'They are not concerning you. And they are not my plans. They are consortium plans. I do not think these plans involve any development that will give you employment. So perhaps you can count yourself lucky to have married what you call a greedy woman who will be rich. Although not as rich as she might have been if she hadn't married a fool. You will write the letter today so that I can show a copy of it to Mr Pandey when he arrives.'

'Have you written the letter?' she asked later. He said he had not. He said he had no time to write such a letter today.

'Then you will write it tomorrow morning.'

'I can't write it tomorrow. Tomorrow it is Management's day off. It is Sunday.'

'You will write it on Sunday evening.'

'I shall be engaged on church business on Sunday evening. It is Management's day off until Monday morning.'

'I shall not speak of this letter again. If it is not written by the latest on Monday morning before I sign the contracts Mr Pandey is bringing up and if he does not have a copy of that letter to take with him back to Ranpur by midday on Monday he will also take back my instructions to institute proceedings for divorce.'

'Disobeying one's wife are not grounds for divorce. You will write the letter yourself if it must be written.'

194

'You are paid to write such letters.'

'I am not paid well enough to write such letters. I have not had a rise in salary since marrying Ownership.'

'Now who is being greedy? Huh? You get your keep. You get pocket money. On top of this sometimes you get sex. You will not get sex again until the letter has been written and perhaps not even then. And speaking of grounds for divorce, I am not thinking about disobedience to wife, but of more serious matters.'

He began to tremble. She laughed. 'Ranpur, for example. You think I do not know what goes on in Ranpur, huh? But I am a reasonable woman. I ask myself, what can one expect when one is married to a man who thinks of nothing but sex. If you write the letter I may forget about Ranpur. We might have sex in Bombay or Calcutta. The consortium is also thinking of Goa. Goa would interest you. It is very sexy in Goa because the white hippies lie around having sex in the open. It is also full of old churches. In Goa there are more churches than houses. And there are many western tourists in search of the real India as well as hippies who have found it and are having sex.'

She began to laugh. The bed began to shake. Her breasts wobbled and her belly heaved. He felt like a beggar, starved and meagre holding his bowl out and under a compulsion to grin and cut a caper and earn a paise or two. 'I am lost,' he thought, as he left the room. 'I do not want to go to Goa. I want to stay here. I want to stay here so long that in a hundred years from now people will be able to point to two worn places in the tiles below the steps to the altar at St John's and say, "Francis Bhoolabhoy was here. *Those* were his knees".'

But even the church was excluding him. He cycled there at seven o'clock on that Sunday morning, April 23rd, and knelt and prayed and then waited for Susy to arrive with the flowers. He knew that Father Sebastian was due to arrive on the night train from Ranpur. He knew Father

195

Sebastian intended to stay yet again at Susy's bungalow. He had hoped that Father Sebastian would stay at Smith's, like old Tom Narayan. Father Sebastian was the kind of man St John's needed and not the sort to seek the most comfortable and prestigious roof under which to shelter. But he seemed to prefer the accommodation Susy offered, and Susy's company to his own.

When it had turned eight o'clock and Susy still hadn't turned up with the flowers he became restless. By nine o'clock he was pacing up and down the path from the lych-gate to the porch. The service was not until eleven. But Susy was overdue. And he had worked out the reason long before she and Father Sebastian at last arrived at ten o'clock in a tonga that looked like a festival float so burdened by flowers that she and the priest were embowered by them. Against Father Sebastian's shining black face her own dark coffee-colour looked so pale.

She had gone to the station to meet him and they had had breakfast together. Now, while Mr Bhoolabhoy stayed in the background, they decorated the church together. When this was done he suggested to Father Sebastian that they might go over some accounts in the vestry but Father Sebastian said casually, 'I'm here until Tuesday, and it's such a lovely morning, let's be outside. There is something I want to ask.'

Susy did not come with them. To show that he was not jealous he said, 'Come on then, Susy, enjoy the sunshine.'

'No, I have one or two things to do in here yet.'

'Tell me,' the priest said when they were outside. (*What* things had Susy still to do?) 'The English lady who was here at Easter with her husband, Colonel—'

'Smalley.'

'Colonel and Mrs Smalley. Yes. Is she not the lady in some of the pictures taken in the churchyard?'

'Yes, the same one.'

'I'm using one of them, and the better of the two interiors, in the article I spoke of. Is she a regular worshipper?'

'Not recently. But then her husband has been quite ill since January.'

'Ah, yes. I see. I'm dining with them tomorrow evening.'

It was the first Mr Bhoolabhoy had heard of it. Tusker had said nothing last Monday. All he'd said was, 'Saw your new chap.' Somehow, Mr Bhoolabhoy thought, I am being left out.

They strolled slowly back to the church. Mr Bhoolabhoy checked that all the hymn and prayer books were in place. From the vestry he heard Susy laughing with Father Sebastian. He stared at the altar. 'I am just management even here,' he said. And hid himself until it was time to go and toll the bell.

It began to toll as Lucy's tonga turned into Church road. 'Send not to ask,' she murmured, 'for whom the bell tolls. It tolls for thee.' The grave and lovely words caused her sadness but no distress. Whenever she thought of them she remembered how at the end of the film Gregory Peck rode off with Ingrid Bergman on a horse. She hadn't liked that film much. All she remembered was the horse with Ingrid Bergman being carried off on it. Descending she paid the tonga wallah off. There were still a number of people arriving. Next week, perhaps on Thursday, she would be here with Mr Turner. She hoped he wouldn't be too much of an intellectual. It would be nice to talk to him about the common or garden things that had always interested her: films and plays and popular music. 'I am an indoor person, I suppose, Mr Turner,' she would tell him. 'It was impossible to enthuse about such things in India in my day, because they weren't recognized as proper subjects for enthusiasm, precisely because they were indoor things. That makes me very middle-class, doesn't it? The upper-classes, and all the people who like to think of themselves as upper-class, are never happy unless they are competing at something in the open air, living what they call a full life. But in these indoor things I can recognize my own life and through them project and live so many lives, not just the one I have.'

She smiled and nodded at the Singhs, went in and this time chose a pew near the back and knelt and prayed.

She could be anything and anyone she wished. Within the darkness of her closed eyes and enfolding palms she was suddenly – how strange – Renée Adorée running after the truck taking Jack Gilbert away to the front in *The Big Parade*, one of the few old silents she had seen. Another was *Seventh Heaven*, which the girl like Clara Bow had taken her to. The twins took her to *The Big Parade* because it sounded a manly film and, she supposed, they had never got over what they called the disappointment of just missing the Great War and were compensating for the missed opportunity to have shown themselves fine fellows. They teased her afterwards for crying when Renée Adorée clung on to Jack Gilbert's hands and then his boots as the truck carried him and his comrades away, and then had to let go because she couldn't keep up, and there had been that lovely shot from the back of the lorry showing her receding into the distance, alone and forlórn on the muddy road. She hated the twins for teasing her and she'd hated them for sniggering during the scene in the shellhole when Jack Gilbert didn't shoot the wounded German soldier but was good to him and then started raving about the horror and brutality of war. 'The poor mutt's only been at the front five seconds,' David had said in a voice loud enough for people to say Shh! She'd hated them for laughing at Jack Gilbert, not because of Jack Gilbert but because of Toole and the fact that Jack Gilbert's doughboy uniform had electrified her with a recollection of Toole.

She uncovered her eyes and resumed her seat, waiting for the service to begin.

Toole had been her first sexual object. She had woken to him, been woken by him, simply by sitting in the back of the Rolls which took them from the Hall to the Church at Piers Cooney each Sunday in those glorious summer holidays of 1919, 1920 and 1921, when she was 14, 15 and 16, and the boys nearly three years older. She had become aware of the back of Toole's neck as she'd never been aware of anything before in quite the same disturbing way. And she hadn't been able to understand why the twins made such a joke of Toole's name: such a secret private joke; but every time they addressed him as Toole she knew the joke was being shared again between them.

In the old days at St John's in Pankot, leaving with Tusker and other officers and wives in strict order of precedence, while the rank and file of British soldiers on station, enduring church parade, had kept their seats to let the gentry leave, she had seen, sometimes, a Toole among them, and carried him away with her in her imagination, as she had without quite knowing why carried away Toole or been carried away by him all those years before.

Toole had been Sir Perceval Large's batman-driver in the war. The twins said it must have been a cushy billet because Uncle Percy (as they called him) had never been to the front. In her heart Lucy disagreed about the cushy billet. She was sure Toole had fought and suffered before becoming Uncle Percy's servant and resented **not** being sent back to the trenches but instead forced to drive Uncle Percy's staff car and clean his boots until the Armistice brought them both back to Piers Cooney.

Toole was a local man, the son of a ploughman on one of Uncle Percy's farms. She sensed from the back of his neck that he was also resentful of the fact that the war had not changed his condition of servitude much, but that driving was better than ploughing or labouring and that he was glad of a job that gave him the chance to exercise a skill acquired as a soldier and at a time when jobs were scarce anyway.

He drove with immense care and assurance. So it seemed to her. When he was not driving he could be seen in his shirt-sleeves in the stable-garage, under the car or bent over its open bonnet, endlessly cleaning and polishing. In the August sunshine the gleaming coachwork of the motor dazzled her. Inside there was never a speck of dust or a stain on the buff corduroy-covered upholstery. The windows were as clear as if there were no glass. These things

199

she noticed, but mostly she noticed Toole, up front, clad in a brown uniform that had a high tight collar with buttons at the front and seams at the back that spread and broadened from waist to shoulder; a uniform that fitted him so closely that it struck her that he must find it unbearably hot and uncomfortable because his neck and his gloved hands, which she knew were brown, suggested a preference for exposure to sun and weather.

He seldom spoke. The twins asked technical questions about the car which she didn't understand and which he answered briefly in words equally unintelligible to her but obviously to the twins' satisfaction although they laughed at his accent too, and were always trying to get him to pronounce the word cylinders. They spoke to him in that haughty young gentleman's way which was a combination of the carefree and easy-going and the arrogant.

She believed he guessed that for them the word cylinders, pronounced with a Somerset richness, was as much a joke between them as his name, which they were always using. Occasionally he found ways of avoiding the word. Toole was no fool. She sometimes felt coming from him, too, a controlled contempt – not for her, to whom he was always gracious and courteous (opening the door for her and leaving the boys to make their own way out) – but for the twins, and at a different level for the three of them who were, he must have known, only the children of a poor relation who had been employed at The Hall to try to put some ginger into the sickly son, to train him to withstand the rigours of Eton during the illnesses that sent him and brought him back from one preparatory school to another, so that apart from the holidays he was often at home during term, in their mother's care. Toole was old enough to know the Little children's history, aware and alert enough to realize that the summer holiday for the three of them was his master's charity towards a distant female cousin who had lived under his roof and then, her task completed, made a respectable marriage with the curate and who if subsequently unblessed by fortune had at least produced two strapping sons of her own and, as an afterthought, a dainty little girl, all three of whom would benefit from the kind of summer holiday their father could not easily afford and which perhaps was granted by Uncle Percy as a memorial offering to the sickly son who had been their mother's charge and who had endured Eton, done well at Oxford, and died in the trenches.

The writing of Christmas and birthday letters to Uncle Percy had been one of her earliest disciplines. Presumably Mumsie hoped for some lasting advantage from the connection, but there was none, and 1921 was the last holiday in Somerset. Uncle Percy, long widowered, died the following Spring and the estate went to a nephew who was not interested in the Little side of the family. Lucy did not regret it. She was almost glad. The 1921 holiday had begun beautifully but ended horribly. Midway through it Toole was suddenly no longer there. An older man took his place – a nasty common little man, smarmy, obsequious but also insolent. Toole's disappearance was a mystery because it was not discussed, but she overheard the twins talk.

There had been a girl, a local girl. Toole and she had been what the twins, shying from the word love, called soft on one another. But the girl was 'a cut above him', a farmer's daughter, promised by her father to the son of another. The girl had wanted to marry Toole and Toole wanted to marry her. They had both disappeared, although not together. Years later, the kinder of the twins, Mark, whom she found one day mooning in the orchard over the loss of the latest girl he and David had vied with each other for but who had been seen off by Mumsie who thought no girl good enough for either of them, said, 'Remember Toole?' and told her how Toole had got his girl into trouble ('Sorry, Luce, but you're old enough to know what I mean') and promised to marry her. Toole had a little flat above the stable-garage, a decent wage, a decent job, a decent employer. They could have been happy, perhaps moved on to better things because the motor business was booming and there was nothing Toole didn't seem to know about motors.

He had gone one evening to face the family but the girl wasn't there. She'd been packed off to a relation in

Cornwall. The father and the father of the man she was promised to, and the man himself, had set on Toole, beaten him up and dumped him unconscious in a ditch a mile from the village. He'd probably lain there for hours. When he got back to the Hall he packed all his things and in the morning faced Uncle Percy. It was mid-month but he wouldn't take a penny of the money owing to him because he was letting his employer down by going at once and not giving notice. He was going to Cornwall to look for his girl. Then he just went and that was the last anyone ever saw or heard of him.

'I hope he jolly well found her,' Mark said. 'I hope they went off together. I've often wished I had his guts.' She said, 'How did you find out all this, Mark?' He said, 'That rotter who took his place told us. And what a rotter he was. Grinning and putting his hand on your knee and telling you not to get involved with girls. Oh, Lord. Sorry, Sis.'

And he got up and went; went, went, as Toole had gone, gone. It was the last of the few intimate conversations she had with Mark, who was in Insurance, but spending his weekends with David (who was an accountant) bent over the open bonnets or under the chassis of what they called flivvers acquired on the cheap from richer friends and which they were making good for Sundays when they roared out of the vicarage, two hulking young men of nearly thirty, on their way to keep appointments with the girls Mumsie always disapproved of and made unwelcome; and roared out one Sunday too often, never to return, finding their own Passchendaele in a pile-up between their flivver and another.

'The grace of our Lord Jesus Christ, and the love of God, and the fellowship of the Holy Ghost, be with us all evermore. Amen.'

'Amen,' Lucy said. The service was over. It had passed her by. She had gone through it automatically, rising, kneeling, singing, or just sitting quiet remembering Piers Cooney.

After the blessing Father Sebastian held his position. His arms were folded across his chest. No one dared move until he moved. The silence was intense. Suddenly there was a strange sound. Father Sebastian smiled, held up one hand, and as he did so a note blared, a true and singular note, an authentic note that took her breath away because it was by her so long forgotten. A wind seemed to stir through the congregation.

The organ was playing. It was playing music she recalled but couldn't name. An anthem, a voluntary, pealing and pealing away. There were falterings. The organ hadn't played for a long time. But it played. She peered. The piano was abandoned. So it must be Susy who was up there in the old organ loft.

When the music reached a climax Father Sebastian took up the great cross and, holding it high, came down from the sanctuary and paced slowly down the aisle to the sound of the organ and the murmurs of the amazed congregation who bowed and bobbed and dipped as he went past them on his way to the West door.

He stood in the porch, holding the cross in his left hand, shaking each hand with his right. The organ still played. It took her a long time to get out of the church.

'Mrs Smalley?' he said, when it was her turn.

'Yes, Father Sebastian. What a lovely Matins. Whatever happened to restore the organ to us?'

'A little technology, a lot of faith and Miss Williams to play.' He had had something for breakfast spiced with garlic. 'You *are* the lady in the photographs?'

'There were some photographs, yes. We shall see you tomorrow? My husband particularly asked me to remind you. Seven-thirty?'

On the spur of the moment she added, 'Do bring Susy with you. I've known her since she was a child.'

CHAPTER THIRTEEN

Walking home she began to regret that impulse invitation
and rather to hope that tomorrow morning when she kept
her appointment at the Seraglio Room Susy would plead
a prior engagement. In all the years they'd known one
another they had never exchanged social visits and Susy
had never called her anything but Mrs Smalley nor Tusker
anything but Colonel Smalley, never taken the least advantage of the fact that they both called her Susy and that
she was now virtually their oldest acquaintance in Pankot
– and, until last year, a regular professional visitor at The
Lodge and as familiar with it as she was with her own little
bungalow.

Regretting the invitation, Lucy was at the same time
ashamed of regretting it; but one of the earliest lessons she
had learned in India was of the need to steer clear, socially,
of people of mixed blood and she had quickly been taught
how to detect the taint, the touch of the tar-brush in those
white enough to be emboldened to pass themselves off as
pukka-born. She'd been told that the Eurasians (Anglo-
Indians as they were then called) were very loyal to the
British, that without them there would have been no reliable
middle-class of clerks and subordinate officials. The rail-
ways, especially, depended on them. With their passionate
attachment to a Home many of them had never seen and
had no prospects of seeing ever, they formed an effective
and in-depth defence against the strange native tendency
to bribery and corruption which, coupled with that other
native tendency to indolence, could have made the Indian
empire even more difficult to run than it already was.
Nevertheless, effective and reliable though they were, they
would take a yard if you gave them an inch; and in any
case – although it was not their fault, individually, as
people who hadn't *demanded* to be born – they did repre-

sent a physical connection between the races that had continually to be discouraged.

Most of them were the off-spring of sad and reprehensible liaisons between native women or women of mixed blood and British Other Ranks who unless you kept them fully occupied, which wasn't easy, did have this tiresome habit of occupying themselves. But then, if a man was stuck in India for years, serving his King and Country, you could hardly expect anything else. It was the way of the world. Unfortunately, many of the liaisons were unofficial, some were instances of bigamous marriage. Whatever the origin, though, the Eurasian population had grown, through inter-marriage, living what Lucy thought of as its own rather sad and self-contained and often pretentious mimic life. It had always touched her when she heard of a soldier who had married his Eurasian girl and taken her back to England, and it had touched her too when she heard of a soldier who had fallen in love both with his girl and the country, signed on for another stint or taken his discharge in India when the time came and stayed on with her.

Susy's father had been potentially such a man. Lucy remembered the widowed Mrs Williams saying years ago, 'Len loved it here.' Mrs Williams, pale though she was, the daughter of a Eurasian mother and a Eurasian father, had never tried to pass herself off. Her elder daughter, Lucille, had not only tried but successfully married her GI when living in Calcutta earning her living as a singer, and gone with him, as the saying then was, Stateside. What had happened to them subsequently, Heaven knew. Susy never said, perhaps because she did not know but could only guess from the infrequent letters she got from time to time. Perhaps the child of the marriage had exposed the great lie. The genes could play cruel tricks. They had played such a trick on Susy herself who was not only not stunningly beautiful, as some of the Eurasian girls could be, but as brown-skinned as Mr Bhoolabhoy.

Susy had learned her hairdresser's trade literally at her mother's knee. Lucy met her first as a skinny-legged little girl in a plaid skirt, white blouse and white knee-high socks, with her black hair done in a plait and tied with a white ribbon (the whiteness emphasizing the coffee-coloured skin which her mother was at no pains to try to disguise. Susy turned up with her mother at Smith's, when Lucy and Tusker were billeted there early in the war. She came to help and watch and learn her mother's skills as a hairdresser.

In those days you had alternatives. You could go to Mrs Williams's bungalow, one room of which was equipped to cope with several memsahibs at a time, or you could have Mrs Williams call. The latter was preferable, the former sometimes unavoidable if there were grand things afoot like a party at the Summer Residence or at Flagstaff House when the demands for Mrs Williams's services were especially heavy. How that woman had worked! How well she had trained the two Eurasian girls she hired. How well she'd taught skinny little Susy.

Towards the end of the war people said Mrs Williams must be making a small fortune; but Lucy watched the decline and fall between 1947 and 1948 when most of the English women had gone home and Pankot gradually filled with Indian wives who washed and dressed their own hair, never had it cut, and many of whom still seemed almost to be in purdah, so shy and retiring were they.

When Lucy and Tusker left Pankot, finished with the army, beginning a new life as box-wallahs in Bombay, Mrs Williams was still alive. When they returned to Pankot in 1961, Mrs Williams was some years dead but Susy was carrying on the business and benefiting from the new wave of modern Indian wives and daughters. She had opened a salon in the bazaar, called Susy's. She could do backcombing and beehives, short cuts, the things young Indian women now wanted. The older ones could still have appointments with her in her bungalow if that was what they preferred. The salon had rather frightened Lucy. She felt out of place there. It was styled on the open-plan. Conversation was free and open; but she could not easily join in. She knew nothing of Dusseldorf, Basle, Roma, Cairo, Moscow, Paris. She could not state a preference for a particular duty-free shop at any one airport. She could not even discuss Fortnums except from a ten-year-old recollection of going in once to buy Tusker some Stilton. She had never been to Washington. Saks in Fifth Avenue was merely a name to her.

'You can come to the bungalow, Mrs Smalley,' Susy said after her second visit to the salon. 'Or I will come to The Lodge if you'd prefer. I do not care for all this togetherness either, but people expect it nowadays once they've been foreign. Gossip, coffee, magazines. All London-style.'

So Susy had come to The Lodge, once a month, bringing her modern portable equipment with her. Lucy enjoyed these sessions. Susy was a film fan too. And liked the old tunes. She liked hearing about London in 1950; and telling Lucy what if anything she had heard from Lucille in the States. When the Blackshaws came to Pankot, Phoebe had shared the sessions at The Lodge. After they went home Lucy enjoyed them again because there was only Susy to talk to and talking to Susy was more interesting than talking to Phoebe Blackshaw who had spent so many years in tea-gardens she could talk of nothing else. Also, Phoebe hadn't treated Susy very kindly. She had been abrupt and distant. Susy never showed any sign of being upset. She'd simply got on with the job, moving from one to the other of them.

It must have been a month after Phoebe Blackshaw went home that Susy stood back one day and looked at the mirror into which Lucy was looking and said, 'Mrs Smalley, have you ever thought of letting it go?'

Lucy had stared at her own reflection and seen how the dark brown dye was beginning to make her look like an old woman who tried to look younger but managed to look older.

'What do you advise, Susy?'

'It's such lovely hair, Mrs Smalley. Very fine and soft. Never any trouble to set. But the colouring is beginning to coarsen it. Also you have such a lovely white skin. Like porcelain. The colour no longer works with it.'

'But grey is so depressing.'

'You will never be grey, Mrs Smalley. You will be white. And don't worry about the transitional period. We can bleach the colour out. It will be perfect when white, cut a little shorter, just gently waved, and given a blue rinse.'

'Blue?'

'Yes, blue. It will bring out the violet in your eyes. I have some good rinse. An American lady brought it from London and left two whole cartons. Man, they are so rich, these Americans.'

That was the beginning of the blue rinse. To perform the initial operation, Susy removed the mirror and only set it up again when she had finished. Lucy stared at herself. She thought, The girl's a genius. Even Tusker said, 'Good God! Whatever's Susy done to you?' but had looked pleased. 'Only English women can carry it off, Colonel Smalley,' Susy told him, 'only English women with delicate features and fine skins and who are not too tall and have not put on weight.'

Thereafter, tending Lucy's blue-white hair, poor Susy's hands had looked even more uncompromisingly *of the country*; and the transformation of Lucy marked the beginning of Susy's professional troubles.

Lucy had supposed Susy owned the bungalow her parents had lived in but she only rented it. Her old landlord died. The new one, down in Ranpur, renewed her lease on condition that no business should be carried out from there. The new landlord already owned the premises where Susy had her salon. Two years later he acquired the concession to run the Seraglio Room in the new Shiraz hotel, gave Susy notice to quit the tenancy of the salon which he intended to redevelop as a shop for the luxury tourist trade (semi-precious stones from Jaipur, furs, silks, local folk-craft from the remoter villages of the Pankot hills) and as a sop (and perhaps recognizing that Susy's skill and reputation could be turned to immediate short-term advantage in terms of immediate cash-flow) made a deal with her that entitled her to take one or two paying-guests at the bungalow (which she was already doing anyway by arrangement with the Indian tourist office) and to continue work as a hairdresser at the Seraglio, although not as its chief coiffeurist – who turned out to be a young man of outstanding good looks (if, Lucy thought, you liked those sort of good looks) called Sashi, who claimed to have been trained in Mayfair, London, who wore wet-look black trousers, high-heeled boots, a frilly shirt open almost to the waist to expose a chest-full of black hair in which nestled a primitive metal medallion on a chain.

Under Sashi's emotional rule at The Seraglio, Susy obviously suffered. Lucy did not know to what extent and did not want to. She was happy to have been able to make a cut-rate deal with Susy which meant that she could just afford the Seraglio Room provided she was there not later than 8.30 a.m. when Susy would let her in, trim, shampoo, rinse and set her and get her under the dryer before 9.30. Nine-thirty was the official opening hour and within a few minutes the first of the smart young assistants' began to arrive to get things ready for Sashi's manifestation shortly before 10 a.m. when the first appointments of the day were due to turn up, usually in the elegant shapes of Air India and Indian Airway hostesses who had spent a night at the Shiraz and had to smarten themselves up for the flights that evening back to Ranpur and on to Calcutta or Delhi.

Yes, Susy had been a good friend. She should not regret inviting her to join Father Sebastian at The Lodge.

When she got home Tusker was on the verandah. Today, or tomorrow at the latest, she would have to tell him about the photographs, about Sarah, about poor Colonel Layton, and about the imminent Mr Turner. He seemed to have nodded off. Bloxsaw, some distance away, opened one eye, then shut it. There was no sign of Ibrahim. It was a quarter to one. At Smith's hotel, Sunday was usually chicken pulao day, and she was very hungry. She hoped Ibrahim had not been sent over for trays, because then it was difficult to get second helpings and the tray-helpings were already small enough. She poured herself a very small gin and tonic and tiptoed out to sit near Tusker and wait for him to wake up.

But sitting, she saw he was awake already. His head was still lowered but his eyes were open, gazing at her.

'Hello, Tusker, dear. Have you had a nice little nap?'

He did not reply. She sipped her drink. 'Would you like a little drink? A very very small gin, because it's Sunday?'

'Why because it's Sunday?'

'Sunday is chicken pulao day. Pulao goes down nicely after a spot of gin. And you have been such a good boy.'

'I'm not having chicken pulao. I'm having poached egg on toast.'

'Oh, dear. How dull. I'm not sure about egg for breakfast and egg for lunch. It's very binding. Aren't you feeling well, Tusker?'

'What I feel's neither here nor there. I'm having poached egg on toast. In fact we're both having poached egg on toast. And we're cooking them here.'

She saw now that he was wearing his malevolent expression. She would have to tread carefully. 'I see,' she said. 'Are there enough eggs?'

'Ibrahim's gone to get some more.'

She sipped her gin. He was going to be *awkward*. Her tummy rumbled with hunger.

'By all means then, Tusker, have a poached egg. But I'm really very hungry, so I shall have chicken pulao.'

'Not today you won't because you're not going to the dining-room and Ibrahim isn't going to fetch a tray from the dining-room. We've finished with the dining-room and we've finished with trays.'

A pause.

'There are a lot of things I could say to that, Tusker, but I suppose first I'd better ask, *why*?'

'Because I say so.'

A pause.

'And what precisely is the connection between what you say and what I do?'

'The connection is that I'm still master of this bloody house.' He waited. 'Well? Am I or aren't I?'

'I can't deny that. No. Indeed, I can't. You are the

210

master of the house. On the other hand I am the mistress. And it is usual for the mistress to decide what shall be eaten and by whom and when, and if the master does not like it there's mostly nothing he can do about it unless he happens to have a talent for shopping and cooking which I'm afraid you haven't. I have seen you attempt to make a curry. In the bazaar I've known you to squander half the week's housekeeping in half-an-hour. I have watched you poach an egg. If you insist on having a poached egg for lunch I am prepared to poach it for you myself in order not to see several eggs wasted, and because as mistress of the house it's my duty to see the master fed. But after that, Tusker, I shall go across and have my chicken pulao. I shall expect to sleep between three o'clock and five o'clock and providing Ibrahim brings back enough eggs I may even poach you another one for your evening meal. Then I'll have to decide whether to have one too, or dine at Smith's or at the Club or at the Shiraz.'

'Afford it can you?'

'No. What we can still just afford is our special arrangement with the kitchen and management at Smith's and this is an arrangement I have absolutely no intention of giving up, unless of course you replace the electric stove with one that works effectively, and hire a cook. I have not stayed on in India to become, in my old age, either a cook or a masalchi. You have always pointed out the advantages people like us enjoy over those who have gone home and have to make do without servants even when they can afford them. If we had gone home I should have welcomed turning my hand to whatever was necessary. But we did not go home and so I don't welcome turning it. Here is Ibrahim now.'

She called him so that instead of going round the back he came round the front. Her hand was feeling a bit shaky. She had not intended to take Tusker up quite in the way she had done. But he had this effect on her nowadays.

'Thank you, Ibrahim,' she said, taking the eggs from him. 'I'll deal with these. Go and get your own meal. Did Burra Sahib give you the money for the eggs?'

Ibrahim said he hadn't. She asked how much was owed, opened her purse and gave him the sum asked. Before going he looked from one to the other of them, then salaamed and took himself off. She took the bag of eggs to the kitchen, switched on the plate that was supposed to heat a saucepan of water. It would do this either in a few seconds or half-an-hour. One could never tell. She smelt the butter from the fridge. It was bit off, but would do to grease the poaching pan and stop the eggs sticking. She searched for this pan, found it, studied it. It was dirty. She went out.

'Will scrambled do? I'm not cleaning *this*.'

'Neither am I.'

'Quite. So you see. You *see* the *difficulties*.'

'I see more than you think,' he said. 'And you're not going to the dining-room. Neither of us will. Ever again.'

She sat down, holding the dirty pan well away from her. 'Then I'll ask you again, Tusker. *Why?* Only this time don't say because you said so. And do for once *think* before you speak. Think for instance of the fact that we have invited Father Sebastian to dinner tomorrow evening. One can hardly offer him a poached egg, so unless you intend to give him drinks here and then take him over to the Shiraz or up to the club – neither of which establishments strikes me as being quite his venue if that's the word – there'll really be no alternative to our dining him at Smith's or arranging for Smith's to serve a special little meal for us here. And while you're bearing all this in mind I might as well tell you that I asked him this morning to bring Susy Williams with him, if she's free. It would make up a four.'

'Susy Williams? In Heaven's name you've known Susy Williams for more than thirty years and not had her to a meal once.'

'Which is one reason for having her now. When she does my hair in the morning I shall confirm the invitation. There's no more to be said about *that*. The only thing there's anything to be said about is where do we feed them? And if you say Ha! Or start obfuscating and mention poached eggs again I shall throw this dirty pan straight at you.'

'Throw it then.'

'I shall if you say Ha!'

'Ha! Ha!'

She threw it. It bounced off him as if he were made of something other than flesh and bone. Bloxsaw yelped, staggered to his feet and loped away to seek sanctuary in the garage. Startled crows shrieked and wheeled in the warm pellucid air. She got up and went inside to get herself another drink.

Only once before had she hit him; and that was at the time of the débâcle in Bombay, when she beat him off with a rolled-up *Times of India,* outraged less by what had been hinted about a relationship between him and Mrs Poppadoum than by what he had just told her: that he had refused Mr Feibergerstein's proposal to send them home to work out the last year of his contract with Smith, Brown & McKintosh, which would mean getting a small pension from the firm to add to the pension from the Indian Government. The alternative was really an ultimatum, little better than the sack. And he had chosen the alternative. 'I'm sixty next year,' he'd yelled at her, grabbing the *Times of India* from her numb hand. 'I'm not spending my 60th birthday in some place like bloody Stevenage. And I'm not going to be blackmailed.'

Somewhere like bloody Stevenage was where Feibergerstein Industries of Boston, London and Amsterdam had acquired Smith, Brown & McKintosh's interest in a pharmaceutical company. Feibergersteins were also big in the chemical fertilizer industry. They had also recently acquired control of Smith, Brown & McKintosh, who had run a shipping and general merchandise agency in India for over 80 years, and employed Tusker on his retirement from the army for ten of them as their administrative manager, at a salary that had sounded to Lucy glamorous in comparison with his army pay and which, together with the paid-for business trip home in 1950 and the prospect of more to come had accommodated her to the idea of staying-on yet again; until she realized that Tusker's personality change on leaving the army involved him in

213

spending money like water, gambling, drinking, getting involved with the tax-authorities, the customs and with the police over the Bombay liquor laws; and finally, it seemed, with Mrs Poppadoum.

In her heart Lucy had never believed that Tusker had misbehaved with Mrs Poppadoum. The Mrs Poppadoums of this world were beyond old Tusker's reach. Sigrid Poppadoum was young, Swedish by birth, a tall blonde beauty who (Lucy was convinced) made eyes at everything in trousers to annoy her prickly little Indian husband (whose third wife she was) who could steer government contracts the way of Feibergerstein and Smith, Brown and McKintosh, and whose nephew, trained at a business school in the States, had become a protégé of Solly Feibergerstein and been placed by him at Smith, Brown & McKintosh in Bombay as a young but senior executive. Mr Feibergerstein's wife, Mary-Lou, had said to Lucy when visiting with him in Bombay, 'Solly railly berlaives in Indian-ah-zaershun, which ah guess you British never railly did.'

For years now it had been clear to Lucy in retrospect that poor old Tusker had been for the chop the moment Solly Feibergerstein set eyes on him and had seen nothing but an old dug-out, an old Sahib whom Smith, Brown & McKintosh should never have employed when there were competent young men looking for jobs. But at the time it had simply seemed to her that Tusker was digging his own grave, complaining that that 'young twit Poppadoum's nephew' was after his job, and that he wouldn't trust Solly Feibergerstein farther than he could throw Poppadoum, but doing nothing to prove Mr Feibergerstein wrong in his assessment of Tusker's own capabilities. The opposite in fact.

And today, drinking another gulp of gin and lime, still shaking from the effort of having thrown the poaching pan at him, she still could not forgive him for the débâcle. There had been that incident at the Taj, when – half-cut yet again – he had bitten Mrs Poppadoum's ear, spilt his wine and said '**** it,' which had made Sigrid Poppadoum laugh and laugh but caused her husband great

214

offence, and Solly and Mary-Lou (and Mr Sylvester, the Managing Director of Smith, Brown & McKintosh) to smile bleakly in that way Lucy remembered the old race of British Sahibs and Memsahibs smiling if you do anything not quite pukka. For this smile to be effective and eloquent the lips had to twitch but turn down at the corners and the eyes be cast down for no more than a couple of seconds, and then raised and a new topic of conversation then introduced. Watching them, Lucy realized that nothing had changed for *her*, because there was this new race of sahibs and memsahibs of international status and connection who had taken the place of generals and Mrs Generals, and she and Tusker had become for them almost as far down in the social scale as the Eurasians were in the days of the *raj*.

'Tusker's worth the lot of them put together,' she had thought but the thought had lasted only a moment and the ghost of it, returning to haunt her now, gave her no comfort. He had been the most awful bloody fool. You simply couldn't survive in the world by speaking your mind and acting as you felt, moment by moment. It was all wrong, wrong. There were times for this, conditions for that. Of this timing Tusker had long ago lost his intuitive awareness. He had thrown his bonnet over impossible windmills. His unreasonable rage, when faced with the consequences, was the rage of a child.

He was right in one thing, though. It had been attempted blackmail: the choice offered of going home to work out the last year and take a pension, or of taking almost immediate separation in India and a piddling sum by way of compensation for loss of office. He had taken the compensation.

She had had no say in it. She had protested. She had cried. She had beaten him over the head with a newspaper. It had been like trying to knock sense into something composed only of temper and vapours and obstinacy and stupidity. And where had the compensation gone? It had gone – most of it on that absurd extravagant trip round India which had ended in Pankot. 'One last look', he said. They were still looking. But the rest of it had gone too.

215

Like his compensation from the army. How was it possible for money to go so quickly?

And where was the written statement she had asked for during their last quarrel? The clear statement of the position she would be in if he dropped dead? Where was *that*? She drained her glass and left the kitchen in a mood to demand it again; but on the way through the living-room something caught her eye at last: a piece of paper stuck under the telephone. The writing was in block capitals so she did not need her spectacles. It was Tusker's hand. The note said: David Turner. Ranpur 34105.

At that moment Tusker came in carrying the poaching pan. He went to the kitchen and started to clatter. A tap was run. A saucepan fell. He swore. She went in to him.

'For Heaven's sake, Tusker, go out and sit down and stop this absurd display of sulks. I'll poach your silly egg.'

'I can poach my own silly egg. I'm not a fool. And I don't like being made a fool *of*.'

'Who in Heaven's name is making a fool of you?'

'You for one. By *that* for instance.' He pointed at the telephone note, then picked up another saucepan. 'Made me sound a proper Charlie, didn't you? May I speak to Mrs Smalley, he says. She's out I say. Is that Colonel Smalley he says, this is David Turner. Who? I say. Turner, he says. So I say, What? And he says Turner. David Turner. Guy and Sarah Perron's friend, so I say are you sure you've got the right number because I don't know anyone called Guy and Sarah Perron, this is Pankot 542. Yes, that's the number I have, he says. So I took his.'

He looked absurd, standing there at the sink, holding a pan under the running tap and not looking at what he was doing, looking at her instead, accusingly, so that suddenly the water caught the rim of the pan and sprayed out, drenching his bush shirt. He flung the pan in the sink but it fell on the side and so he got drenched again before turning the tap off.

She sat on a stool, both hands clasped to her mouth, the telephone note crumpled between them, trying to stop herself laughing out loud.

He grabbed a towel, rubbed his shirt, grabbed a glass, poured gin, then lime, and stalked out, leaving her amid the ruins of an abortive attempt to cook an egg. She cleared the mess up, dried a saucepan, felt the hot-plate by putting her hand near it. It wasn't even lukewarm yet. She put some butter into the pan, then beat up two eggs in a bowl; left bowl, pan, salt and pepper and milk ready on the draining board; poured herself another gin and went out to join him.

She sat down. 'I was going to explain about Mr Turner today or tomorrow, but he's earlier getting in touch than I expected, so let me tell you about him now.'

'No need. Told me himself.'

'Yes, I see.' She sighed – sitting there, ankles neatly crossed, glass held in two hands resting on her lap. 'It's another of those mornings when I have to be endlessly patient. I mean with *myself*. I mustn't let myself become frustrated by evidence of my increasing inability to comprehend what is said to me.' She gave a little laugh. 'Do you know, Tusker, it's so strange? I'd somehow managed to get the impression that a young man unknown to you had telephoned, that you had a short conversation with him which ended abruptly with your taking his number and subsequently becoming crosser and crosser at the thought that he might have put the phone down imagining he'd been talking to someone not fully in possession of his senses and that this was entirely due to the fact that your wife had forgotten to warn you about him and therefore made a fool of you? However did I get that extraordinary idea?'

'Irony doesn't suit you.'

'Nothing does. I'm coming to that conclusion. Nothing suits me. Since I apparently can't tell you anything about Mr Turner you don't know, however, and you're obviously not in a mood to tell me what you *do* know, I think I'll go and ring him now.'

'You can't very well, can you?'

She thought that out for a few moments. 'You mean he's not in for the rest of the day? Something like that?'

'I mean you can't ring him because you haven't got his number.'

She closed her eyes, gently.

'I'm sorry, Tusker. I'm afraid I didn't have my spectacles on again. All I could read was a telephone number in Ranpur, written in block capitals with the little Biro I gave you for your birthday. I must have failed to notice something written in smaller print. For example something to the effect that the Ranpur number is the one to reach him on a certain date but not before because he is in transit just now?'

'He's not in transit. He's in Delhi.'

'He rang from Delhi?'

'He said he was in Delhi. Presumably he rang from there.'

'I know he *was* in Delhi because he wrote to tell me so. He said he expected to be in Ranpur on Tuesday and would ring me then, which is why I said he's a day or two early getting in touch.'

'So what are you making a fuss about?'

'I suppose it's my stupid little way. Just as it's your stupid little way to obfuscate. So shall we take a short cut and try to establish between us some mutual understanding about the reason he left his Ranpur telephone number, for instance whether we are trying to ring him, or he is to ring us, and what his intentions are about arriving in Pankot, and when, and whether he wants us to make his hotel booking for him?'

'Which of that lot do you want establishing first?'

'I have no particular preference, Tusker. It seems to me a simple enough list. But if it confuses you let's start with his expected time of arrival in Pankot.'

'Wednesday morning.'

'Good. That means he's coming on the night train and since the night train comes up from Ranpur we can take it he'll be in Ranpur by Tuesday evening at the latest.'

'Tuesday morning.'

'So some time on Tuesday I can ring this number in Ranpur should I wish. Either that or he may ring us. Now,

Tusker, perhaps the only remaining point to be settled is the reason why he may want to ring us or us to ring him. Let me hazard a little guess. Could it be he'll want to know whether we have been able to book his hotel room? Perhaps, since you seem to have had such a long and friendly conversation with him after all, you even volunteered to do that and it's just a question of letting him know by phone on Tuesday whether he should tell the taxi to bring him to the Shiraz or to Smith's.'

'He said he'd prefer Smith's because he's heard all about it from Sarah.'

'Yes, that fits in, Tusker. That's also why he's chosen to come by train. He wants to do everything in the *old* way. How long is he staying?'

'Two nights.'

'That's about what I thought. I hope you agree, Tusker, that although we can't put him up here, we must still treat him as a guest, and pick up his bill. And that one, sometimes both of us, must give time to him and take him around and see that he's fed. We must treat him as the friend of an old friend, because that's what he is.'

'Ha!' he said. 'I suppose you mean Sarah. You used to criticize her. You used to suggest she was unsound.'

'There was a time when she gave one cause to wonder. She more than made up for it later by standing by her family through all their little troubles. I'm not going to discuss that with you, Tusker. I hope you've said nothing to Ibrahim?'

'I haven't said anything to Ibrahim.'

'He would only tell Minnie and I want it to be a surprise to her. Mr Turner is bringing her a present from Sarah and Sarah's sister Susan.'

'He's got your blue rinse too.'

Her cheek became a little warm. 'How nice. Lovely. Susy can use the whole of my very last packet and not just the halves we've been using to eke it out.'

'Perhaps you'd get to the point.'

'I'm glad you realize there is a point, Tusker. The point as I see it is that I don't see how we can afford to pick up

Mr Turner's bill at Smith's and feed him at the Club or at the Shiraz, both of which are so much more expensive than our eating arrangements with Smith's. You've said that you will never eat in that dining-room again, nor have trays sent over from that kitchen. Now I'm quite prepared to humour you tomorrow by somehow rustling up in our own kitchen a dinner for Father Sebastian and Susy. It will be difficult, but not utterly impossible. What will be utterly impossible is attempting to do the same for Mr Turner to whom I'll have to devote quite a lot of personal attention. While he's our guest we shall either have to have trays sent over or keep him company in the dining-room. He will think it very odd if you don't join us. He will think it even odder if I meekly accept your unexplained and incomprehensible statement about no more trays and no more visits to the dining-room and he finds himself eating alone while you and I exist on a diet of poached eggs here at The Lodge.'

He did not reply but continued to stare at her. She drank what was left of her gin and got up.

'Where are you going?'

'I am going to scramble your egg.'

'I don't want an egg now. I'm past eating.'

'In that case, Tusker, since I am *not* I'm going now to have my chicken pulao, late as it is. Perhaps later today you'll let me know whether you can afford to feed Mr Turner elsewhere as well as pick up his bill at Smith's. I have no idea how near or far we are from bankruptcy, moreover' – she hesitated, felt for the brooch in her lapel, for courage – 'I still have not had the clear statement I asked for some time ago about the position I'd be in if left alone. So you see my difficulty. I have tried very very hard, Tusker, to go along with you and to make things as comfortable as I can for you, and I am old enough not to worry much that the clothes I'm standing up in are the only decent ones I have. You are just as shabby. I'm not complaining about the past, but I *am* frightened about the future because it's an unknown quantity, chiefly because you have never shared your hopes and fears with me but have simply taken your anger out on me without my know-

220

ing why or what causes it, which can only leave me feeling that *I'm* the cause and it seems awfully unfair after more than forty years of marriage.'

'Why are you crying?'

'I'm not crying. If I were I'd have a perfect right to. For the last time, Tusker, do you want an egg?'

'No. I told you, didn't I? I'm past it.'

'Then I'm past cooking it for you.'

She went to the head of the steps.

'Where are you going?'

'To get my chicken pulao, and to make Mr Turner's room booking. He can at least be assured of bed and breakfast even if the bed strikes him as motheaten and the breakfast as rotten and the bathroom as disgusting.'

She went down the steps, still holding the brooch. With her other hand she shielded her eyes from the glare and walked, thus, down to the hotel compound. The lame one-eyed *mali* who had been old *mali's* assistant was crouched over one of the pots of starveling plants. The grass on the verge of the path needed trimming. She entered the hotel. The place smelt of stagnant water and ancient damp : pervasive smells that attached to everything – the cane chairs, the faded cretonne-covers of the ruptured sofas, the potted palms, the cloths on the tables in the dining-room. Only one table was occupied – by two men who looked to her as if they had escaped from the Shiraz to discuss a deal and not be overheard. Having given her a brief glance they resumed their muttering and their chicken tandoori. She took her usual place and banged the brass-bell. After a while old Prabhu padded in.

'Good morning, Prabhu. I'll have a gin and lime and then the chicken pulao.'

'Sahib not coming?'

'Not this morning.'

Prabhu went. She asked herself: How many years have I sat at this table and watched the hotel settle imperceptibly on its own foundations? So much weight. Too much weight. The foundations must have sunk by now at least a foot.

221

Someone opened a door. Someone passed by. She looked up and recognized Mrs Bhoolabhoy's lawyer's clerk, Mr Pandey, who sketched a bow and went into his room. The gin and lime came. It might be bad for her to have another one. She didn't care. It might be fun to get a little merry.

The chicken pulao came. Here in India it would feed several starving families. A jug of water came. She sent it back. The jug had smears on it. She began to tuck in. After the second or third mouthful there was an eruption – a shriek from within, a great draught as the door opened and Mrs Bhoolabhoy emerged, a moving mountain of flesh in pale salmon pink and clacking sandals that billowed past, pushed into Mr Pandey's room waving a sheaf of papers. The door banged shut. More shouting. Then silence. A minute or two later when Mrs Bhoolabhoy came out again she and Lucy were face to face.

'Oh, Mrs Bhoolabhoy,' Lucy began, 'we're expecting a guest on Wednesday. I wonder if you'd kindly book a room—'

'I have already told Colonel Smalley I can't be bothered with that. You must speak to Management tomorrow. I have other things to deal with. All I want to know is about the shears. Have you dealt with the question of the shears?'

Mrs Bhoolabhoy stood over her, like something formidable created by a new disturbance in the Himalayas where the gods and goddesses of Hindu mythology were supposed to have originated.

'Shears?'

'Shears. Shears. Shears!' Mrs Bhoolabhoy raised her arms and made motions. *Snick-snick*. 'Shears!' she shouted. 'Kindly I give permission for your *mali* to use mower, shears, watercan. But this morning when I am telling my *mali* to cut the verges he says there are no shears because your *mali* has taken them away somewhere. I will not have my property taken off the premises.'

'I know nothing about your shears, Mrs Bhoolabhoy,' she said, though guessing where they were: with Joseph up at the church.

'You know nothing about shears. Colonel Smalley

knows nothing about shears. Colonel Smalley is even telling me he knows nothing about a *mali* because he says you do not have a *mali* only I have *malis*. Dear God! Am I crazy or is everybody else crazy? Who has been using my mower and shears and watercan for weeks if not your *mali*?'

'I suggest we discuss this elsewhere and at some other time, Mrs Bhoolabhoy. I am in the middle of my lunch.'

'I am not discussing it. I have not time to discuss trivial matters. I am simply saying that the shears must be brought back. I have more important things to do than argue about shears.'

She waddled away, leaving behind her a trail of sandalwood perfume which, to Lucy, was like the pungent smell of her own smouldering outraged dignity. When Mrs Bhoolabhoy had banged her door shut Lucy poured a glass of water and then continued very slowly to eat her meal. She did not look at the two business men. An Englishman, of course, would have intervened. Midway through Mrs Bhoolabhoy's tirade he would have risen quietly, come across and said, 'Mrs Smalley? My name's Smith. We met at HE's garden party last year. Can I be of any assistance?' And she would have indicated just by a look how grateful she was to be reassured of the help and protection of a gentleman whose intervention would have deflated Mrs Bhoolabhoy, reminded her of her place and sent her silent away to repent, to repent.

But that was at another season and in a distant country. She found it difficult to raise a glass of water without betraying an unsteadiness of hand which she felt the two Indian business men were watching out for, as if for further evidence that times for them had changed for the better and that their own old humiliations were being adequately paid for by new.

One of them called the bearer, causing her to start. Prabhu came in, gave them a bill which was checked through item by item before being paid in small bills peeled off a thick wad of larger ones. When they had gone she asked for her own bill to sign and said she'd have her

coffee in the lounge. She sat for a long time on one of the
wicker chairs, drinking the coffee, trying to work out the
best way of explaining operation *mali* to Tusker who had
obviously found out about it by having a similar row with
Mrs Bhoolabhoy. Poor Tusker. Poor silly Tusker. He
hadn't been cross about Mr Turner. He had come right
away to book him a room. And what had just happened
to her had happened to him, only more so, because there
had been that ridiculous argument about whose *mali* was
whose. Poor Tusker. Yes, poor silly Tusker. Maddening,
aggravating Tusker. Unpredictable Tusker. She bent her
head, supporting it with a hand across her eyes, elbow
supported by the chair and arm, and smiled, because she
couldn't help seeing the funny side of it.

CHAPTER FOURTEEN

It was four o'clock when she got back to The Lodge. Ibrahim was waiting, squatting on his hunkers below the verandah.

'Colonel Sahib gone out with Bloxsaw,' he announced.

The tea tray was prepared. In the kitchen there was evidence that for lunch Tusker had boiled himself an egg. The gin bottle was still at the level she had left it. There were still plenty of eggs in the fridge. There were some mixed herbs in the cupboard. There were two tins of tomato soup, bread, milk. On second sniff the butter didn't seem too bad.

'I shan't need you again this evening, Ibrahim. I'll make the tea when Burra Sahib comes home and we'll probably have an omelette this evening. Some soup first. Yes, that will be nice. How are we for beer?' They checked. 'Good. Tonight I can cope. Tomorrow we shall need all our energy. Somehow or other we have to conjure up dinner for four. But I think that may be fun, don't you? I shall have to be up early. Really quite early because I'm going to have my hair done and while I'm having my hair done you will have to go to the bazaar and buy things for salad, and get hold of a chicken which somehow we must roast and then have cold. Oh, and some mayonnaise from Jalal-ud-Din's. And they have anchovies, don't they? We could make a small hors d'oeuvre. Hard-boiled eggs, sliced, anchovies. And tomatoes. Perhaps some ladies fingers cooked, but cold and in french dressing. Mustard, do we have mustard? If we don't Jalal-ud-Din's will. Oh, and tinned corn. Sahib likes tinned corn. Where are the little hors d'oeuvres plates, Ibrahim?'

He opened a cupboard and showed her.

'They'll have to be washed. Dear me, how busy we're going to be.'

'Memsahib?'

'What is it, Ibrahim? Salt, how are we for salt?'

'Chicken very difficult.'

'What nonsense. There are always hundreds of chickens.'

'First to be killed though. Then plucked.'

'Yes, of course. Can't you get that done by the man you buy it from?'

'Perhaps, Memsahib. But then cooked. This stove not good for cooking. From this stove only burnt offering.'

'Does it have to be?' She absent-mindedly reached for a glass and poured another small gin. He offered her the lime bottle. She observed his parched lips. She got down another glass, poured a small measure in and gave it to him. He took it.

'Memsahib, it is forbidden.'

The glass was very steady in his hand. Her own, tipping in lime, was not.

'God will forgive us, Ibrahim. Cheers.'

'Salaam.'

He had good eyes.

'I am beholden to you, Ibrahim, for looking after us.'

The eyes melted.

'And you see,' she went on, bustling about the kitchen, bending, stooping, looking into this and that, opening drawers, 'Burra Sahib has for the moment and for quite inexplicable reasons taken against having anything to do with the hotel kitchen and the dining-room. So we're going to have to try to cope for a while, because I've rather taken against them too. We could have savoury. Cheese on toast.'

'Anchovies on toast better, Memsahib. Anchovies for savoury, not with hors d'oeuvres. Eggs and anchovies not good mixture. Much wind is resulting.'

'Yes, that is good advice. But what of the chicken?'

She straightened up from a stooping position, felt giddy, reached for support.

Ibrahim was there. He assisted her to the stool. 'Memsahib not to worry about the chicken. Ibrahim will make pukka arrangements.'

'Thank you, Ibrahim. I really am sorry to put upon you.

But Burra Sahib and I have these sudden social commitments. And, silly me, I seem to have overdone things before we've even started. I'll be perfectly all right in a moment.'

She accepted the glass of water he gave her and let him assist her to the bedroom. 'I'll have a little nap, then I'll be right as rain. Well I'll have to be. There's the dinner tomorrow evening that you're going to help us with, and a day or two later a visitor, an English visitor. Tomorrow morning I'll give you a list of things to buy. Meanwhile could you do something about the shears? *Mali* must have taken them to the churchyard and Mrs Bhoolabhoy is very cross with me.'

She was aware of him helping her to sit on the edge of the bed and take off her shoes; then, as she lay down, of the sound of the curtains being drawn.

It was dark when she woke. For a moment she thought it must be the middle of the night, but light was coming into the bedroom from the living-room and Tusker's bed was empty. Someone had covered her with a light blanket and she was fully clothed. She reached for her bedside clock. It wasn't quite eight o'clock. She had slept for nearly four hours. She put her shoes on and tottered into the bathroom, splashed her face, combed her disordered hair and dabbed cologne on her temples.

'Tusker?' she called lightly as she went into the living-room.

Ibrahim came in from the verandah. 'Sahib not in.'

'Not in? Whatever can have happened to him?'

'No, no Memsahib, nothing happening. Sahib came back for tea, now gone out again. He has left a note.' He went to the escritoire and brought her an envelope marked *Luce*. 'I make tea?'

She fetched her spectacles and sat at the escritoire, switched on the lamp, turned the envelope over to open it and found something written on the back:

227

'Thought I'd dine at the Club tonight so booked a table when out for my walk. Couldn't wake you. So gone on. Table for 8 p.m. but I'll hang on until 8.30ish in case you want to join me. Otherwise back about eleven. The enclosed is the clear statement you asked for.' It was signed T, and marked 7.30 p.m. Perhaps it was Tusker, not Ibrahim, who had covered her with the blanket.

She got her ivory paper-knife and slit the envelope. In it were two sheets of paper, fairly densely written. When she had finished reading them she began to read them again.

'Tea, Memsahib.' Ibrahim placed the tray on the Kashmiri carved wood table. 'Then I fetch tonga?'

'Tonga?'

'Tonga to take Memsahib to the Club?'

'No, Ibrahim. I'm not feeling up to dining out.'

'I make supper?'

'No, I had such a heavy lunch. And I have an early start tomorrow. I shan't eat again today. May I have my morning tea at seven instead of seven-thirty? Just mine. Sahib's at his usual time. I must be off by eight-fifteen.'

'Yes, Memsahib. Memsahib?'

'What, Ibrahim?'

'Shears are returned to Bhoolabhoy *mali*.'

'Oh, yes. I'd forgotten. Thank you.'

'Burra Sahib now knows about *mali*?'

'I don't know. Perhaps. Why do you ask?'

'Prabhu says there was much trouble today with Bhoolabhoy memsahib over use of tools. That she is shouting first at Burra Sahib and then at you, Memsahib, and telling Burra Sahib Joseph is not her *mali* but Sahib's and Memsahib's.'

'Well. Perhaps she did. But she would be wrong, wouldn't she, Ibrahim? Joseph is *your mali*.'

'I give him the push.'

'The push? Why?'

He put his hands behind his back. 'I cannot afford to pay Joseph unless Memsahib pays me to pay him, especially as rise not yet forthcoming. If Burra Sahib now knows truth and gives *hukm* that no more money is to be spent

228

on garden and Memsahib not to pay a single paise for what Mrs Bhoolabhoy should be paying for, then it will be kinder to Joseph for me to give him what is owing to date and the push, and leave garden to go jungly.'

'I think, Ibrahim, that whatever he says Sahib would not like to see the garden go jungly again. In any case I do not wish it to go jungly. I have no intention whatsoever of letting it go jungly. It is as much my garden as it is Colonel Sahib's or Mrs Bhoolabhoy's. And I don't want to discuss the garden tonight. Perhaps you'd just leave out the makings of Sahib's cocoa in case he wants it. I shan't have any myself tonight.'

When Ibrahim had gone for the night she drank her tea, now lukewarm. To occupy herself she began to write out Ibrahim's shopping list. When she had done that she put a batch of records on the old radiogram and waltzed, fox-trotted, quickstepped round the room with an invisible partner until the batch ran out. Then she made herself a cup of coffee, put a coat on and sat out on the dark verandah, warming her chilled hands round it.

'Bloxsaw? Bloxsaw?' she called softly. No answer. Ibrahim had put him in the garage for the night. Come back, little Sheba, she murmured.

The lights from the Shiraz made the middle of The Lodge's garden darker because of the contrast between the part where the light reached and the part where it didn't. Down to the left Smith's was dimly lit. But there were more night-illuminations in Pankot than there had been in the old days, and this made the stars look farther away. The outline of the hills was no longer so distinct against the sky, perhaps just an indication of how poorer her sight was now than then. The air was coming quite coldly from the mountains and she shivered, went in to make another cup of coffee and longed for the telephone to ring.

While the kettle was boiling she read Tusker's note again:

229

'You asked for a clear statement of yr posn if widowed. Far as I can see y'd get from IMWOF about £900 pa plus a RW supplt of maybe £600. Say £1500 in all, adjustable from time to time to cost of living index. The Smalley Estate income dries up on my death but y've always known that, Luce, and for the past ten years quite apart from the fall in value of the capital investment it's also yielded less interest because some bloody fool at Coyne Coyne persuaded the trustee to reinvest some of it in so-called Blue Chip equities (young Coyne, I reckon). Been getting less than £200 a year out of it since about 1964. Always tried to keep some of that money back in London but gradually had to have it all transferred as it came in to the Bank in Bombay. Present bank balance here approx £500, maybe £200 in London. Life Insurance only £2000 but the policy's with profits and been going long enough maybe to double that value at maturity. What it all comes to Luce is you've enough to take you home if that's what you want though in yr posn I'd prefer to stay here, considering the sort of income you'll have. At home you can't starve really, what with supplementary benefits, and things like Distressed Gentlefolk (Ha!). Also they've got the Nat Health and Old People's Homes. Perhaps for a white person being poor in England's better than being poor in India, though by average Indian standards we're rich if not by the standards of the Indians we mix with. I'm sorry, Luce, if I seem to have made a mess of things. You'll be wondering where some of the money we've occasionally managed to get our hands on went and I don't really know. It was never much anyway. About £3000 compensation when my army career petered out with Independence and I was too old to transfer to British service. We spent a lot of that on that trip home for Smith Brown & McKintosh (because they only paid *my* expenses) but I'm not making that an excuse. I know I was a fool, Luce. The profit I made on the car we brought back from the UK and sold to old Grabbitwallah as I used to call him, in the days when that sort of gimmick was still legal was really no profit because it was paid for in black money, in one hundred rupee notes which I couldn't very well bank, and nothing goes quicker than hundred rupee notes. Some of them quick on the Bombay racetrack, as you know. In those days nearly everybody was bringing cars out from home free of UK tax because they were being exported and then selling them to Indians who couldn't get cars any other way except by waiting years. But I was playing out of my league because I thought of money like that as fairy gold whereas to people with a real instinct for turning a fast buck it was plain solid cash. Some of my separation pay from Smith Brown & McKintosh went on paying up arrears on my contributions to IMWOF, I'd got a bit behind, but I never mucked about with that, Luce, because I knew it would be your mainstay. Most of the rest went on that round-India trip before settling here. I know for years you've thought I was a damn' fool to have stayed on, but I was forty-six when Independence came, which is bloody early in life for a man to retire but too old to start afresh somewhere you don't know. I didn't fancy my chances back home, at that age, and I knew the pension would go further in India than in England. I still think we were right to stay on, though I don't think of it any longer as staying on, but just as hanging on, which people of our age and upbringing and limited talents, people who have never been really poor but never had any real money, never inherited real money, never made real money, have to do, wherever they happen to be, when they can't work any more. I'm happier hanging on in India, not for India as India but because I can't just merely think of it as a place where I drew my pay for the first 25 years of my working life, which is a hell of a long time anyway, though by rights it should have been longer. But there you are. Suddenly the powers that be say, Right, Smalley, we're not wanted here any more, we've all got to bugger off, too bad you're not ten years younger or ten years older. I thought about this a lot at the time and it seemed to me I'd invested in India, not money which I've never had, not talent (Ha!) which I've only had a limited amount of, nothing India needed or needs or has been one jot the better for, but was all I had to invest in anything.

Me. Where I went wrong was in thinking of it that way and expecting a return on the investment in the end, and anticipating the profits. When they didn't turn up I know I acted like an idiot, Luce, for years and years. The longest male menopause on record. One long Holi. Can't talk about these things face to face, you know. Difficult to write them. Brought up that way. No need ever to answer. Don't want you to. Prefer not. You've been a good woman to me, Luce. Sorry I've not made it clear I think so. I'm not going to read all this rigmarole through when I've finished – if I did I'd tear it up. So I'll just stick it in the envelope and forget it. Don't want to discuss it. If you do I'll only say somehing that will hurt you. No doubt will anyway. It's my nature. Love, Tusker.'

She went into the kitchen. The kettle was boiled almost dry. She managed to make about a half-cup of coffee. She took it out to the verandah, still wrapped in her coat. Intermittently, from the Shiraz, she felt and heard the thrum and drum of the band in the Mountain View Room. The stars sparkled. When the band stopped she could hear the calls of the jackal packs in the hills. She drank up her coffee and went indoors, put the wire screen in position, closed the door and left it on the latch in case Tusker had forgotten his key. She rinsed the coffee cup, checked that his cocoa-tray was ready, then went into the bedroom, undressed and went to bed. She put Tusker's letter under her pillow and turned off her light.

She would be sixty-seven next birthday. If Tusker died she would be lucky to have £1500 a year. For capital, there would be only the £2000 plus profits from the insurance. She would have enough to take her home, but what then? She dropped off, woke, tossed, turned. Presently she switched the light on to see the time. It was gone eleven. In the dark again still juggling with figures and possibilities she remained alert, for a while. Then she must have dozed. She was woken by voices and identified Tusker's and Dr

Mitra's and Mrs Mitra's. God forbid that they stayed. Presumably they'd brought him home and he'd invited them in. Within a few moments she was relieved to hear their goodnights, Tusker locking up after them, going to the kitchen to make his cocoa.

Peace enveloped her. She turned on her side away from the light from the living-room and let her sleepy fingers find their way to the envelope that contained the only love letter she had had in all the years she had lived.

CHAPTER FIFTEEN

At 7.15 on the morning of Monday April 24th, Lucy finished her bed tea. Over at the hotel, Mr Bhoolabhoy heard Mrs Bhoolabhoy moan in Room 1. Fifteen minutes later Lucy tiptoed out of the bathroom, having dressed in there in order not to disturb Tusker who had had a restless night and was now asleep. She went to tell Ibrahim to delay Burra Sahib's tea until 8.15, when she would be leaving for the Shiraz. While she was telling Ibrahim this and giving him the shopping list, Mr Bhoolabhoy, summoned by Minnie, was tiptoeing into Mrs Bhoolabhoy's room. He too had spent a restless night, after a strangely puzzling and taxing day with Father Sebastian, Mr Thomas and Susy. Entering, he found Lila as he'd expected to find her: prostrate, moaning gently. They had not spoken since the row on Saturday.

'Shall I send for Dr Rajendra, Lila?'

The mouth shaped the word No.

'Dr Taporewala, perhaps.' He moistened his lips. 'What about Dr Battacharya?'

She moaned again, then murmured, 'You have written the letter?'

'I am about to.'

'Do it. Then bring it. I will sign it.'

'There is no need for you to be bothered with trivial matters of detail, dear Lila. What am I here for?'

'Sometimes this is a question I ask myself.'

'Lila, it will have to be typed.'

'Naturally.'

'The machine will make a noise.'

'One has one's crosses.'

A moment or so later, sitting in his cubby-hole, Mr Bhoolabhoy inserted a sheet of hotel notepaper plus carbon and flimsy in the old Remington and began: April 24th, 1972. My dear Colonel Smalley—

From Dr Pandey's room there came the sound of All India Radio. He ran out, opened Mr Pandey's door, switched the radio off, indicating the state of Mrs Bhoolabhoy's head. Then he went back to his office.

Writing the letter would put the seal on his total and abject surrender to Lila. He knew he had already surrendered. But it was still a difficult letter to write. It was like composing a warrant for the execution of an old friend. To hack the halting sentences out he had to keep reminding himself that it was also like composing a warrant for his own life-long imprisonment. He and Tusker were both victims of a system. He would spend his remaining years like a little dog at Lila's heels, panting after her all round India and perhaps beyond the black water, wagging his tail, until she decided it was time to have him put down. A merciful release? This morning it was one he almost welcomed.

He should have been told about the organ. Yes. For years he had gone on and on about the organ. He had once tried himself to raise the money for its restoration. Mr Thomas knew this. Susy knew it. The sudden pealing of the organ yesterday which should have been a joy had been a shattering blow to his self-esteem. 'We wanted it to be a surprise for you, Francis,' Father Sebastian said. 'A little reward for all your past endeavours.' *Past* endeavours? 'How kind,' he replied. And looked from one to the other and noted their smiles. Smiles of pity? Gradually the explanation of the organ's otherwise miraculous resurrection had been unfolded. Father Sebastian had had a look at it. He knew something about organs. He suspected that things were not so bad as they had been allowed to seem. (Allowed?) He also knew of an expert technician, in Calcutta. The man had come up. He had stayed with Susy. Mr Thomas had let him into the church with the spare key. Within ten days he had worked the miracle and for days afterwards Susy had been practising.

'We wanted to surprise you,' she said, echoing Father Sebastian. 'But, oh, goodness, what we didn't have to get up to. We thought you'd catch us at it any time. During

235

day time Mr Thomas's kids kept watch with orders to divert you if you put in an appearance while one of them went to warn Brother John in the organ loft. And at night when I practised Joseph kept watch to run and warn me, just in case you took it into your head to visit and see nobody had run away with the Church.' They laughed. Joseph had known, too, then. Only he had not known.

'It must have cost a great deal of money,' was all he could say, but trying to look pleased, as happy for himself as they seemed to expect him to be.

Susy said, 'Father Sebastian is on a Grants committee for things like this.'

'And not everybody,' the priest said, 'is interested only in money these days. It was much a labour of love. Brother John said it was not technically difficult. He and his assistant soon had it fixed up. At Whitsun we hope he will come up again and give a recital.'

'He played so beautifully,' Susy said. 'Oh, I felt such a nincompoop in comparison. His Bach was out of this world. Miles better than poor old Mr Maybrick's, who taught me when I was quite a little girl and could hardly reach.'

I too am out of this world, Mr Bhoolabhoy thought; and thought it again as he typed, 'Yours very sincerely.' I am no longer needed here. I do not know about organs. I cannot play organs. I take other people's word for it when they say organs are u.s. I inquire gently year after year about restoring organs and say to people please may we not do something about this organ. But the only organ I know anything about is the one that has contributed to all my difficulties and does not need restoring but having a cloth put over it.

It was eight o'clock: the old witching hour in the days when Smith's was an hotel he was proud to manage.

'I shall be off in a few minutes,' Lucy told Ibrahim. 'I've made another little list, because while we're at it we may as well have in a few extra tins of stuff from Jalal-ud-Din's.

Here is the extra money, and do, Ibrahim, please get a tonga back, because you can't possibly carry it all. If you find things more expensive than I've put down tell Jalal-ud-Din I'll settle the balance during the week.'

'Memsahib, what of drink?'

'Well, yes, we'll need more drink, but I think that is Burra Sahib's responsibility. I'll discuss it with him when I get back, round about 10.15 or 10.30. What I want you to do directly I've gone is give him his tea and then make his breakfast, and then go down to the bazaar. We can all meet up again at about 10.30 and have a little conference, and then Sahib can take Bloxsaw for a walk and buy the booze.'

She checked her handbag. She had the money to pay Susy. She had the scarf to put round her newly set head in case there was a breeze when she came out of the Seraglio. She collected her things, went down the steps to the path – and paused.

The canna lilies are in bloom again (she thought) *such a strange flower*. That was from *Stage Door*: that lovely scene when Katie Hepburn had just been told that Andrea Leeds had killed herself because she'd so badly wanted the part Katie was to play. She was told just before she made her entrance; and went on to a personal triumph no one had expected.

'Ibrahim?' she called.

'Memsahib?' He came down.

'Shouldn't those have been watered this morning? They look so terribly dry and parched poor things.'

'I will tell *mali*, Memsahib.'

He watched her go. She took the side path to the side entrance where the Shiraz loomed. She paused again, bent and touched the petals of a potted petunia. Then he went indoors, put a kettle on, set up Smalley Sahib's breakfast tray. At eight-thirty he took the bed tea in and opened the curtains. He went to the garage to let Bloxsaw out. The creature slunk to the verandah and lay down again. Then he cut bread for toast, put the water for Sahib's boiled egg on to simmer in a pan. Simmer or boil over. Who could tell?

Ten minutes later Mr Bhoolabhoy was back in his cubby-hole with a flea in his ear and the letter to retype. He said to himself: I do not care. It is all up with me, too. Why should I bother myself about Colonel and Mrs Smalley?

Dear Colonel Smalley,

Beg to inform you this hotel and annexe currently subject of planning development under new company ownership and notice hereby given that as from July 1st next coming tenancy of Lodge only extendable on weekly basis with one week's notice. I therefore advise you in good time to look for alternative accommodation in very near future. Meanwhile please accept this letter as notice to be prepared to quit on June 30th next coming.

Yours faithfully,
L. Bhoolabhoy. Prop.

Even this short version took him a long time and several attempts to compose. By the time he'd got it right and had nothing more to do than to make a clean top copy for Mrs Bhoolabhoy to sign, plus an extra carbon for Mr Pandey to take back to Ranpur on the midday train, it was nine o'clock.

'Sahib,' Ibrahim called, placing Tusker Sahib's tray on the verandah table. 'Breakfast.'

Tusker Sahib, dressed but not yet shaven, was down in the garden, just below the verandah, looking at the canna lilies. Bloxsaw was meandering, dogging Tusker's footsteps. 'Oh, for God's sake bugger off,' Tusker Sahib said, and pushed the creature with his foot. 'Ibrahim!'

'Sahib?'

'The canna lilies haven't been watered. Why the hell not?'

'Memsahib asking same question, Sahib. Answer from

mali is that pukka watercan this morning not available. He has found old watercan, but badly leaking. Now being repaired. Presently he will water canna lilies.'

The Sahib clumped up on to the verandah. He had to kick the dog out of the way again. 'You don't need a watering can just to water a bed of lilies. There's such a thing as a bucket or is there a hole in that too? And why isn't the pukka watering can available?'

Not wanting to get involved in a discussion about the availability or non-availability of tools or about whose *mali* was whose he said, 'Perhaps leaking worse than old one. Sahib, breakfast.'

'Well I'm not blind. Where's Memsahib?'

'Gone to hairdresser. Back 10.30. Sahib has all needed? Tea, toast, marmalade, four-minute egg. *Times of India*?'

'*Dak*?'

'No *dak* this morning yet, Sahib.'

'Why not? Not even a bill? Never did enjoy breakfast when there's no *dak*. Go and write me a letter you lazy sod. Better still get this damned dog off me and take him for walkies.'

'Yes, Sahib. Soon I will do. Just now I shut Bloxsaw in garage.'

'I said take him for a walk, *now*. You can get me a new stick of shaving soap in the bazaar while you're at it. And hurry back.'

'Yes, Sahib. I will do this. I will take Bloxsaw for a walk. But not in the bazaar, Sahib. He is not a well-trained dog. If not on lead he runs hither and thither after other dogs and gives trouble to all and sundry because thinking only of copulation.'

'Then put him on the lead.'

'Sahib, the point is that I cannot for the moment take Bloxsaw for a walk on or off the lead. To begin with there is the live chicken to bargain for and I would not put it past the shaitan of a dog to gobble it up on the way home.'

'I asked you for a stick of bloody shaving soap not a live chicken!'

'This is understood, Sahib. It is Memsahib who ordered

the chicken.' He got the lists out of his pocket. 'And all these many things. Many arms full, many baskets. Memsahib has said I must come back with them in a tonga. I do not see how I can buy all these things and come back with them in a tonga with the dog sitting at the front or trotting behind.'

He smiled, assuming that Tusker Sahib would see the point and smile too. But the Sahib didn't smile. He said, 'Show me the list.'

'Dinner for tonight, Sahib,' he reminded him. 'Also stocking up for visitor from Yookay.'

Tusker Sahib studied the list. He said, 'Did Memsahib give you the money?'

'Yes, Sahib.'

'Give it to me.'

Ibrahim did so.

'You can forget all this. Just take Bloxsaw for his walk and buy my stick of shaving soap.' He poured himself a cup of tea. *'Bus.'*

Bus. Meaning that's all. Bugger off. Get lost. Scram.

'Sahib?'

'I said *bus*. And get this sodding dog from under my feet.'

Shaitan, Ibrahim thought. Male isshovanist pig. Like his own brother-in-law. In Finsbury Park his sister had cried and begged him to bring her back to India with him that time the law caught up with him because he'd outstayed his welcome and his visas. His brother-in-law was a shit. Eight pounds a head from twelve tenants and only one loo, none daring to complain because from time to time there were more heads in the house than there should have been, some living in cupboards. His brother-in-law was a blackmailing swindling bastard who treated his wife like a servant. Englishmen like the Sahib were just as bad. As bad as Muslim bugger-fellows, Brahmin bugger-fellows, Western Punjabis, Banyas, Bengalis and Rajput princes. All bugger-fellows.

'I said *Bus!*' Smalley Sahib repeated.

'Ibrahim is not yet deaf, Colonel Sahib.'

240

'Well sod off then, and take the bloody dog with you. And get my shaving stick.'

'Sahib, it is a question of shopping first and walking dog afterwards. Also Memsahib is saying Colonel Sahib will take Bloxsaw for walk when going to get the booze.'

As if cued by an invisible and ill-intentioned prompter the dog began to whine and pace up and down. Tusker Sahib shot out of his chair, grabbed the dog's collar and dragged it down the steps and into the garage and there locked it in. When he got back he said, 'You're fired.'

Ibrahim sighed and put his hands behind his back. 'Yes, Sahib. But shopping for Memsahib first, then fired, then three weeks' pay due.'

The next bit amazed him. Tusker Sahib took his wallet from his trouser pocket, counted money, handed some notes and said, 'Now get out. Go on get out. Pack your things and go.'

Ibrahim did not take the money at once. 'Why are you doing this to me, Colonel Sahib?' he asked. 'What is a man to do who is told this thing by the mistress and another by the master? One moment it is imperative to go to the bazaar and bargain for chicken and have its throat slit and feathers plucked and get it dressed and by the will of Allah get it cooked and serve it cold with salad and hors d'oeuvres and anchovies on toast to follow and the next moment it is a question of shaving soap and taking the dog for a walk. Ibrahim can have coped with all these things but not all at once. Whose orders is he supposed to obey?'

'If you'd ever been a soldier you wouldn't ask that,' Tusker shouted. 'The last order. Always the last. And you know what that is. Get out!'

Ibrahim picked the money up from the table where Sahib had thrown it. It was best not to prolong these scenes. 'May Ibrahim ask before he gets out how Memsahib will manage to arrange dinner for four this evening?'

'No, Ibrahim may not ask. It's no bloody business of Ibrahim's. Who do you think you are? I've paid you off. Get off. Get out. Piss off.'

Ibrahim went. He glanced at his watch. 9.15. He waited

241

for a moment inside the bungalow in case the Sahib cried for help because the egg was off, but the only sound was that of Bloxsaw beginning to whine. He went out to find Joseph and tell him to pack his bags too. *I do not want the garden to go jungly. I have no intention of letting it go jungly*, Memsahib had said. In spite of being paid off on the spot for once, the business of reinstatement should not take long. 'He is, after all, my *mali*,' Ibrahim murmured. 'One out all out.'

At the back of the bungalow he came face to face with Minnie. She gave him an envelope which was addressed to Smalley Sahib.

'Much trouble,' she said.

'Good. Good. For me also, my dove, much trouble. Sacked again.' He nibbled at her ear and tweaked her nipples and muttered his tale so that she laughed, pressed herself against his hardening organ and ran. A little stooped, he went back to the Burra Sahib.

'A letter, Sahib. Just now come.'

'I told you to get out! You've got your money, so go, now. *Ek dam.*'

'From management,' Ibrahim said, putting the letter on the breakfast table. 'Shall not trouble household further. Only performing last duty. The world collapses around one's head. So it is written. Salaam Aleikum.'

Bloxsaw was now banging the garage door. Ibrahim waited inside The Lodge for a few moments. Then he heard Burra Sahib shout, 'The bitch! The bloody bitch!' and scrape his chair back to go and sort her out. Smiling, Ibrahim left by the back way, found *mali* behind the garage still at work on the watering can and said, 'Leave that. We are dismissed. One out all out.'

Fifteen minutes later they were squatting outside the Shiraz, with bed-rolls and token luggage, waiting for the Memsahib to emerge so that negotiations could begin.

Mr Bhoolabhoy backed away from the bed of crimson canna lilies where Tusker lay, dead eyes open, face purple,

242

one hand stretched out, the letter clutched in it, so that the hand looked like something alien planted among the lilies and the letter like the white flesh of its unexpected, unplanned for flower. And Mr Bhoolabhoy ran wild. He ran wild through The Lodge and found it empty so ran out again to the garage where the howling creature he had been sent to complain about suddenly began pounding on the door. This terrified him. He backed away and turned, was again confronted by the body in the canna lily bed. He ran wild across the garden, back into the hotel, pushed into Lila's room, pushed Minnie out, slammed the door and approached the bed on which his wife lay writhing like an enormous pink caterpillar. He gathered her into his arms.

'My Love,' he whispered, 'My Love, my Lila. He is dead, he is dead.' He closed his mouth on hers before she could protest and got his hands round her neck, shaping them for strangulation or adoration. He pressed his body on her with all his strength to keep her pinioned. But she was the stronger. He felt himself being lifted and heaved. He fell on the floor with a thud. She sat up.

'Who is dead?'

He told her. He described it.

'Where is the letter?' she demanded, leaning over and breathing into his face.

'In his hand.'

She reached down and grabbed his shirt. 'Get it!'

'Get it?'

'The letter, you fool. If he is dead there is no need of the letter.'

Her moustache was pricked by sweat. A drop fell off, trickled down her chin and on to the transparent material that covered her breasts but did not disguise the structure and colour of the nipples. 'Indeed I am lost,' he thought. 'She will make me do it. I am not a Christian at all. I am a Hindu and she is my goddess. Every orgasm is an offering to her, and every erection a manifestation in me of Shiva-*langam*.' He shut his eyes so that he could not see his idol. He tried to conjure a different image. It would not come.

'Lila, I cannot rob the dead.'

There was a great disturbance. She was getting off the bed. Her massive thigh pushed him sideways. 'Fool!' she shouted. She made for the door.

'Lila! Come back. Do not do it.'

But she had gone. He staggered up and followed her, then paused, struck by something like a revelation. She was frightened! And that meant that she was a fool too. She was in a panic. She had lost her grip on reality. At least three other people knew the letter had been sent. Minnie who had taken it, Ibrahim who had received it, Mr Pandey who was waiting for a copy of it. And the letter was only a notice to quit. It had killed Tusker but who could be blamed for that?

Running after her he began to exult. 'Now I've got something to hold over you!' he said. 'Scared were you? I'll say. Got the wind up did you? Now who's the fool, my love, my Lila, my life?'

Rising from his second inspection of the body of the patient he had just called in to say good morning to, Dr Mitra saw Mrs Bhoolabhoy flabbing towards him, and her little husband trotting in her wake.

'Doctor Mitra, thank goodness,' she cried at him from some distance. Reaching him she stopped, breathing heavily from the exertion. 'My husband found him a moment ago and panicked. He said he thought he was dead but perhaps he is only fainted and in need of help.'

'I'm afraid he is dead.'

'Oh! Oh!' She doubled her fists and thumped her bosom as if about to beat it. Her husband stood behind her, wringing his hands, staring at Tusker's now empty hand.

'I'm afraid he was due for it,' Mitra said. 'But he knew that, I think.' He stood up. The letter was in his pocket.

Mrs Bhoolabhoy rounded on her husband and this time did beat her breast. 'It is the shock of the letter!' she moaned. 'You should have brought it personally. You

244

should have told him days ago. You who were his friend!
You should have broken things more gently. Oh! I blame
myself. It is no good leaving things to you.'

She bowed her head and waddled away, one hand clasped
to her brow.

'Well, now Mr Bhoolabhoy. Would you help me get him
into the house? There seems to be no one in. When we've
done that I'll ring the hospital. Do you know where Mrs
Smalley is? We ought to get a message to her if we can.'

'It is not true!' Mr Bhoolabhoy suddenly cried.

Deliberately misunderstanding, Dr Mitra glanced down
at the late Colonel Smalley and said, 'I'm afraid it is. Come,
Mr Bhoolabhoy. Give me a hand. We can't leave him here.'

'There we are, Mrs Smalley. A cup of coffee and some
magazines. The dryer's not too hot, is it?'

'It's fine Susy. I'm so glad you can come this evening.
I'm afraid it will be rather pot-luck.'

'Oh, pot-luck, good-luck, my mother always said. I'm
really looking forward to it. Father Sebastian is too.'

Lucy shut her eyes, the better to enjoy the caressing
warmth of the drying-helmet. I should not be ungenerous
in my thoughts (she told herself) but of course in the end
this is what it comes to: that one is into the Indian-
Christian scene and into the Eurasian scene. Perhaps it
will make a change.

She drank her coffee and noted in the mirror that the first
of the smart young assistants had arrived, which meant it
was gone half-past nine. She looked down at the magazines
on her knee. Toole stared up at her in his Steve McQueen
persona. Paris-Match: a paper left by a tourist, presumably. She flipped through the pages, trying to read the cap-
tions. She had never had any gift for languages. Her first
French school book had been called *Le Livre Bleu*. She
could remember the first sentence. 'On m'appelle Jet.' My
name is Jet. Or Blackie. Black cat. Lucky cat. The French
mistress at the Girls' High School was a Miss Hoad. Known

245

as Miss Toad, or Froggie. Nobody had liked her until she was ill. Mysteriously ill. A hysterectomy, probably. Then all the girls sent flowers to the cottage hospital. Her own box full had been culled from the vicarage garden. Syringa. Cabbage roses, white and crimson and sweet smelling. A spike of delphinium. Lupin. A peony. June–July flowers. Rita Chalmers's parents had ordered a bunch from the florist. Everything Rita Chalmers did was elegant. She had married a man whose parents had a Rolls. Lucy wondered whether Rita had been happy. She had not thought of Rita Chalmers for years, nor of Miss Hoad, nor of the box of flowers. She remembered how superstitious her mother was of dreams about flowers. 'If I dream of flowers,' Mumsie had said, 'I inevitably have news afterwards of a death.'

She turned back to the front cover and met Mr McQueen's not-looking eyes. Toole. Toole. Are you still alive, Toole? If not, were you happy? Did you make a good life? Did either of you ever regret, if you found one another? All I remember about you really is the back of your neck. It seems that my love, my life, has never had its face to me and that I have always been following behind, or so dazzled by sunlight that I could not see the face when it once turned to me. Did you see the green bag, Tusker? Did it glitter in the sunshine that dazzled me? How will you remember me? What is your image of me? Does it amount to anything at all? You say I have been a good woman to you. But what does that mean? What does Luce mean? Is it an endearment? Or just shorthand? I'm sorry. I mustn't ask silly questions any more. The years of asking questions are over. You have written me a love letter and I kept it under my pillow all night long.

All night long.

'Mrs Smalley?'
She woke. 'Oh, am I done already?' The drying-helmet was off her head. The first roller was being taken out. Sleepily she felt the hank of freed hair with her finger

246

tips. 'Are you sure, Susy? It still feels just a trifle too damp. I don't want to catch cold.'

'You won't catch cold, Mrs Smalley. You've had a stronger rinse than usual. It's best not to overheat. It's a smashing colour.'

That wasn't Susy's voice. She focused on to the images in the mirror. It was Susy who was taking the rollers out but it was Sashi, the young male stylist, who had spoken. He was standing behind the chair. When Susy moved away to put the rollers to one side Lucy could see, at the far end of the salon, two or three of the smart young lady assistants. They were watching. How strange.

'I'll comb Mrs Smalley out, Susy love,' Sashi said. 'Bring another nice cup of coffee, there's a dear.' Susy went. In the mirror Lucy saw that when she got to the group of girls she hesitated and one of them spoke to her and then seemed to help her out of the salon. The young man was combing deftly. Very deftly. Beautifully, in fact. As he combed he did clever things with his fingers and talked to her all the time. He had scarcely taken any notice of her before.

'Is Susy unwell?' she asked.

'Susy? No, Susy's fine. What beautiful hair, Mrs Smalley. We must do something different with it one day.'

'Thank you. I think I'm too old to change, though.'

And I could not afford to change. I can only afford Susy. At cut rates. Before the Seraglio Room's busy day begins. Susy, bless her, does not have this superior young man's undoubted talent and touch. Which is making me strangely uneasy.

'There, Mrs Smalley. Will it do?' He held up a mirror for her to get a closer view.

'It will do very well if it will hold. Yes, very well. You *do* have a gift.'

He handed her a perfumed towel. 'Please. Just while I spray.'

'Oh, I see.' She held it lightly against her face to protect her eyes. She heard the short bursts of the aerosol; smelt the heavy scent, felt the frosty little zephyr-breaths on her head. And then his fingers again, making some kind of final adjustment. She gave him the towel back and looked at her image.

She was an old woman. An old woman with immaculately dressed hair the colour of very pale violets and a blanched face whose every line and crack showed very clearly in the blaze of the salon's working lights. Old Mrs Smalley. Not Little Lucy Little. Old Mrs Smalley's eyes had no depth to them. The stronger colour of the hair did nothing for them. Her neck was scrawny. The handsome young Indian was gazing down at his handiwork as if seeing nothing but that. As handiwork it was good. Better than good. Their eyes met in the mirror.

'Thank you,' she said. 'It was kind of you to look after me. Now I must be off because I know you're very busy people, which is why I come early. Perhaps Susy will let me have my bill.'

She had her bag on her knee and opened it with her veined misshapen fingers. In it was the letter from Tusker which she had meant to read again under the dryer.

'Oh any time will do for the bill, Mrs Smalley,' he said, busying himself at the bowl, rinsing, wiping, setting things to rights for the new customer. Susy arrived, carrying a cup of coffee. She put it down and the young man left. In the mirror she saw him chivvying the girls away, out of the salon, so that in a moment she and Susy were left alone.

CHAPTER SIXTEEN

As the daylight began to go so too did her capacity to cope with people, with their charitable instincts. The Lodge had been under a kind of siege. From somewhere she had found the nervous energy to deal with it. Hour after hour people had turned up. The telephone had rung. Someone had answered. It rang again. Again someone answered. The table in the living-room became covered by chits delivered by hand by servants which Ibrahim brought in.

He had had so many friends, really.

The Menektaras came. The Srinivasans. Dr Mitra had been there at the beginning but had now come back with Mrs Mitra. Susy and Father Sebastian were in the kitchen making coffee and tea. Mr Thomas handed it round. People said they would not stay but she said, 'Oh yes, please stay.' Some bunches of flowers arrived. She looked at the cards but never quite took in the names and knew that anyway the flowers would have to go elsewhere to be ready for tomorrow. The club secretary came, with the little old Parsee widow who ran the Library.

'Oh,' Lucy told her. 'I'm afraid we still have Mr Maybrick's book. Long overdue. I'll see it gets back to you.'

'Come back with us, Lucy,' Coocoo Menektara said, as the daylight faded and people began to leave. 'Spend the night. As many nights as you wish.'

'Thank you, Coocoo, but really I'm quite all right, and I'd rather be here, if you understand.'

Coocoo kissed her and said, 'Ring if you change your mind. We'll come and collect you.'

The Srinivasans said, 'Come back with us.'

The Singhs (how nice they were) said, 'Put up with us for a bit.'

The Mitras were the last to go. No, not quite the last.

249

Father Sebastian and Susy and Ibrahim were still busy in the kitchen.

Dr Mitra said, 'Will you be all right? You're welcome to stay with us.'

'I'd prefer to be here. Really I'm quite all right.'

'I've left just one pill on your bed-side table. Take it. Get some sleep. Susy says she'll stay with you if you want her.'

'I'll be all right. Ibrahim will look after me. When Tusker was ill that time, he slept in the living-room. Poor Ibrahim. He looks so tired. He's been on his feet all day.'

'There is just one thing that troubles me, Father Sebastian.' She was alone with him in the living-room. She had switched a fire on because she felt rather cold. Ibrahim had gone to get some logs to build a proper one. Susy was still in the kitchen, washing up. Father Sebastian had brought her a bowl of hot soup and a glass of Golconda brandy. 'Tusker had this strange kind of passion for *place*. I mean he was happy here. After tomorrow, could the ashes be kept for a while, not here, I mean in the crematorium chapel and then when it could be arranged buried in the churchyard? He mentioned a south-west corner.'

He nodded but said nothing.

And later a little stone, she thought. With just one word on it. She smiled. Tusker. What a funny name.

'Drink your brandy, please Mrs Smalley.'

'Will you be here tomorrow?'

'Yes, I shall stay until Wednesday.'

'What is tomorrow?'

'Tuesday.'

Tuesday. There was something she had to do on Tuesday. She drank her brandy. 'I think I'll go to bed now, Father Sebastian. It's so good of you to have given so much of your time. And you, Susy.' Susy was by her side. Susy followed her into the bedroom, and helped switch on the lights in there and in the bathroom.

Lucy sat on the edge of Tusker's bed because her own already had the mosquito net down.

'It was the letter, of course,' Lucy told Susy as Susy bustled to and fro doing things. 'It was the letter that killed him. It must have been a great shock. Dr Mitra wouldn't let me see him. He wasn't going to let me see the letter either, but I knew I had to see that.'

'Don't worry about the letter,' Susy said. 'So long as I have a roof over my own head, Mrs Smalley, you always have a home with me.' She paused, stood, looked down at Lucy. 'People like us must stick together,' she said.

After a moment Lucy put out her hand but Susy had already moved away, busying herself again.

'Would you like me to stay?' Susy asked.

'Thank you all the same. Perhaps you'd ask Ibrahim if he wouldn't mind staying in the house, as he did when Tusker was ill. I'll feel safe then. I think I'll go to bed now, I'm very cold and tired.'

'Don't forget your medication. I'll bring you a cup of cocoa when you're in bed.'

She undressed in the bathroom. She left the light on in the bathroom. She got into bed. Susy brought the cocoa.

'Minnie is here too, Mrs Smalley. They have made a fire and will be next door if you want either of them. Shall I turn off the lights?'

'Only the overhead. I'll turn my own off when I'm ready to sleep. Please leave Tusker's on.'

When she felt the sleeping pill beginning to work she clicked off the lamp and lay on her side away from Tusker's light and shut her eyes. Now my own, my love, she thought. Now my own. Now.

And slept.

Woke, shivering. Her watch showed 3.30. She should not have gone to bed so early. The pill had worked, but worn off. She got out of bed, put on her gown and slippers and was shattered by recollection, Tusker's empty bed. Going past it to the living-room she switched his lamp off. The living-room was unlit except by the light coming from the bedroom. She trod gently. Curled up near the almost dead fire were two shapes in blankets. Minnie and Ibrahim, one on each side of the fireplace. Going gently past them she caught her breath because there was a third shape, huddled with its back to the wall.

Joseph.

The three of them.

No, she told herself. It is very moving, but I mustn't cry. If I cry I may not be able to stop and that will never do, will it? There is such a lot to think about and attend to. She stood in the dark kitchen until her eyes were used to it and she could make out the shape of the brandy bottle and a glass, probably a dirty one, but that didn't matter. She moved cautiously back through the living-room with bottle and glass, anxious not to disturb the sleeping watch.

Back in the bedroom she poured a stiff measure of brandy. To drink it she sat on Tusker's cold bed and stared through the net of her own to the lamp on the other side of it, and then remembered what it was that she had to do tomorrow as well as go to Tusker's funeral. She gulped some of the brandy. She had to ring Mr Turner in Ranpur and put him off. Or, rather, she would have to ask someone reliable like Dr Mitra to ring and tell Mr Turner what had happened. He would be disappointed, but he would understand. He would write to her from Calcutta, probably. When she replied she would suggest that they kept in touch because he would be in India for some time yet, and there might well be a chance of meeting later, when she had recovered from the shock.

The shock. She gulped more brandy. It was very strong. She went into the bathroom to run some cold tap-water into it. She ran too much. Now it was too weak. She went back to the bottle and topped the drink up and then back into the bathroom because she suddenly felt sick, and her bowels were stirring. She stood by the basin, waiting to be sick. She was unable to be sick, but her bowels were still moving, so she went over to the thrones and sat on hers, with the brandy glass on the floor within reach. She heard herself moaning quietly and at once stifled the sound with her hand over her mouth. She did not want to wake the servants. She had forgotten to put a towel over the shutters. Not that it mattered. If Ibrahim heard a sound he would not come bursting in once he had seen her empty bed, He would send Minnie in to call out and ask if she was all right.

Now that she was alone she would have to have the catch put back on the shutters. Tusker had had it taken off for the same reason that he had insisted on two loos. In India, he had said, you could never tell when you'd get taken short. And who could tell if you both might not get taken short at the same moment? If they could only have one bathroom, they could at least have two loos in it and no catch on the door. Actually it had only happened once, the time they'd both eaten something that disagreed with them. She'd always sworn she'd never undergo the indignity of sitting on her loo while Tusker was sitting on his. But, this once, she'd been driven to it, and half way through the performance Tusker had begun to laugh and after a while she had begun to laugh too, so there they had been, enthroned, laughing like drains.

She began to laugh now, silently. She put her hand out to hold his so that they could laugh together.

'Memsahib?'

A woman's voice. Minnie. She must have been standing well away from the louvred shutters. There was nothing to be seen of her head or her feet.

'It's all right Minnie. Quite all right, thank you. Go back to sleep and get some rest. I shall be back in bed very soon.'

She coughed, to underline her self possession. After a while she drank more of the brandy. Swallowing it, she realized something: that she could not put Mr Turner off, because he was bringing a present for Minnie from Sarah and Susan and, in a sense, from the young man who had been baby Teddie. One could not think only of oneself. It didn't matter about the blue rinse, because now she would let her hair go. But it mattered about the present for Minnie. It would be a big thing in Minnie's life to find herself remembered as the little ayah. In the morning she would send a chit to Mr Bhoolabhoy, by Minnie, asking him to book Mr Turner's room and to ring Mr Turner personally in Ranpur to confirm it and say nothing about what had happened. By Wednesday, when Mr Turner arrived, everything would be over and she might be suffering from delayed shock. Mr Turner's presence could be a godsend to her.

She had another swig of the brandy.

It would be difficult of course. She would have to keep very firm control when taking him round Pankot, pointing out this, pointing out that. All the places which had for her associations inseparable from memories of Tusker. She might not quite manage to accompany him to the churchyard. It would be difficult for him too, of course, the moment he discovered that Tusker to whom he had spoken only yesterday, was now, on Wednesday, gone.

'I didn't put you off coming, Mr Turner,' she would say, 'because quite honestly, it is good for one to talk, in all the circumstances, especially to strangers. Come, let me show you round The Lodge. Let's go into the garden first. There's not much to see either of the garden or the bungalow. He loved the garden. Well, you can see, can't you Mr Turner, how nice it looks. We have a good *mali*, of course. From here, just here, before they built the Shiraz, one could see almost to the top of Club road. We'll go that way this afternoon. Perhaps Coocoo Menektara will give us tea at Rose Cottage, then we might have a drink at the Club. We'll go by tonga because then you get the best view of the valley.

'Tusker and I went everywhere by tonga in the old days. But I'm afraid he was really rather naughty because he used to pay the wallah off when we arrived, in the hope that we'd get a lift home in someone's staff car, either that or somehow the wallah misunderstood and didn't come back at the right time. I remember one party when we seemed to be absolutely stranded. Perhaps that was symbolic, Mr Turner. I mean everyone else gone and just Tusker and me, peering out into the dark waiting for transport that never turned up.'

She drank more brandy. Straightened her body, leant back against the support of the raised lid, head against the wall, glanced at the empty throne beside her, then shut her eyes.

But when we went to parties, Tusker, just before we went in, you always took my arm. You helped me down from tongas and into tongas. Waiting on other people's verandahs for tongas, then, too, you took my arm, and in that way we waited. Arm in arm. Arm in arm. Throne by throne. What, now, Tusker? Urn by urn?

It's all right, Tusker. I really am not going to cry. I can't afford to cry. I have a performance to get through tomorrow. And another performance to get through on Wednesday. And on Thursday.

All I'm asking, Tusker, is did you mean it when you said I'd been a good woman to you? And if so, why did you leave me? Why did you leave me here? I am frightened to be alone, Tusker, although I know it is wrong and weak to be frightened—

—but now, until the end, I shall be alone, whatever I am doing, here as I feared, amid the alien corn, waking, sleeping, alone for ever and ever and I cannot bear it but mustn't cry and must must get over it but don't for the moment see how, so with my eyes shut, Tusker, I hold out my hand, and beg you, Tusker, beg, beg you to take it and take me with you. How can you not, Tusker? Oh, Tusker, Tusker, Tusker, how can you make me stay here by myself while you yourself go home?

ALSO AVAILABLE IN PAPERBACK